Heady Sensations

Mark's potent, knowing smile intensified, while his voice became a seductive purr. "I will give you a foretaste of all the honeyed delights awaiting to be savored by lovers." Slipping a hand beneath Elysia's wealth of dusky silk-soft curls, he cupped her tender nape and prevented her from stepping farther away.

Stunned by the shocking awareness of what an intimate danger Mark could be, her brown eyes widened as he bent gently to brush his mouth across her lips once, twice, and once again. In Elysia's soul, a faint alarm bell heard earlier now tolled in earnest warning of devastating peril.

But the latent power of his touch proved too strong an enticement, and Elysia sank headlong into a blaze of heady sensations, melting against their source, while a tiny whimper escaped her tight throat. . . .

Books by Marylyle Rogers

The Dragon's Fire
Wary Hearts
Hidden Hearts
Proud Hearts
Chanting the Dawn
Dark Whispers
The Eagle's Song
The Keepsake
Chanting the Morning Star
Chanting the Storm
Twilight Secrets

Published by POCKET BOOKS

For orders other than by individual consumers, Pocket Books grants a discount on the purchase of **10 or more** copies of single titles for special markets or premium use. For further details, please write to the Vice-President of Special Markets, Pocket Books, 1230 Avenue of the Americas, New York, NY 10020.

For information on how individual consumers can place orders, please write to Mail Order Department, Paramount Publishing, 200 Old Tappan Road, Old Tappan, NJ 07675.

MARYLYLE ROGERS

TWILIGHT SECRETS

POCKET **STAR** BOOKS

New York   London   Toronto   Sydney   Tokyo   Singapore

This book is a work of fiction. Names, characters, places and incidents
are products of the author's imagination or are used fictitiously. Any
resemblance to actual events or locales or persons, living or dead, is
entirely coincidental.

An *Original* Publication of POCKET BOOKS

A Pocket Star Book published by
POCKET BOOKS, a division of Simon & Schuster Inc.
1230 Avenue of the Americas, New York, NY 10020

ISBN: 0-671-87186-2

First Pocket Books printing November 1994

10 9 8 7 6 5 4 3 2 1

POCKET STAR BOOKS and colophon are registered
trademarks of Simon & Schuster Inc.

Cover art Sharon Spiak

Printed in the U.S.A.

To the Ladies Sharon, Heather, and Jennifer:

Friendship is a rare and precious treasure beyond price—
Thank you for giving me that gift!

Author's Note

When William the Conqueror died in 1087, he left his most proudly held possession, the duchy of Normandy, to his eldest son, Robert, and the kingdom of England to the next elder, William (who was known as Rufus for his ruddy complexion). A third son, Henry, was left with little but in the end claimed and held it all.

Henry's ascendency began in the summer of 1100 when while hunting in the New Forest King William Rufus was killed by a stray arrow believed to have been shot by a friend, Walter Tirel. Although there was never any proof, people then and history today look skeptically at this "accidentally" shot arrow. Particularly when added with Henry's all too opportune proximity and amazing readiness to seize the throne.

The event's timing also was suspect. It occurred while the oldest brother, Robert, was away on Crusade. By the time he returned, Henry had solidified his hold on the kingdom. Nonetheless, Robert laid plans to take England by force and in July of 1101 launched his invasion. However, after landing in Portsmouth, he could make little headway despite having the aid of the rich and brutal earl of Shrewsbury, Robert of Belleme.

Unlike the vast majority of people in his age, Belleme had no religious feeling. Though known for his greed, he consistently refused to follow tradition and exchange captives taken in war for ransom. Instead, Belleme kept his hostages imprisoned for the pleasure of savagely torturing them.

History records this man as Robert the Devil. And the term *wonders of Belleme* was used in a manner that make it roughly equivalent to wielding the threat of the bogeyman ... except Belleme's danger was very real.

Rarely was Belleme loyal to anyone but himself, and despite his merciless nature and vicious habits, he was ultimately an impatient pragmatist. Upon finding that the lord of property he wished to plunder was able to withstand his initial attack, Belleme wasted no time in siege but turned aside to seek easier prey.

King Henry never trusted Belleme and systematically set about the task of breaking him. In 1102 the king stripped his enemy of English lands and titles before banishing him forever. Belleme spent another decade in the comfort of his extensive continental properties. However, when he foolishly returned to England in November of 1112, Henry seized and tried him before the royal court. In the end Henry had Belleme imprisoned and held so closely that the day of his death is not known.

In Norman England not only were the underage

male heirs of men who held lands direct from the king kept in his lucrative wardship but surviving heiresses owed their sovereign the service of marriage throughout their lives. In other words, the king could and did see them married to whomever he chose and if that husband died, the king had the right to do it again. These royal rights were not limited until the Magna Carta was signed by King John in 1215 (whose first eight clauses are largely addressed to this issue).

It may be useful to know two additional facts: First, religion during this era was an important influence in people's lives and to them a literal devil was as certain as the existence of God. Second, despite the above, in this period it was an unmentioned but common practice to "suppress" unwanted or imperfect babies by abandoning them in the deadly darkness of a night forest or meadow.

TWILIGHT SECRETS

Prologue

*T*hree short blasts of the huntsman's horn pierced quiet morning air. It summoned anticipation from the party of hunters who began stealthily moving through mists held low by the New Forest's dense vegetation and close-grown trees. Each intent on being first to spot a stag at bay, none were prepared to be prey himself.

Zwi-i-i-ing! Thwack!

As a heavy body thudded to the earth, a shriek tore brutally through the woodland's peace. "The king's been struck!"

A moment of stunned silence followed. Then came the rattle of a dozen swords unsheathed and the sound of men rushing to their fallen leader's side.

From the green shadows of a well-hidden covert, Mark had seen the arrow shot. Yet he waited and watched confusion consume the king's horrified companions until one man in the outer ranks of those huddling over King William Rufus's inert form directly met his gaze. Only after Sir Walter Tirel gave a bleak smile and slight nod did Mark carefully edge back from his thick-leafed shield of tangled bushes and quickly slip away.

In a copse not far distant stood Mark's destrier, motionless and patient. But once Mark swung with ease onto the stallion's back, the beast demonstrated his power with a hasty dash to deliver news of the royal death to a waiting prince.

Mark was confident that his steed was strong enough to carry him onward to join his friend and liege lord in a mad rush first to seize the nation's treasury at Winchester and then on to Westminster to claim the ultimate prize—a crown.

Chapter 1

June 1101

$\mathcal{A}$ dense forest had gone quiet against the intrusion of humankind while beams from a sun half done in its descent shafted through lush green leaves. Although the only sound heard was the steady thud of his destrier's hooves over a narrow lane's soggy surface, Mark was alert to possible dangers lurking near.

A rain shower quickly come and gone had left abundant moisture on the thick foliage overhead. Thus, despite a clear sky, droplets of water continued to fall. But Mark paid small attention to either the odor of his cloak's damp wool or the chill it lent. Penetrating gray eyes constantly shifted from the muddy path ahead to delve into the green shadows on each side, leaving him prepared for what was too likely to come.

Of a sudden Mark's way was blocked by armed men who planted themselves two deep in the narrow passage a brief distance in front of him. The sharply honed edges of their bared blades glittered with stray gleams of sunlight.

"What have we here?" Mark's sardonic half smile appeared but his silver-ice eyes went so cold they threatened to freeze those daring to stand against him. "A welcoming party from Wroxton Castle? Or did you issue from Kelby Keep?"

"What matter can it be to any man fool enough to approach alone a destination surely known to be hostile? Even wolves move in packs." Short, broad, and completely bald, the sneering speaker narrowed his eyes on the image of a black wolf emblazoned on the lone rider's shield. "Never will we permit that the Lady Elysia be wed to a bastard like you!"

Mark startled onlookers by laughing freely, head tilted back until his hood fell away to reveal a thick mane of raven-black hair unprotected by the helmet he disdained. The waiting was done. In a single swift, graceful movement he unsheathed and thrust his broadsword toward the heavens. "Valbeau to me!"

The stocky challenger dashed forward, blade slashing. But before his weapon could crash against his mounted prey's, the forest erupted with a mass of armed warriors. These newcomers immediately surrounded the smaller band confronting their leader. However, the trapped men refused to easily cede the victory. Soon the forest echoed with the sound of blades meeting in earnest conflict.

Unwilling to put his favorite steed at risk in a battle with a foe afoot, Mark exercised amazing agility in dismounting while continuing to meet a relentless assault. Despite the ground's treacherous layer of mud, once on the same level, he fiercely met his opponent's onslaught. Mark's powerful defense became a mighty attack that sent the bald man's weapon flying harmlessly into dense undergrowth. In desperation the man jerked a dagger from its position behind his belt and lunged forward, but Mark twisted to the side and the man tumbled headlong into a briar patch.

Superior skill joined with the sheer force of greater numbers to bring an end to the conflict. While an eerie silence settled over the woodland, Mark towered above where his once sneering foe lay flat with sword-tip pressed against the base of a vulnerable throat.

"Hugh!" Without shifting attention from his defeated opponent, Mark called out to the taciturn man who'd been his loyal friend since the day they'd met as boys come to foster in the Conqueror's Norman court. "Help me see my quarry and all of his companions safely trussed."

Habitually stingy with words, the bearded Hugh curtly nodded a head as dark as that of the one in command. He immediately set about fulfilling the ordered deed with the lengths of rope brought in expectation of this likely need.

As the leader of their erstwhile foes was pulled to his feet for the tying of wrists behind his back, Mark wryly mused at the sorry sight.

"Seems the priestly messenger successfully delivered King Henry's decision." An errant ray of sunlight slid over ebony hair as Mark tilted his head to one side while returning a captive's ridicule of his parentage with a jeer of his own. "We can only pray that even your sort refrained from the wicked villainy of harming a man in holy orders."

The bald man glared but refused to respond.

Though Mark had expected no answer, the lack deepened his cynical amusement—and regret. Both this man's unwillingness to speak further and the actions he'd led others in taking to forestall the king's proclaimed intent made Mark's goal of smoothly assuming his new position as lord of Wroxton more difficult to attain.

Mark would far rather have arrived unannounced, but Henry had insisted upon dispatching a priest to Wroxton Castle with a royal decree certain to be resented. The wily new king had argued that it was best to enter any conflict with one's enemies unmasked. Thus Henry had sent his messenger ahead for the purpose of smoking out the snakes in a thicket of traitors. Mark could not dispute his friend and sovereign's logic yet would've preferred to work toward the same end with a lighter touch—particularly where he was expected to wed with one of their number.

"I won't do it!" Pulling away from the brush wielded by her childhood nursemaid and long-time companion, Elysia twisted about to lift a brown gaze gone near black to the comfortably plump female at her back. "I shall simply refuse."

Ida patiently watched while the younger woman rose yet again from the three-legged stool where she'd perched to have tangles smoothed from dusky locks prior to their braiding. Knowing the maid was already aware of the futility at the core of heated claims, Ida wasted no breath in stressing their folly. The message sent by Prince Henry (Ida hadn't yet come around to thinking of the Conqueror's youngest son as her king) had put the whole of Wroxton in a tizzy but her lambie worst of all.

Elysia fair stomped from one side of her bedchamber to the other, loose curls tumbling in a dark cloud to her hips. "I am to wed with Gervaise! And I would soon have been but for the ruthless slaying of King Rufus by those who think to force another upon me."

"Ah, lambie . . ." There was no point in disputing Elysia's words when Rufus's death rendered the question useless. Yet Ida knew it was doubtful the avaricious king would ever have allowed the rents drawn from the maid's heritage to flow into the pockets of another man—unless the prospective groom were in such a position as to compensate for the loss either with wealth or military support. Gervaise was not such a one. Indeed, Ida had never trusted the neighboring landholder. Marriages between those wellborn were commonly arranged for the sake of procuring property and titles, but an infatuated Elysia believed Gervaise's motives far more personal. Harboring serious doubts, Ida feared her lambie doomed to disillusionment.

"Calm yourself." Ida stepped forward to wrap a thick, comforting arm about the young woman who'd been gifted with little rest in the hours since the arrival of a priest bearing an unwelcome royal decree. In truth, Elysia had slept not at all until dawn peeked over the horizon. As a result the maid's fiery spirit simmered too near the surface. It was also the reason that at this late hour of an afternoon Elysia had only just completed what should've been morning ablutions and why wild curls had yet to be tamed into braids.

"You *have* sent my missive to Gervaise?" Elysia asked this same question for near the hundredth time.

"Aye." Again Ida quietly repeated a reassurance. "I dispatched it a full day and more past."

"Then why has he not come to me?" Doe-brown eyes soft with anxiety met the hazel gaze of the woman who'd stood as mother since Elysia's own had left while she was but a toddling.

"Mayhap your beloved is taking steps to see the mischief undone." Ida knew the success of such an action to be impossible but saw no reason to further burden her sweet, already agitated charge with unpleasant facts.

"Elysia?" A quiet voice tentatively called from the doorway. "Have I committed some wrong that you are so angry?"

Forcing an upward curve to frowning lips, Elysia turned and moved toward the timid girl hesitating in the shadows of a barely open portal.

"Of course not, Evie." Elysia put an encouraging arm around the maid's shoulders much as Ida has so recently done for her. "I am upset by actions threatening to alter my life's path. But they are deeds in which you have no part and for which you can no more bear the blame than you ought for any wrongs done within Wroxton's borders."

With the latter pointed statement, Elysia cast a meaningful glance over her shoulder to the woman behind. Ida had unaccountably joined near all castle inhabitants in rejecting the company of this innocent woman-child bearing both the visible and unseen scars of a sin not her own.

Head ever lowered to ensure that loose flowing hair the shade of unripened wheat would cover her disfigured cheek, Eve nodded while quietly giving the news she'd come to impart. "Lord Gervaise awaits you in the great hall."

Elysia flashed a smile bright enough to warm the chamber's early summer chill. Heedless to the impropriety of appearing with hair neither bound nor covered, she hurried from the chamber. With as much haste as safety permitted she rushed down a narrow, steeply winding stairway whose gloom was lessened only by resin-soaked torches placed in rings widely spaced and driven into stone walls.

Pausing beneath the arch where the stairwell opened to a sizable hall, Elysia fondly studied the tall, wiry man standing with his back to her. Gervaise's russet head was bent toward the central hearth while he peered into flames leaping beneath a huge caldron of stew and several spitted birds. She smiled. Never would he admit it, but his sight was not as keen as once it had been. A failing that bothered her not one whit. 'Twas to be expected of a man who carried the age of two score and several years more—an age that brought with it a restraint and wisdom she admired.

Although a contemporary of her parents and more than twice her age, Elysia had idolized Gervaise since childhood. She'd been thrilled when, some little time after her father's death, he had proposed an alliance between them. The offer had been delivered with a listing of dry facts upon which Gervaise based his belief that joining her inheritance to his lands would be advantageous for them both, despite Kelby's lesser size and importance. Choosing to believe the passionless nature of his proposal born of respect for her chastity, Elysia told herself that a longing for fervent words and deeds was merely proof of her own impetuous immaturity.

Once granted the happiness of dreams come true by Gervaise's proposal, she'd been left with but a single block to her happiness. But it had proven an immovable rock: King William Rufus's greedy determination to ensure Wroxton's sizable income would continue flowing into his own coffers by keeping its heiress unwed and in his ward even though at twenty she was years past the age most maids wed.

When Rufus died and his brother Henry seized the crown, Elysia had hoped the change would ease their position, but Gervaise had warned her their new monarch's cooperation would be even more difficult to win. Her shoulders slumped. Gervaise had spoken true. With King Henry matters had grown infinitely worse!

"Gervaise," Elysia quietly called. "Tell me you've had word that the past day's events were merely some horrible mistake. Better still, tell me that a scribe's error in naming the groom has been corrected and 'tis our wedding rites which soon will be performed."

As the man turned to face the willowy creature hastening toward him with arms outstretched, firelight glinted over the white threads in his mane and left the fleeting impression of winter's first frost on autumn leaves. Once within reach, Gervaise took Elysia's hands into his, halting her headlong rush and restraining the maid to stand demurely a brief distance from him

Elysia could feel her cheeks burn with bright color. Once again, as too oft in recent months, Gervaise had wordlessly staved off another of her impulsive actions.

'Struth she would've thrown herself into his arms had he not prevented her from making a private matter public by enacting a passionate scene before the small army of curious houseserfs laboring to set up trestle tables for the meal to come.

"Nay, Elysia. 'Tis all too real." Gervaise's lips thinned into a tight smile as he shook his head. "But I have dispatched a messenger to plead the cause of our betro—"

"I *won't* marry him!" Elysia tamed her voice to a mere hiss. "Not this stranger, this bastard—"

With a pained grimace, Gervaise squeezed Elysia's fingertips to end this too closely watched discussion of personal matters, but it was another man's words that stole her voice and banked the coals of her temper.

"If the king wills it ..." Mark stood in an open portal. He'd left his guardsmen and their prisoners in the walled bailey below to climb wooden steps leading up to this entry on the massive stone tower's second level. "If I will it, then, milady, wed me you *shall.*"

Startled by the unfamiliar voice, Elysia spun around to find a stranger silhouetted against twilight's purple haze. As the unwelcome visitor stepped further into the hall, she took one look at hair dark as night and black-lashed silver eyes and inwardly named the man far too handsome to be trusted. Even before her father's death, Elysia had seen enough of such men to be wary. And to see the image of a black wolf on his shield seemed to confirm the rightness of her distrust. She'd heard of the Black Wolf, King Henry's champion. How was it that no one had warned her it was this famous warrior to whom the king thought to wed her?

Mark found amusement in the critical appraisal of her hostile brown gaze. Having wondered if others hesitated to describe his bride for fear of being forced into an honest report of severely limited attractions, he was relieved to find that suspicion utterly unjustified. She was elegantly slender, and her large, dark eyes were beautiful. Moreover, her thick mass of curls—unbound as few wellborn women would permit—caught and reflected ever shifting gleams of firelight while framing the pale oval of a delicate face. This quashing of erroneous apprehensions brightened Mark's mood, and his lips slowly curled upward in an action of honest warmth whose rarity she could nowise appreciate.

However, that potent smile did deliver a physical impact that caught Elysia's breath. Under its power she was instantly convinced her worst opinions had been confirmed. This devastatingly attractive man would expect every woman to fall weak to his charms. But not she! She was already bespoken, and best he learn it was so!

"I am betrothed to another."

Black brows scowled. "Betrothed?" No mention had been made of any such bond. The next moment Mark's forehead smoothed, and a mocking half smile lifted one corner of his mouth. That he hadn't been warned was surely proof no alliance had been formalized and lent reason to doubt the truth of the maid's desperate claim.

"Aye." Gervaise spoke, uncomfortably aware that a hall recently filled with the dull roar of activity had gone so silent it seemed even the walls had sprouted ears. "Eighteen months past a betrothal was performed between Elysia and me, Gervaise of Kelby Keep."

For the first time, Mark turned his penetrating gaze full upon the lanky man at the heiress's side. The threads of gray liberally sprinkled through red hair reminded Mark that the man he'd known during his first years in Normandy was a decade older than himself. Henry had warned Mark to be wary of this man whose loyalties near certainly lay with the Conqueror's oldest son and inheritor of his French duchy. The warning was unnecessary as Mark well remembered the bond between Gervaise and one of Duke Robert's most committed supporters, Robert of Belleme, earl of Shrewsbury. Yet for all that Mark had expected Gervaise's opposition, he hadn't expected to face this adversary of old as suitor to his proposed bride.

"Have you documents bearing King William Rufus's seal as proof of her guardian's assent to the match?" Mark sharply asked. "Without his approval, the bond you claim is meaningless and one I need not honor."

"Would you make that decision for *your* king?" Gervaise was quick to parry the thrust.

Mark immediately shook his head. "I've no reason to fear King Henry's decision and am willing to lay the matter before him." He intended to add another fact but was forestalled by a maid annoyed with two men debating her future as if she were some inanimate object.

"Then you must leave now." Elysia wanted this dangerous man gone with all possible haste. "You have no right to tarry here."

"Have I not?" With unhurried calm Mark reached

into his tunic and pulled out a leather packet from which he withdrew a crackling parchment. Against a creamy surface the royal seal was clearly visible. *"Our* king has placed the heiress of Wroxton in my ward."

"You've been named Elysia's guardian?" Gervaise's hazel eyes narrowed while his face went so pale his hair flamed the brighter.

Mark could almost see the wheels of his opponent's mind at work. "King Henry would not drive me into a commitment I found unpleasant. Yet he took action to ensure that Wroxton rests in my care no matter my choice of bride. The decision of whether I wed with Elysia or hold her as my ward is mine to make. Thus, no matter my choice, remain here I and my army will."

That this man was to wield power over her future lit golden fires in the depths of Elysia's dark eyes that even tears of anger could not quench. Facing him with clenched fists firmly planted on slender hips, she repeated the heated declaration he'd earlier heard her make to Gervaise.

"I will *not* wed you!"

Silver eyes gleamed with delight while Mark's potent smile returned. Few women had ever refused his attentions and many had sought the honor this fiery maiden would spurn. Elysia's action caught his interest and promised to hold it as few women had for any length of time in recent years. Although he'd seen little in the martial state to recommend it and was no more certain he wanted to marry her than she him, this unexpected beauty's temper might well add spice to the tasteless gruel of a struggle to find and eradicate traitors.

Elysia burned with fury over the amusement the Black Wolf found in her heartfelt denial. "You cannot take control of Wroxton Castle!"

"I already have." With the deep purr of his claim, Mark's mocking smile deepened. "By my defeat and capture of those sent to forestall if not slay me, my hold over this fiefdom is an accomplished fact."

While Elysia radiated antagonism at the amused stranger, Gervaise's eyes narrowed and his hands slowly curled into fists. If this man had defeated all those sent to take him, it meant few remained in Wroxton who obeyed his commands. Few but . . . Gervaise told himself he was sharp-witted enough that even were only one left still he would win this struggle too important to lose.

Chapter 2

Mark moved restlessly atop a bed whose heavy drapes were open. Wearied by the many trials of a difficult day, he'd fallen atop the wide bed still half dressed only to find the sleep once so invitingly near had grown elusive.

Silver eyes narrowed on a portal rare in any sturdy Norman castle. This lord's bedchamber on the castle's highest level boasted a window rather than the usual arrowslit. He'd been startled by the dangerous oddity upon first entering the room and had investigated. It was, he discovered, a safe luxury as beyond shutters thrown wide lay a steep descent down stone tower walls and the sheer cliff upon which it perched above the sea's pounding waves.

Gaze shifting to lingering clouds drifting across the face of the moon, Mark's thoughts turned to plans for the next day's initial steps toward asserting command over Wroxton and in uncovering the traitors harbored in its midst. Already he had ordered Hugh to take a small band out into the demesne to judge its mood as well as its needs. He meant to assess the same with regard to those residing in the castle and the small adjoining village by summoning their leaders to a meeting the next afternoon.

Light from the sky's silvery orb fell across Mark's bed—and glittered on the sharp-honed edge of a dagger raised with deadly intent.

In one of the two smaller chambers across the narrow corridor bisecting this floor Elysia found no easier peace. A vision of the stranger laying claim to her lands—and to her—picked remorselessly at the restraints both her father and Ida had trained her to wrap about a too ready temper. The lord's chamber, vacant during the almost two years since her father's death, had become near a shrine to the memory of the quiet, educated man once its inhabitant. And, save for absent floor rushes, since his passing, it had been as neatly kept as if he might return at any moment.

At the mere thought of the vital, too powerful stranger daring to sleep in her father's bed, the banked coals of Elysia's fiery spirit threatened to flare free. The prospect of Sir Mark's insistence that she join him there fanned the first flickering flames. She refused to acknowledge the unwelcome possibility that the heat of her reaction was not due solely to disgust for the darkly handsome man . . .

"Valbeau to me!"

Elysia sat bolt upright. After a shocked moment of immobility, she jumped from her bed. Then, while feet thundered up stone steps in answer to the call, she snatched up the fine linen undergown laid out for her to don as a first layer on the morrow. Unlike serfs who slept fully dressed in the great hall, she went to bed nude, making it necessary to jerk the thin white garment over her bare form before hurrying to the door.

Sturdy oak planks opened to the view of the Black Wolf's armed men massed in the corridor and crowding the opposite chamber's entry. These strangers in her home parted to allow the lady of the castle to move forward until she stood framed in their leader's doorway.

By the light of a torch taken by a young, curly-haired guardsman from an iron ring in the stairwell, Elysia saw her most unwelcome visitor. He was stripped to the waist and the muscles across his powerful back bunched while he held a bared broadsword menacingly above midnight dark hair.

Something gleamed beneath the brand's flickering light and caught Elysia's eye. For a fleeting instant her gaze dropped to a horribly familiar dagger lying on the chamber's bare plank floor and then flew to the youth huddled against a far wall.

"Jamie, what have you done?" Elysia gasped.

The attention of all shifted to the young beauty's white face but Elysia's remained fixed on the frightened youth. She watched as he leapt up and launched himself through the unshuttered window. Immediately dashing across the chamber, Elysia gazed down to where foam-tipped waves crashed against a rock cliff.

"Never would I have punished the boy so cruelly as he has done himself."

Startled, Elysia tossed a doe-soft glance of puzzlement over her shoulder to the man who'd come to stand a short distance behind. Would he really not have done so? In her experience, admittedly limited, for fear of appearing weak, few men would even claim such benevolence.

But this man ... weak? Elysia gave an infinitesimal shake to her head while instinctively taking quick stock of his powerful physique's undeniable brute strength and the hard planes of a face too handsome to trust and as cold as the silver ice of his eyes.

"I pray pardon." One side of Mark's mouth tilted up in a mocking smile that did nothing to warm his freezing gaze. "By your appraisal of me it seems you are less concerned for the boy than I'd thought."

Furious with herself for giving the appearance of any personal interest in him, Elysia turned to truly face her new guardian while straightening to her full height—woefully less than his. She was thankful for the chill window ledge pressed against her spine as in that first moment's awareness of his overwhelming size she might elsewise have fallen a much rued step back.

"Of course I fear for Jamie. How else but that?" As Elysia spoke, honest fear shook her voice. However, its source was less concern for her friend's physical well-being than alarm over the possibility that she might've unwittingly betrayed her confidence that their childhood game had seen Jamie safely free.

Mark saw the swift succession of emotions chase across Elysia's expressive face before settling into an honest anxiety. Her mercurial mood shifts were disarming while at the same time he remembered how quickly the golden fire glimpsed in the depths of soft brown eyes could flash to the surface. She was a rarity—a woman he could not easily understand and mentally assign an identifiable label.

His sardonic smile deepened. This talent for shielding her thoughts was the more remarkable for being born not of the ability to don a blank expression but rather by virtue of hosting so many emotions he could not easily delve through their layers to the truth at their core. From a personal view it was exciting, but on the practical level it was both dangerous and annoying.

Eyes narrowed to silver slits, Mark turned toward the openly curious men watching this odd exchange between their leader and the maiden garbed in a gown of cloth so fine spun it barely preserved her modesty. Mark had only just met the damsel, but his men's attention to the enticing vision of her lush beauty unaccountably irritated him, and he took immediate steps to see them busy elsewhere.

"Before the tide begins to ebb, find boats and make your way to where water strikes the cliff. Recover the boy's body . . . if you can." Mark had little doubt but that his adolescent assailant's action had sprung from a desire to protect his lady. It was an honorable motive and one Mark found difficult to disdain. "I would leastways see he is buried in hallowed ground."

Mark's attention returned to the wary damsel at his side. Were no body found, the niggling suspicions roused by her surely intentional shrouding of true responses beneath layers of shifting emotions would warrant deeper investigation.

To Elysia it was all too plain that her response to Jamie's action had roused unwanted questions. Feeling pierced by penetrating gray eyes and feigning unconcern to cover an inability to directly meet the steady assessment of the man too near, her gaze dropped to the broad expanse of his chest. Elysia gulped hard. Her action had been ill-conceived as, to her disgust, she found this view of his raw power intimidating. But, refusing to reveal the panic it caused, she stood motionless rather than further betraying herself by whirling about to again stare through the open window. She was torn by an inward battle to stifle fierce words while at the same time stilling the urge to simply turn and flee. But even amidst that unpleasant struggle, her attention was caught by the crimson blood trickling from a wound on his shoulder.

Elysia saw immediately what course she must follow, unpleasant as it might be. As a first step, she acknowledged that Ida was right. During her initial confrontation with this man, she'd both looked and sounded like a shrew. Moreover, her frozen manner at the high table during the meal that followed had been an insult to Ida's training of her as a lady. Now she must confound this wretch by proving what a lady she truly was.

"While your men conduct their search as you bade them, I will bind your wound." Sincere worry for Jamie's safety put a genuine strain beneath the soft concern in Elysia's voice. This sham would allow her to do her best for Jamie and his mother on one hand and to distract the Black Wolf's suspicions on the other.

Mark was barely aware of the minor scratch. With the experience of many battles and having survived far more serious injuries in places where no gentle maids were near to tend them, he could easily have cared for it himself. However, he wouldn't dream of forestalling this unexpected offer although his suspicions were deepened by her sudden good will, and he would be wary of any potion she thought to apply on his open wound.

"I will hasten to fetch bandages and medicinal herbs to staunch the blood flow." Before Mark could respond yea or nay, Elysia slipped from the chamber.

Rather than going to the alcove where bedclothes and medicinal supplies were stored, Elysia rushed down winding stairs to the level below. It was here that the tiny chamber built into the width of the castle wall was shared by Ida and her son. Elysia had hoped to reach her old friend before the news of Jamie's actions was delivered by others. But once she entered the room, quiet sobs proved Elysia had come too late to prevent minutes full of painful loss.

After carefully closing the door to ensure privacy, Elysia hurried forward and sank to her knees beside a sturdy wooden bed. She shared the hurt of this beloved woman but doggedly bolstered her own flagging spirits by telling herself there was no need for such distress. It was necessary to believe it herself before attempting to inspire such confidence in Ida.

"Hold tight to the hope that your sorrow is unnecessary," Elysia whispered and then with all the self-assurance she could muster added more. "I am almost certain Jamie is safely hidden from his pursuers."

Lying in a weighty ball of misery atop the straw-stuffed mattress resting over a bed's simple rope webbing, Ida seemed oblivious to Elysia's presence and even less aware of her words. Elysia gently patted a hunched back, patiently waiting for the meaning of her statement to sink through the clouds of Ida's despair.

Slowly Ida sat up and turned to Elysia, tear-drenched eyes brimming with an anguish afraid to believe.

Anxious to lighten the atmosphere and lead the other into accepting Jamie's safety as a credible possibility, Elysia forced to her lips the impish smile of childhood—a reminder of past mischiefs.

"Surely you can't have forgot how oft you rebuked Jamie and me for diving into the sea from ever higher perches on the cliff wall."

A glimmer of Ida's usual merry self brightened pain-dulled eyes as she gruffly answered. "The pair of you near scared the life out of me and more than a time or two."

Relieved by this hint of revived hope, with an unrepentant grin Elysia promptly attempted to reinforce progress made. "Our misdeeds may have, instead, saved Jamie's."

Deeming this a dubious dream at best, the older woman's gaze again clouded. "But never did either of you attempt such a fool stunt at night. Nor did you dive from a point so high on the castle walls."

" 'Struth." Elysia solemnly nodded. Nowise could she deny any fact to this woman who knew both her and the castle so well. "Yet, still I much doubt the strangers who search will find Jamie's body."

"Oh, they must! They must!" Horrified by the prospect that her son's lifeless form might be forever lost, Ida's pudgy hands came together as if in prayer. "With all my heart I beseech God to let me lay my boy down for his final rest in hallowed ground."

Elysia hadn't expected Ida's fervent reaction and bit her lower lip hard. How could she have failed to consider Ida's response to the horrible prospect she'd unthinkingly raised? Annoyed with herself, she took Ida's joined hands between her own and gently squeezed them as she hastened to correct her error with encouraging words. "You don't want Jamie to be found if searchers are unsuccessful only because he has survived."

Ida slowly shook her head although her fear-widened gaze remained locked with the compassion in Elysia's eyes. "If Jamie is found alive, a punishment far worse than quick death is certain to be exacted for his crime against Wroxton's new lord."

Elysia opened her mouth to make a denial, but the grieving woman pulled hands free and dropped her face into them as she sobbed out her greatest dread. "They'll bring Jamie back only to leave him moldering in some dank dungeon cell."

Elysia wrapped slender arms about the agitated woman and waited for her sobs to lessen. She feared Ida was correct in thinking her loyal son would be called to endure a lonely lifetime of misery. Yet once the other's grief subsided into silent tears, Elysia again anxiously sought to instill a measure of peace.

"Don't dwell on bleak speculations. Rather, think on brighter possibilities. Should the Black Wolf's men fail to find Jamie"— Elysia bit off the words *alive or dead*—"merely does it mean he's found safety within the secret hideaways of our childhood. And, truly, you must put your faith in that bright prospect! The high tide into which he dove could easily carry him there.

*　　*　　*

Elysia was later than anticipated in making her promised return to tend the Black Wolf's wound. Concern for what suspicions might be roused by her tardiness or, worse, by a failure to appear kept her oblivious to the fact that her garment was considerably less than adequate for so late a night visit—or visit of any making with a man not of her blood. It was a mistake she rued the moment the thick oak door swung open.

"Milady, pray enter."

A wry half smile appeared as Mark waved his visitor into the room. He was amazed that this pure maiden had dared come to a man's bedchamber alone and at night. 'Struth, a number of faithless wives had thus boldly offered themselves to warm his bed even while assiduously guarding their daughters' chastity. He wondered who was responsible for so serious a lack in training that this lady-born would commit such a misdeed—and apparently without a moment's forethought.

"I've come—" Elysia paused to still the shaming wobble in her voice. Although expected, the abrupt nearness of this powerful man and his too personal, too appreciative gaze was more intimidating than a nervous Elysia could handle with aplomb. "I've come to treat your injury." Holding a damp cloth square in one hand and in the other a small basket containing rolled bandages and a pottery jar of herbal balm, Elysia stepped into the room with more courage than she could honestly claim.

Elysia heard as behind her the guest-turned-host quietly shut the door to close her inside—alone with him. Save for the great hall, the lord's chamber was the largest single room in the castle yet this stunning man's mere presence seemed to shrink it to uncomfortably small dimensions. She felt caught like some simple-witted lamb who'd aimlessly wandered into a wolf's den.

Resting broad shoulders against the sturdy door, Mark watched the inadequately garbed beauty with curls tumbling free to her hips nearly stomp to the center of the room. With the instincts of a hunter he sensed the trepidation this spirited woman attempted to hide beneath a proudly uptilted chin. He'd been surprised when at the scene of the minor wound's infliction Elysia stated her intent to treat it and was amused to see she now undeniably rued that offer.

With her back subjected for long quiet moments to the penetrating touch of silver eyes, to Elysia it seemed the devastating man was attempting to strip her thoughts and emotions bare. She sent a speaking glare over her shoulder. *Bloody oaf!* With this assuredly sinful oath, silent but fervent, Elysia released a measure of pent-up irritation. It was an irritation bred of resentment for both his ability to make her feel threatened and this proof of the truth in Ida's many warnings that her impetuous nature would one day thrust her into peril.

Catching a glimpse of soft-bowed lips firming into a resolute line and golden sparks flaring in dark eyes, Mark nearly laughed. Elysia's determined bravery—despite the apprehension she couldn't conceal—earned a measure of his respect. Here was no simpering, coy court beauty worthy of little more than disdain. And yet he'd be a fool not to wonder what purpose lay behind her determination to care for the wound of a man at best resented. He'd been sent to unmask dangerous traitors to the crown lurking within Wroxton's boundaries. Was she the first? To Mark's surprise, that possibility made him uncomfortable.

Mark knew the wiser course lay in limiting such close contact betwixt them until he'd time to gain a sense of how the land lay and the truth in the natures of those creatures who inhabited it. Toward that end, he moved to face the fair damsel while attempting to relieve her of a clearly unwanted chore.

"As you can see, the bleeding has stopped." As was his wont, a thread of wry laughter lay woven through the words.

Already resenting the threat she perceived in the sensual grace of his approach, Elysia misheard his amusement as a jest at her expense. A faint frown marred her smooth forehead while brown eyes narrowed on stains now dark. "Aye, 'tis dry but I said I'd tend your wound and tend it I will."

Elysia's first instinct was to gladly accept his excuse, to turn and flee from certain danger—but never had she run from any challenge. And the last thing Elysia would willingly do was betray so pigeon-hearted a response to this stranger whose mocking smile she recognized as both potent lure and insult. Nay, after saying she would perform this task, even were he the devil himself and she required to walk into hell to see it done, see it done she would!

Mark lifted his hands palm up in pretended surrender and backed toward the window. Beneath its shutters resided both a sturdy trunk hosting a platter of clustered candles and a three-legged stool. He settled on the latter to lessen the difficulty of the maid's chore by putting his wounded shoulder more easily within her reach.

Elysia bit her lip to bolster courage, and yet to her consternation hands wielding a damp cloth to dab at dried blood trembled. It was difficult enough to divert her gaze from the wedge of black curls arrowing down from the wide expanse of a muscular chest to the drawstring at the waist of homespun chausses without his cynical smile and the silvery glitter of a steady gaze.

It was the custom for the lady of any castle to welcome all wellborn guests by attending to them with waiting baths, but Ida had always performed that duty in Elysia's stead. Thus, until came the clamor that had drawn her to his open door earlier this eve, Elysia had never seen any man even partially nude. And then she'd been so concerned for Jamie's actions that she'd paid little heed before announcing her intent to return. Now was a different matter entirely. The power in his magnificent form was frightening. In truth, the big, dark man was all blatant masculinity and frankly threatening.

Mark watched the fascination mingling with resentful fear in Elysia's widened eyes and his crooked smile deepened. While yielding to her surprisingly tentative attentions with apparent unconcern, he asked, "Was your marriage to Gervaise arranged by your father?"

"Nay." Elysia's hands went still. She could easily claim it was so, but falsehoods were too often inadvertently exposed by even the most loyal of friends. Possessing one huge, desperate lie that must be kept, she wouldn't risk speaking more for fear of loosing all. Her care for his wound resumed with unnecessary fervor. "My father succumbed to a sudden illness two years ago and before that was unwilling to see me leave his side."

"Ah." Ebony hair caught and reflected candleshine as Mark nodded. Knowing the damsel's age, he quickly calculated that she'd have been eighteen when the man died, an age several years beyond that at which most maidens were married. "It was by your sire's difficulty in parting with his only child, his beloved daughter, that you remained unwed before his death."

Pretending a need to peer closer at her work, Elysia tilted her head and sent a cloud of dusky curls cascading forward in a vain attempt to shield an expression of joined anxiety and annoyance. Elysia was unaware that his probing eyes had already seen what she thought to hide. She was even less aware that the sole result of falling curls was the drawing of his attention to creamy flesh inadequately covered by delicate white cloth.

"Then it was your choice alone to accept the planned alliance with Gervaise?" Dark brows arched with the question that was no question. Mark knew this must be true as Gervaise had said the union was agreed upon a mere eighteen months past.

"Aye!" Elysia firmly stated, taking a step back to glare at the unsettling man. "The choice was mine to make and make it I did."

"Putting aside the fact that you were in the king's ward and unable to wed without his approval in the first instance, did you truly think to make such a decision without sage counsel from any source?" Mark deemed his cynical view of the matter confirmed by the fires beginning to flare in brown eyes against the implication that she was in need of another's advice.

Elysia felt the steam of a simmering temper rise to fog the clarity of her view. Plainly this man, like all others save for her father, believed no female was capable of thinking for herself. In the next instant he unknowingly delivered a crippling blow to the scorn of her wordless condemnation of him.

"What did your diligent shepherdess, Ida, have to say about her 'lambie's' choice?" A gleaming silver gaze narrowed on the damsel startled by his question. "By what I saw of her at the table this eve, she seemed a woman of good sense."

This proof of the Black Wolf's ability to steal the heart out of her every argument increased Elysia's ire. Golden temper drove gentle brown to the outermost edges of glaring eyes.

"Did you not seek Ida's counsel?" Mark was unfazed by her mute anger. "Mayhap you were so caught by some misguided infatuation with a much older man that you disdained her opinion in order to justify surrendering yourself—and all that you possess—to him?"

Elysia's lips thinned. At her advanced age she was irritated that the intruder come to complicate a well-planned life should assume her emotions so immature and refused to explain her actions to him!

"Did you not wonder why after waiting so long he suddenly became your suitor?" With the instinct of a hunter, Mark struck at this vulnerable point. "Has he demonstrated the grand passion of an impatient lover which would explain his surely belated wish to claim you as bride?"

"What passes between Gervaise and me is private and none of your concern!" The moment the words left her tongue Elysia regretted the impulsive, heated response too certainly a betrayal of the accuracy in his assumption of her betrothed's cool restraint.

"I thought not." To Mark her claim was an admission, and the sardonic glitter in silver eyes increased. "The Gervaise I've known for most of my life hosts a passion only for wealth and power."

This news that the Black Wolf had met Gervaise before this day startled a gasp from Elysia although later and on closer thought she'd realize it was only to be expected.

"Ah, you were unaware that I and your erstwhile betrothed have known each other for a goodly number of years? Decades, in fact." Mark could near laugh over the beauty's amazement. Clearly she knew little of the other man's past. " 'Struth, although leastways ten years older than me, Gervaise dwelled in Normandy with then Prince Robert while I was fostered at the same court and in the company of the Conqueror's youngest son, Henry."

As the unwelcome guest continued speaking with wry humor, Elysia absently twisted wet cloth between her hands until water dripped unnoticed to puddle on the plank floor.

"It was a common jest among my peers that the ice at Gervaise's core had driven all the fire in his soul to his furthermost extremities." Mark spread his hands wide. "Hence, the flame of his hair. Think on it and you'll have to admit he does nothing without cold and calculated planning."

The even deeper tone of distaste that crept into a

black velvet voice when Mark spoke of Gervaise made Elysia defensive. But suspecting his goal was to wear away loyalty to her betrothed with dark logic, she refused to give him the satisfaction of an outburst. Elysia instead gazed steadily down while busying nervous fingers in neatly folding the thoroughly wrung-out cloth streaked with deep crimson stains.

Mark studied the masses of shiny curls flowing from a determinedly bent head while the methodical movements of dainty hands betrayed more than she would admit.

"Gervaise's apparent failure to so much as kiss you in all the months since your sham betrothal is surely proof that the chill in his soul would smother your fiery spirit."

Elysia was annoyed no end that this mocking stranger had so thoroughly analyzed Gervaise—and to his detriment. Beneath the blustery winds of anger sounded a faint warning bell. Might what this too attractive stranger suggested be true? The mere fact that Mark's assertions had roused such a disloyal thought was frightening. Elysia suppressed it by launching into the heated statement she'd earlier refused to give.

"You are wrong! Gervaise *has* kissed me."

"Ah, but only a single kiss?" The underlying thread of laughter in Mark's voice was calculated to provoke a further confession from this defiant protagonist. She was proving to be more daring and thus more interesting than he'd expected when King Henry had given the right to take her as bride.

"Was it a burning lover's kiss? Or simply a short, dry peck to seal the advantageous bond he sought? Surely one so passionate as you must want more."

Could it be true? Were all her fears based on fact? The abused cloth square fell free as Elysia's hands rose to lie crossed below the vulnerable curve of her throat. Could the Black Wolf's penetrating eyes peer deep enough to uncover all her secrets? She was flustered and nearly convinced it was so. How else could a stranger know her private disappointment?

"But how"— Mark slowly rose to his feet—"could a virtuous maiden possibly recognize the lacks in Gervaise's embrace?"

Saints he is tall! Elysia's heart stopped and then raced wildly. With the dangerous man towering a mere whisper away, a rare panic sent her thoughts into chaotic disarray and she pulled back.

Mark's potent, knowing smile intensified while his voice became a seductive purr. "I'll prove both how unnatural is Gervaise's coldness and the folly of wasting passionate fires on a man capable only of smothering that flame." Slipping a hand beneath Elysia's wealth of dusky, silk-soft curls to cup a tender nape, Mark prevented her from stepping further away. "I will give you a foretaste of all the honeyed delights waiting to be savored by lovers."

At his touch Elysia went as still as if she were a rabbit mesmerized by the approach of a wolf. Stunned by the shocking awareness of what an intimate danger he could be, brown eyes widened while he bent to gently brush his mouth across her lips once, twice, and once again. As if each touch of his mouth was the first tentative flicker of a fresh-lit fire, sparks of pleasure spread through Elysia.

Mark continued his sweet assault until soft lips went pliant beneath his. Then deepening the kiss, he searched and found an indescribable berry nectar inside. Here was the taste of a true and untutored passion, and Mark gloried in this rare treasure never shared with him before.

In Elysia's soul the faint alarm bell heard earlier now tolled in earnest warning of a devastating peril. Intending to hold him back, she pulled a whisper away and laid balled fists against his intimidating chest. But the latent power beneath her touch proved too strong an enticement. Cool mists of rationality evaporated under the heat of desire. Small fingers flattened against satin skin, then instinctively moved to savor crisp curls and the iron thews beneath.

As brown eyes became molten amber, Mark was startled to discover himself vulnerable to the unexpectedly intense appeal of this innocent maiden on whom he'd meant to practice no more than a little light seduction. Steadily drawing Elysia full against his muscular frame he became all too conscious of her single garment's delicate fabric. Worse, with tempting awareness of how easily that negligible barrier could be sundered, his pulse thudded harder.

Sanity scattered by Mark's unanticipated gentleness, Elysia also felt the forbidden excitement, the devastating need to be closer still, to touch flesh to flesh. Sinking headlong into a blaze of heady sensations seemingly able to dissolve her bones, she melted against their source. The overwhelming man welcomed her surrender with an even more intimate kiss. And as another searing bolt of delight shot through Elysia's trembling body, a tiny whimper escaped her tight throat.

But with that intoxicating, hungry sound, Mark

found the limits to his control. He forced himself to lift his mouth from the liquid fire of hers. " 'Tis as I thought." Mark whispered into the downy curls over her ear. "Never before had you been truly kissed."

Though it required near the whole of the willpower honed over a lifetime of difficult challenges, Mark put a brief distance between himself and Elysia's honeyed beguilements. With eyes darkened to charcoal, he gazed into the enchanting vision of a face passion-rosed and lips slightly swollen from his kisses. "You *are* as chaste as a newborn babe."

Few things had Mark wanted to do more in his life than yield to Elysia's guileless enticements. But he was certain that for such sweet play he would later pay the price with her bitter resentment—and likely an honest hatred for him. To his own surprise, he found that prospect unbearable—a fact that earned a strong dose of self-mockery. How was it that no price was demanded for a night's dalliance with any of the abundant willing partners among the ranks of other men's wives. But guilty regret was sure to follow were he to enjoy the same with this maiden whom he'd the right to take as his own bride. In reality, it was the very fact that to take this virgin he must wed her, which made the deed impossible. He was in no way convinced that he wished ever to marry, even less at this point in his life or to this likely traitor to his sovereign and friend.

Under his steady gaze, Elysia felt shamed and abandoned. No matter what the man's intent had been, his ability to coolly pull back while leaving her lost in passion's fires was surely proof of a willingness to use others to serve his own ends. It was a fact reinforced by the mockery in his crooked smile. 'Struth, the Black Wolf was a predator and she his innocent prey. Once ... but never again!

Elysia stiffly bent to pick up the fallen rag and the basket of unnecessary ointments and bandages she'd carried into the chamber. Only pride lifted her chin and held her pace steady as she departed. Only pride prevented the wretched display urged by an impulse to bolt from his presence as if a den full of ravenous wolves were nipping at her heels. With fingers tight on the basket's handle, she moderated her steps though she could believe herself escaping just such a wicked creature.

Chapter 3

$\mathcal{E}$lysia's heart pounded, pounded near as loudly as the waves crashing against the cliff below. In the decade since last she'd defied wiser counsel to rashly dare this hazardous journey between precipice and secret havens, she'd learned a measure of caution. And with awareness of how near lay certain peril, she took great care while maneuvering her way over the narrow path descending a sheer rock wall.

The drifting mists of a gray predawn made it unlikely that anyone glancing from the castle above would see her. Elysia was sharp-witted enough to do her utmost to see it remain so. Toward that end she wore an undergown of cream with a kirtle of dove gray, both able to blend with the shroud nature provided her surroundings. Even, she reassured herself with more zeal than she felt, the heavy black satchel firmly strapped from right shoulder to left hip would go unnoticed.

As Elysia cautiously made her way down the ragged pathway invisible to any save one who had learned it as a fearless child, she clearly recognized the danger of her actions. And yet in the midst of danger's tapestry was woven a thread of excitement that appealed to the impetuous nature her father and Ida had long attempted to subdue.

The scent of sea and feel of damp rocks beneath slender fingers flooded Elysia's mind with memories of daring adventures. All of which had been brought to an end by the gentle father horrified to discover his young daughter leading an even younger Jamie on one such madcap escapade. Then when he'd learned from Ida that the youngsters made a game of diving into the high tide from ever higher points on the cliff wall, he'd put an immediate halt to such play by imposing a tight leash upon both.

The forlorn smile beckoned to Elysia's lips by the clear image of her beloved father's terror for their safety slipped into a curious blend of hope and triumph. As she ducked into one of many shallow caves pocking the cliff's face, Elysia prayed that the games her father had named a wicked wrong had now resulted in a right by providing Jamie escape from the Black Wolf's retribution.

Elysia gave scant concern to the fact that this unpromising cave was empty. As she stepped back out onto the path, her thoughts centered on the fact that it was all well and good for King Henry's renowned champion, Sir Mark of Valbeau, to claim no wish to punish the lad so harshly. 'Twas a thing easily said when he believed the matter permanently ended with the boy either drowned or dashed upon rocks.

But trust the Black Wolf's word? That Elysia would not! Although silent, the assertion was fervently made while Elysia entered a much larger cave.

"Jamie ..." It would be impossible for anyone outside the cave to hear her voice above the sound of ebbing tide breaking against rocks at the cliff's base. Still Elysia held it to a sibilant softness. "Jamie ... Jamie ..."

"Elly!" Surprise and excitement made the answer considerably louder. "Elly, is that you?"

Her playmate's pet name warmed Elysia's mouth with an affectionate smile as she followed the sound deeper into the dimly lit haven. At length she spied Jamie in the cave's furthermost recesses. The grinning adolescent four years her junior was sitting up, back resting against a rough wall.

"I knew you'd be somewhere in these caves." With a relief so strong it betrayed the depth of her worry, Elysia rushed forward and sank to her knees beside the friend she could barely see. The gloom was so dense it stole even the bright sunstreaks from his golden brown hair. "I knew you wouldn't throw yourself through that window without a plan."

Jamie was thankful for the murky half light to hide his sheepish blush. He'd rather face the torment of a dozen wicked foes than admit to his lifelong heroine that, in truth, he'd jumped from the window on impulse. Only by instinct had he turned his long fall into the dive that saw him not only survive but within swimming distance of their old hideaways. And an escape at the cost of but a small injury surely soon healed.

"I've brought you food and a blanket." Elysia

shrugged free of the burdensome satchel. "Also, a fresh set of clothes which your poor mother packed with prayerful hope to replace sea-soaked garb. You scared the life out of her . . ." Pausing, a solemn Elysia met Jamie's instantly penitent gaze. "Me, too."

"But I did it for you." Jamie's words were a soft plea for understanding.

Elysia grinned. "Not the leap from the window, I hope." Her teasing response lightened an atmosphere threatening to grow so serious as to quell any hint of the justified joy for his survival.

Jamie grimaced in return.

"Were you hurt?" Elysia quickly went on, purposefully misinterpreting his wince until he clasped a clearly swollen ankle. Then she suffered more than a twinge of guilt for being grateful to have this excuse to change the subject.

"I see you were injured. Is it sore?" She frowned in concern. "Against that possibility I brought a salve able to lessen the ache of tender joints or mend torn flesh." She dug inside the still packed and overfull satchel to pull out the same pottery jar of ointment she'd taken to the Black Wolf's chamber only hours past. This she handed to the young man.

In silence Jamie watched as his courageous friend continued emptying the bag. Elysia laid folded clothes on the dusty stone floor. Next, atop them she piled a loaf of bread, two apples, and a thick slab of cheese. Delving back into a seemingly empty bag, she triumphantly pulled out the final item.

"When nightfall approaches the mists will rise." Elysia displayed a flint cupped in her palm. "Then, it'll be safe for you to build a fire and defeat the chill."

"I could ..." Jamie nodded, a merry gleam in his eyes. "If only I'd the power to turn rocks into wood."

Elysia blinked against the abrupt glare of harsh truth. Bringing a flint to this place where no kindling existed was the action of a goose-wit. In the next instant the absurdity of the situation unleashed a sudden mirth that burst through the inner wall of tension heightened by a multitude of difficult trials. She dissolved into helpless giggles. Under that infectious sound her companion's strained mask, too, was shattered by gales of laughter.

Conquered by unruly gusts of merriment, Elysia fell weak against the same stone wall as Jamie to fight for control. Only after she'd tamed her breath into a normal pattern and wiped tears from the corners of her eyes did Elysia realize how quickly time was passing. Sufficient sunlight was slanting its way into the cave that she could quite clearly see Jamie's pleasant face. This was a frightening fact. It meant the sun had fully crested the eastern horizon and would doubtless quickly dissipate the concealing haze so important to her safe passage. She must delay no longer elsewise the intimidating man King Henry had sent would note her absence and without the mists' protection ... Fearsome possibilities effectively quashed every hint of foolish drollery.

"I must go but"—Elysia flashed Jamie a reassuring smile while hastily reaching for the empty bag—"I promise to fill this satchel with firewood before I return. And return I will ... when the mists rise again at twilight."

Jamie sobered at her mention of the mysterious time between sunset and full darkness. It was an unintentional reminder of a request made and a promise given.

"I was in the stable when Lord Gervaise departed last eve." Jamie hurried to pass on a message to the maid wasting no moment in settling the satchel's strap over one shoulder. "He bade me tell you that when the mists of twilight descend, he'll be awaiting your coming in the same glade where you and I once practiced the skills of an archer."

Elysia went still but only for a moment before firmly shaking her head. "Nay, I'll send a messenger to Kelby Keep, telling Gervaise to meet me there before the morrow's dawn." She was confident houseserfs would be as busy then as they'd been this morning, permitting her to again slip away unnoticed. "Nothing will keep me from returning here tonight."

Jamie was struck by a twinge of guilt for feeling relieved but none for being pleased that when presented with the choice between himself and Gervaise, Elysia had chosen him. And yet, if not this night, then she would go to him the next. Worse, go to meet him in that assuredly cursed glade.

"Tell him to meet you at the old mill. Or anywhere but that place." Elly's eyes narrowed in response to his muttered plea and in defense against her certain disapproval, Jamie's chin firmed into a stubborn line. " 'Tis a glade of ill omens."

Elysia knew why he believed this was so. And knew why, although she'd chided him for such foolishness, he hadn't gone back with her since she'd first stumbled upon a shy, untamed girl while fetching arrows overshot into the woodland.

"Eve was sorely abused as a child and wrongly

blamed for that misdeed and from that day for near every misfortune that befalls anyone." Elysia unwaveringly repeated an oft-stated defense. "She is *not* an ill omen of anything!"

"But if Eve is not a witch, not truly a minion of the devil, why was she living in the forest like a wild creature?" Having heard all the superstitious tales woven about the strange young woman *rescued* by the lady of Wroxton Castle, not even Elysia's defenses had convinced Jamie of Eve's innocence. "And what of her ..." Jamie motioned toward his cheek.

Elysia firmly interrupted. "Eve was in the forest through no fault of her own!"

Jamie scowled, caught between his mother's distrust and Elysia's affection for the peculiar maid.

Annoyed by the youth's reaction, hot words escaped Elysia's throat without wise forethought. "Already I have told you how Eve was cast out as a child—same as you are now an outcast. The greatest difference between the pair of you is that by your actions you are more worthy of the punishment than ever she was."

A stricken expression instantly froze Jamie's face.

Elysia just as quickly flooded with shame for reminding the boy of his peril and the reason why.

"Nay, Jamie." She took his hands with hers. "Your escape from the Black Wolf is a great relief, and I could never think you worthy of punishment for what you honorably attempted in protection of me."

Distress mollified by her acknowledgment of the "honorable" deed done for her, a shy smile warmed Jamie's face.

Heartened by this sign of her friend's trusting forgiveness, Elysia added, "Even your target claimed himself unwilling to punish you so harshly as you did yourself by jumping into the sea."

"How can you trust his word?" A frowning Jamie grudgingly wondered aloud. "Is it just because he's handsome? Has he *done* something?"

To Elysia, suspicious questions were a reminder of the thrilling feel of strong arms and a devastating kiss. In a prompt denial of his words and the betraying blush heating her cheeks, she said, "The unwelcome intruder's good looks and actions only give me more reason to distrust him!"

Elysia immediately turned toward the cave's opening. "Watch for me tonight." Her words faded as she briskly departed.

"Witch!" The shrill scream pierced the gentle calm of a chill morning. "Witch, go back to the devil! Go back!"

Despite the slipperiness of dew-damp sod, Hugh hastened around a corner to where a reserve well had been dug between outer castle wall and the bailey's tall barrier. He paused some distance from the back of a small group and took in the cruel sight of three boys pelting a kneeling maid with stones. Her slight figure hunched over a water bucket while thin arms defensively curled over a lowered head.

A brief moment later Hugh's long strides carried him into the boys' midst. He jerked the speaker up by the scruff of his neck and held him helpless a handsbreadth above the ground. At sight of the huge, bearded stranger seizing their friend, the other boys fell back to cower against the unyielding stones of the bailey.

The boy in Hugh's grip squirmed desperately. "Let go of me! Take her!" he howled. "Take her, not me!"

Hugh roughly dropped the boy's feet to the ground but maintained a tight grip on one flailing arm.

"Aye, to the castle I'll take you. And there for your vicious taunts and wicked blows you'll meet the justice of Wroxton's new lord."

Although the young miscreant stilled, he glared mutinously at his captor. "Isn't you the devil come to get her?"

Hugh's brows shot up and a harsh smile of no humor curled his mouth. "I am Sir Hugh, last of Valbeau in Normandy but now Wroxton Castle's guard captain." Clearly the lad was torn between his own fear and the need to prove himself worthy to be the leader of terrified companions by showing himself able to bravely face a new danger. "But who are you and what excuse have you for your cruelty?"

"I'm Thad, the ironworker's son. And you can't chastise me for doin' what the priest says ought rightly be done t'every witch," the urchin belligerently defended his action.

"What?" Hugh's brow settled into the same dark scowl that had struck terror into many a strong man's heart. "A priest told you to assault an unprotected maid?"

"Aye! Father Padric says the only way t'be rid of such wicked ones is t'burn them or, if'n that fails, t'stone them." The boy glared at the woman, thankful for the excuse to look away from the fearsome knight still restraining him. "Already she has survived fire. Means stoning is the only way for us t'be rid of her."

Hugh glanced toward the pitiful figure to find light

green eyes peeking at him through the shield of widespread fingers while a curtain of pale brown hair near hid the rest of her face. "She doesn't look capable of being a danger to anyone. And even less of being a creature possessing the mighty powers of a witch."

" 'Tis only the false face she dons t'fool you." Despite his own perilous position, Thad sarcastically answered this man plainly too thick witted to ken the depth of a witch's evil ways. "Witches can make anything into another thing entirely, you know. And in a blink they can change themselves t'trick a person."

"If what you claim is a truth, then it proves what you say of her is false." A coldly smiling Hugh turned the boy's logic back on him. "Were the maid a mistress of such powers, she'd surely have turned your stones into harmless flowers and you into a slimy toad."

"Must be a witch!" Thad heatedly defended his earnest belief and with the fervor of a proselytizing monk produced a final, irrefutable proof. "She's got the mark of the devil on her cheek plain as plain can be. 'Tis a sign she can't hide and a dark warning t'us all."

Still holding tight to the boy with one hand, Hugh reached down his other to help the abused and wary maid stand.

A reluctant Eve gazed apprehensively first at the open hand and then up into his encouraging smile. Though quaking with fear, she gave into his care fingers that looked all the smaller for the size of the palm into which she entrusted them. Rising, she stood defenseless before him. Eve looked like some wild bird on the verge of taking flight, but she remained steady even when a huge but amazingly gentle hand reached out to brush aside the swathe of hair ever used to conceal a ghastly blemish.

Despite Hugh's long training in the skill of quelling emotion, he was touched by the single tear laying a silver path down a creamy satin cheek viciously marred. A tide of rose shame brightened the abused cheek, leaving the circled five-point star even more apparent. But Hugh had seen enough of scars left by battle wounds to be certain than a dagger wielded by human hands had carved that emblem.

With deceptive restraint Hugh turned and softly snarled at the boy. "The devil deals in stealing souls, not scarring flesh. It was a human fiend who did this to her. And it's that wretch who ought to pay for his foul deed, not her. She has suffered enough."

To ensure complete attention, Hugh lightly shook the boy before issuing his own warning. "Hereafter leave her in peace or face a wrath rightly to be feared—*my* wrath."

As the last two words rumbled forth, Hugh pushed his half-sized captive away. Thad was certain he'd done enough to earn his companions' admiration and lost no moment in leading their escape.

Convinced the boy would think twice before committing any further such wrong, Hugh bent his full attention upon the still trembling maid.

Eve anxiously eyed her massive defender standing motionless, unthreatening within an arm's distance. Her dealings with all humankind, save Elysia, had taught her how brutal and untrustworthy they were. After spending near half her years surviving alone in the wild, Eve had earned a level of courage and confidence unknown to most women. However, the previous year she'd found endless fears upon returning to the world of man.

Under the steady gaze of this stranger, imposing yet the source of unexpected compassion, Eve gathered together the courage nearly destroyed by the mistreatment of many to whisper "Thank you."

In response to the simple statement, Hugh's stern mouth once more softened into a smile. Again, he saw her as some shy, untamed creature, skittish at any hint of danger. While he still held her fingers in one hand, slowly so as not to alarm her, he lightly traced the circle of her scar with his other forefinger.

"Who did this to you? And how was it that no one was there to protect you?"

"I remember little for certain sure . . ." Green eyes darkened with a wordless and confused plea for belief and release. When he continued to clasp her hand, she struggled to disclose one further memory from the tiny store she had of the ghastly event. " 'Twas there after the fire wherein my mother and father perished."

A slight frown returned to furrow thick black brows. How could anyone fail to remember so vile a moment in their life?

Eve shrank from the abruptly glowering man. Would he, too, now blame her for the deadly fire?

Quick to realize his hostile expression was the source of the maid's alarm, Hugh attempted to atone for having unintentionally driven her into retreat by giving the timid maid another gentle smile. But hoping to learn one thing more without deepening her distress, he quietly asked a further question.

"How old were you when it happened?"

Feeling trapped by endless questions, a stricken Eve

gave a slight shrug. She'd already told him her memories were scant and to this stranger refused to confess herself unable to tell which scenes were memories and which were from the night terrors that constantly haunted her sleep.

Unmindful of the bucket left behind empty, she fled from the huge, gentle man and his painful questions.

Hugh rued the skittish maid's inability to identify the person responsible for the harm done her. Although they'd only just met, he found himself host to a fervent desire to find and make the vile toad pay a high price for his wrong.

Chapter 4

*M*ark! Tarry a moment." After hailing his leader, Hugh hurried to where the man had halted with a foot on the bottom step of the stairway leading up to the castle's entry.

Mark turned a questioning frown toward the friend he'd dispatched at dawn to lead a small force in checking the status of Wroxton's outlying farms. Though the sun had reached its day's zenith, he was surprised to see Hugh so soon returned.

"Don't look at me with such disgust." Hugh gave a short bark of laughter. "I left trusted men to finish the assigned task and only hastened back to report on findings of interest already uncovered before your meeting with village leaders begins."

Mark had faith in Hugh's judgment. If the man thought his news would be useful, then it likely would be. A fact that did not keep him from responding with feigned amazement, " 'Struth, it must be news of great import to make one as dutiful as you break off amidst an incomplete chore for the sake of delivering it immediately."

Hugh's smile became something nearer to a grimace. He wouldn't shock the friend who knew him so well by admitting that he'd have arrived even sooner but for the delay caused by his encounter with three boys and a mistreated maid.

Impatient to reach the great hall and prepare for the soon coming meeting, Mark allowed it to show.

Realizing stray thoughts of the timid maid had caused further delay, Hugh dove directly into his report. "No matter who I spoke with or how many words were said, at core lay the truth that their lord had little to do with Wroxton's management."

Hugh had spoken the truth, but he recognized the difficulty Mark would have in believing such a statement when men blessed with lands, whether by virtue of birth or might, rarely failed to maintain tight control over them. To validate his statement, he gave a brief account of the facts learned in his morning's work. He told of how an inordinate percentage of the previous year's crops was taken; of how animals needed for work were hauled away for slaughter; and, worst, of a tax so burdensome it could only weigh on the people so heavily it must threaten their ability to survive.

"But, despite the decline which Lord Aldreth's abdication of duty wrought on their lives," Hugh drew his report to a close, "the people of Wroxton seem to have held him in affection—as if he were some aging, absent-minded uncle."

Mark stared blindly at a point beyond Hugh's shoulder. There had to be more to the tale than yet told. "How is it that the people failed to protest—loudly?"

"Aye," Hugh nodded. "That's the crux of the matter. Lord Aldreth was good to them when their needs came to his attention. However, it seems the man gradually withdrew and became absorbed in other interests, allowing his much resented seneschal to have ever greater success in preventing such meetings. And after the lord's death, that seneschal took unchecked control of the fiefdom."

"Who is this seneschal?" While asking, Mark wondered what could possibly hold any lord's attention so completely that he failed to notice the declining state of his patrimony. It was a matter that bore looking into, but only after good headway had been made in correcting the ills Lord Aldreth's distraction had wrought.

"The man's name is Dunstan Buchard." Hugh was pleased that he'd had the foresight to have a quick answer for this question.

"Is this Dunstan among those we took captive yesterday?" Mark began mentally sifting through plans for dealing with the greedy man.

Hugh tugged at the short curls of his beard. He rued the fact that he hadn't an equally ready answer for this question. "I've asked after the man, but no one seems to have seen him since yestermorn."

"Find Dunstan," Mark's deep voice went silky. "And if possible, have him brought before me in the great hall while the village leaders are still gathered there."

Hugh was inspired by the sardonic gleam in Mark's eye to expend twice the energy to find the man.

As Mark continued up the steep stairway, through an open doorway, down a hallway through thick stone wall, and into the great hall, he pondered the further implications of Hugh's information. The villagers might have had more opportunity for access to their lord and thus have achieved better treatment while he lived, but they would certainly have been aware of the woes of those outside city walls. And after their lord's death, likely the seneschal had treated them with equal avarice.

The houseserfs had nearly finished clearing the vast room of benches and trestle tables set out for the meal past. Mark made his way to the high table permanently in place on the dais and took his seat at its center to await those he'd summoned. It was a youth found laboring to haul firewood into the hall that he'd dispatched to call village leaders for a meeting with Wroxton's new lord. His choice of messenger had been made with the certainty that the boy would know better than any new arrival who was meant by the term *village leader*.

Gazing absently into the shadows beyond the arch where a corner stairway began, Mark thought of the vision he'd caught of a dainty figure moving through predawn mists. Despite a late night, he'd risen early to see his men set off on their survey of the demesne. He had climbed to the parapet walkway to watch them fan out only to find his purpose foiled by dense fog. Nonetheless, he'd walked from above the front gate to a point halfway around the bailey where another stairway would lead down near the castle's postern door. It was as he rounded the sweeping corner at the back end that he'd briefly glimpsed Elysia.

One moment she'd been there, the next she seemed to have been swallowed into drifting vapors. He wanted to know what had awakened and called Wroxton's lady out into the chill air so early. Having come to this fiefdom to uncover traitors and their plots, Mark viewed Elysia's furtive actions with just suspicion. But as the first step in what type of misdeed? One merely against an unsought spouse. Or as treason to a king?

"My lord." A lanky man with a mouth full of inordinately large teeth called yet again. He'd attempted thrice before to summon the man's attention. Losing patience, he no longer tried to keep irritation from his voice.

Mark's attention abruptly focused on the speaker who fell back from the unexpected power of a silver gaze suddenly bent upon him. He shared the villagers' irritation over the wrongful bemusement that had prevented him from being immediately aware of their arrival. Self-mockery whispered this was another wrong to lay at Lady Elysia's door.

Rising to stand tall and meet their measuring gaze, Mark turned his thoughts to his goals for this gathering. All of which would be best begun with an exchange of simple facts.

"I am Sir Mark, Lord of Valbeau." This mention of Valbeau was meant to show he was accustomed to lordship and well able to take command of their lands. "I have been given the wardship of your lady and control of all Wroxton.

"Now, tell me who you are and what position each of you holds in the village." The fact that these men wore much patched homespun to an important meeting with a new lord went far in support of Hugh's report of the people's poverty.

"I am Jasper, the miller." The man who'd called for Mark's attention spoke first. While waiting Jasper had scrutinized the famous warrior who was the hero of a tale whispered throughout the village the past evening. It was the story of how the Black Wolf had soundly defeated those sent to prevent his coming. Because this man's opponents had all come from the ranks of unruly guardsmen who'd earned the hatred of the villagers, Jasper and his companions had arrived, wary but willing to give him a fair hearing.

"I am Osbert." A burly man with an unruly thatch of drab brown hair immediately spoke to show himself the equal of Jasper. "And the ironworker."

"Both are trades of great importance on any demesne." Mark nodded as sign of his willingness to give them their due respect. But he took note that the two men stood shoulder to shoulder—doubtless the sign of a rivalry and something that bore watching. Petty jealousies were too oft manipulated to meet a foe's unpleasant goals.

Accepting the lord's acknowledgment of their worth, both men took turns to present the four standing a pace behind. No sooner had the last been introduced than Osbert, plainly host to little of either patience or tact, demanded their new master explain one of the first things he'd told them.

"You say you've been made Lady Elysia's guardian? Only that? Have you not come to wed with our lady?"

The brash question earned a mocking smile from Mark. He liked the man whose forthrightness was unlikely to host the talents of a sly traitor. But Mark suspected that neither his trust nor his loyalty would be easily won although unwavering once given.

Mark gave an answer as direct as the question. "King Henry granted me the choice of either wedding with the maid and thus permanently becoming lord of Wroxton, or I may merely hold both the lady and her lands in my ward for a time."

With the easy confidence of one tested and proven worthy, Mark maintained an enigmatic smile and stood steady before the critical appraisal of the six men.

"From my guardsmen returned after speaking with those on the farms and in the hamlets of Wroxton, I've learned of unreasonable taxes, wrongful seizures, and other practices harmful to the fiefdom's health. To improve its strength, I will investigate further and make needful changes."

Mark was near certain that the seneschal, allowed to satisfy personal greed without his lord's restraining hold, had taken for himself the majority of monies and goods demanded from serf and freeholder alike. Thus, he felt one sweeping change must be made immediately.

"Today I begin the task by halving your taxes." He'd yet to see the records, but the taxes demanded were so far beyond what was necessary to meet normal needs, Mark was confident this action would not harm the beast he sought to cure.

The villagers greeted the welcome news with broad smiles although they were tinged with skepticism. Their leeriness of unjustified hopes seemed proven wise when a shrill voice pierced the air.

"That you dare not do!" Two members of the guard had roughly escorted the speaker from his hiding place in a shed beside the stable and into the hall in time to hear Mark's decree. He broke free to rush forward and shoulder his way through the small group facing the dais. "I won't permit such a foolish deed!"

"You are wrong, Dunstan Buchard." Mark had no doubt of the man's identity. Only one who'd treated Wroxton as his own would dare such a foolish challenge. Remaining relaxed, although gray eyes glittered dangerously, Mark took an unnervingly slow tour of the portly figure below. Despite straw caught in fine woolen garb and wildly mussed iron-gray hair, the man's stance was arrogant and his head tilted to an impossible angle in his effort to look down a prominent nose at his protagonist. His attitude left Mark to wonder if Dunstan were somehow unaware of all that had transpired in the past day. Surely the fool who'd hidden himself couldn't think to proclaim himself the master of Wroxton? Mark soon smothered any such delusion.

"You have no power to prevent it."

Convinced of his own importance, Dunstan refused to easily yield. With hands primly folded over a well-fed belly, he countered, "Your king will surely find treachery in your decision to cut by half the duty owed and thus his income from Wroxton."

"Ah, but the king has received only a small part of the taxes you collected. Thus, I've no doubt I'll be able to send him a larger amount and still not leave the demesne as short of all it needs as you've left it while lining your own pockets with ill-got goods." Asides, Mark knew Henry would gladly accept less if in return he earned the loyalty of lands much needed to block one source of danger in a possible invasion.

Rather than sputter hopeless defenses like a fool, Dunstan stood silent with hands tightly clenched. He tamed an instinct to pack his belongings and storm off to seek refuge and support from a cohort at Kelby Keep. Such an action would make the goal they sought more difficult to attain. No matter the cost, he must remain within Wroxton's walls. Dunstan was disconcerted when the Black Wolf's next words proved the man might as well have read his mind.

"The question is less what Henry might in future do if finding wrong in my choices and more what I will do this day about a man so ready to steal from both his overlord and his king."

Mark recalled Henry's talk of the greater ease in dealing with traitors unmasked and took a long, penetrating survey of the one standing utterly bared before him. Assuredly, he would be justified in consigning the man to the dungeon or exiling him from Wroxton. Yet the latter would only make it harder to keep track of his dangerous actions and the former would hobble a potential guide down the likely convoluted trail to the spider at the center of a web of treachery.

"I will seize all that you possess save for two changes of garb and your steed, mail, favorite sword, and dagger. All else will be reapportioned to those from whom so much has been taken by you."

The village leaders watched with growing approval and cautious hope that this lord's word would prove an honorable thing. But their trust was not so easily won. They knew little of Lord Mark. Although men of his station on the whole might willingly spill their life's blood to keep an oath made to a fellow noble, seldom would they hold their word to a common man as dear. They could but watch and wait to see the truth of this famous warrior.

While Dunstan's face grew ruddier, Mark closed his judgment upon him. "You have the choice either to forever leave both Wroxton and England to return to your family in Normandy or remain as mere guardsman, subject to the command of either me or my guard captain, Sir Hugh."

Despite the glee many a guardsman would derive in retaliating for his every slight over near a decade, Dunstan had no choice but to remain and submit to the humiliation.

Mark watched the man struggle with an unwelcome option. He agreed with the king in strongly suspecting one powerful, cruel, and treacherous man who'd dishonored every oath ever made. And it would be foolish to waste so obvious a possible trail to him as Dunstan provided. To do elsewise would also make more difficult the forestalling of further and more dangerous actions. Nay, Mark silently reaffirmed his decision, his intents would be best served by stripping Dunstan of all honor but leaving him to act as an inadvertent Judas.

The next moment Dunstan's disgust overcame his craven nature. He leapt onto the dais, snatched up the lord's crockery mug, and tossed its contents into the man's face. Fervently hoping the liquid was wine and that it would burn Lord Mark's eyes, Dunstan made a mad dash toward a door in the wall built directly behind the dais. The wall closed off a strip of the castle's lowest level to form a private solar for the lord's family.

Dunstan's action won a startling response from the lord assaulted. Despite the spring water running down his face and soaking his tunic, Mark's dark head fell back while rich, deep laughter echoed against the hall's stone walls.

"Who did this to you?" Setting a bright-hued bundle aside in her lap, Elysia took a thin, badly bruised forearm into her firm but gentle hold. Eve had come to the family solar to deliver a requested skein of silk thread. Without experience of other castles where no such chamber existed, Elysia took for granted the privacy of this room.

Eve gave a brief shake to thick, straight hair and bit her lip, unwilling to share yet another example of others' hateful resentment of her. Though never would she speak it aloud, she feared unrelenting resistance to her company would end with her again being exiled to fight alone for existence in the forest.

"Evie, be calm." Elysia recognized the wild panic in green eyes and released the injured arm to lightly squeeze the girl's hand in comfort. "Surely, I've proven myself worthy of your trust?"

In answer, a soft smile warmed Eve's winsome face.

While maintaining a reassuring expression for Eve's sake, Elysia's temper simmered. With each such example of the unyielding intolerance of Wroxton's people overflowing into violence against one innocent of wrong, her temper burned higher. She struggled to banish ire from her voice for fear of further upsetting the much abused maid before saying, "You know I can do little to put a halt to such wickedness if you refuse to tell me its source."

"The big, dark stranger already terrified the boys who hurt me into fleeing," Eve promptly responded, shy smile blooming.

"What?" Elysia's head abruptly lifted, and dusky curls that escaped from her braids' inadequate restraint caught the late afternoon light falling through a long, narrow arrowslit.

Eve saw the other woman's face cloud and thought the blame lay in an inability to speak her meaning plainly after years without talking with another human. "The man warned them that he'd punish them for more."

"The Black Wolf stopped their misdeed?" Elysia was stunned by the prospect.

"Nay!" Green eyes widened. " 'Twas the other one."

"The other one?" Elysia had no notion of whom Eve spoke and saw that lack as a further demonstration of the disruptive effect the Black Wolf had on her rational thinking. His ability to so completely hold her attention that she failed to truly notice any of his companions was an appalling fact, one that stoked her temper to a brighter flame.

"Aye." Eve was too caught in her memories of an unexpected defender to be aware of her friend's discovery and shared a small bit of kitchen gossip overheard. "The one Lord Mark named captain of Wroxton's guard."

Knowing neither of the appointment nor of to whom the position was given, Elysia was puzzled. She opened her lips to seek more information, but the solar door burst open and a furious Dunstan stomped inside.

"Lady Elysia, you must do something! Halt that bumptious toad's actions else he'll see Wroxton's bounty reduced to famine and you made a pauper on your own lands!"

"What?" Elysia rose, and the small tapestry already lying unnoticed in her lap drifted to the rush-covered floor. "Tell me what's happened to leave you so overwrought?"

"He'll ruin all that I've spent a decade creating." With little grace Dunstan dropped his ungainly body to one knee while extending joined hands in a plea toward his lady. "I beg you to intercede."

Elysia motioned him into silence. "Tell me what he has done."

Without need for thought, she knew precisely who Dunstan meant by the term *bumptious toad*. She had paid little heed to indistinct sounds of the Black Wolf's voice coming from beyond the wall. Elysia knew he'd been meeting with village leaders, but as a woman's ability to publicly interfere with decrees made by the king's representative was severely limited, she chose to remain in the solar rather than tempt her unruly temper before it was done. After his actions were known, she'd be free to work out a method to undo whatever ills he had wrought. She had congratulated herself for her wise control and logical plan, both of which proved useless when confronted with Dunstan's wild plea.

"Exactly what has Lord Mark done?"

"He's deeply slashed the taxes!" Dunstan fumed,

looking near to exploding. "And he threatens to make even more sweeping changes."

Elysia frowned, annoyed with herself for knowing too little of such matters. Her father, a much learned man, had taught her to read and love books near as much as he. But he'd seen no reason to teach a daughter how to conduct duties best left to men. Lord Aldreth had been satisfied with Dunstan's management of Wroxton. And if her father had been, then Elysia believed it behooved her to do the same. That meant that the *bumptious toad* must be stopped!

Dunstan misinterpreted Elysia's frown. "Don't you see. By cutting the tax levied, he makes it near impossible to send the king the monies demanded. And the king can call Wroxton forfeit to the crown. Mayhap that's the wretch's plan?"

Elysia understood this logic and it infuriated her. Stop the Black Wolf before he could rob her of Wroxton? That she assuredly would!

Chapter 5

Mark rose from the high table and stepped down from the dais. Village leaders had departed, leaving him free to climb to his chamber and find a dry tunic to replace the one Dunstan had soaked. He left the great hall to the swarm of houseserfs delayed in preparing the large room for the day's next meal by his meeting. As he moved through the archway to where stone steps began spiraling upward a quiet voice called him to a halt.

"Lord Mark—" Ida spoke from shadows on one side of the opening. From this dim-lit haven she had listened to his speech and peeked around the corner to watch Dunstan act the fool. "I beg a moment of your time."

Surprised, Mark turned toward the agitated woman. He'd caught a brief glimpse of her while he stripped the seneschal of his proud position. Had she some relationship with the man that she was so clearly bothered?

"I fear this is as private a place as we are like to find so late of an afternoon." Mark waved at the gloom all about them. Despite Elysia's visit the past night, it was not his habit to invite wellborn women to enter his chamber alone—leastways not one of Ida's age and virtue.

Ida wrung her hands together, struggling to frame an earnest defense and ruing more than ever her lack of a glib tongue.

"Lord Aldreth was a good man," Ida got out at last. Expecting a plea on Dunstan's behalf, this raising of the former lord's specter caught Mark momentarily unprepared. Yet only a slight lift of dark brows betrayed that fact and for but an instant so quickly past that Ida saw only his nod of encouragement for her to continue.

"Pray don't think ill of Aldreth." Ida gulped, knowing she'd made a poor start. And even though beyond the initial block of a weak beginning, the pace of her following words was near as halting. "He was a much learned man ... a caring lord and a loving father."

Having lived amidst a royal court since boyhood, Mark had years of experience in surviving court intrigues and by that training was alert to subtle nuances. Thus, he took note that Ida spoke of the former lord by his given name rather than his title. Was such easy familiarity merely the product of long service to the man? It was possible—but unlikely.

Mark's cynicism showed in his next question. "How could a gentle, *caring* man allow his people to fall into misery?"

Drawing her plump frame to its full if diminutive height, Ida found courage in roundly championing the honor of a man no longer able to speak for himself. "Lord Aldreth has been gone two years and cannot be blamed for Wroxton's decline."

A mocking smile curled Mark's lips. This woman reminded him of an indignant hen, feathers ruffled in defense of her chicks, but he could only admire her loyalty.

"I've no doubt the damage has increased since his passing, but to be in its current impoverished state it must've begun before Lord Aldreth's death."

Ida's hands renewed their wringing. In decades of watching Dunstan she had seen little about him to admire but in this moment wished for his easy words and ability to spout believable excuses. And then Ida remembered that when standing before this man, even Dunstan had failed. With that disheartening thought, she embarked on an awkward speech.

"I pray you will believe it was as a consequence of love that Wroxton's downward slide began."

Dark brows arching over penetrating gray eyes made a verbal request for explanation unnecessary.

"Lord Aldreth loved Lady Anne with the whole of his loyal heart." Ida gazed directly into solemn gray eyes for assurance that Lord Mark continued to listen closely. Taking a deep breath, she added, "But Lady Anne loved God more."

Again, dark brows rose in an unspoken query.

"She was an acolyte in a nunnery when her father agreed to formalize an alliance between himself and Lord Aldreth with a union between the English lord and his youngest daughter—Anne."

"The bride was a nun?" Although removing from holy orders for secular gain the children promised in service to God was done (at the price of a sizable offering), it was uncommon enough to cause surprise.

"Simply a postulant who had yet to take final vows." Ida's feathers were clearly ruffled again. "Thus the way was clear for her to marry." She paused and peered at the man to be certain he understood the significant difference between a *nun* and a *postulant*, but his face was unreadable. "I accompanied the bride from Normandy and lingered to stand as companion in a foreign land."

"But how did Lord Aldreth's love for his wife end in Wroxton's decline?" Mark appreciated learning this background of the former lord but standing in the chill stone stairwell in a soaked tunic was not the time he'd have chose to hear it.

"By the time Elysia was born, Aldreth knew the depth of her commitment and gave his beloved wife the gift she wanted most. He permitted her return to the nunnery of St. Marie de Alcun in Normandy." Ida spread pudgy hands wide. "And there she lives today."

"She is still alive?" Few things truly startled Mark, but this news did.

"Oh, aye." Ida nodded her head so fervently her headcloth was in danger of slipping off. "Anne thrives within those hallowed walls."

Mark tamed his surprise and shifted his attention back to the yet unanswered question. "But that in itself provides no reason for Wroxton's decline."

"After allowing Anne's departure, bereft of his much loved wife, Aldreth sank ever deeper into treasured books. And, believing Dunstan capable, he happily left the management of Wroxton in his seneschal's hands, asking only for sufficient income to purchase new texts."

"He spent all of his time reading books?" Having seen too much of treachery within court circles, Mark early had seen the wisdom of being able to read any document before affixing his seal to it. And after learning to read writs had come the joy of books. But never to the exclusion of far more important realities.

"Not reading alone." Ida shook her head as earnestly as she had earlier nodded it. "Lord Aldreth gloried in the time-consuming chore of translating Greek and Latin texts into our native tongue."

Mark was impressed. Although a few wellborn men saw the wisdom of learning to read, most nobles refused to waste the time required and preferred to leave such sedentary pursuits to monks and scribes while they honed their skills for war or the hunt. Aye, some lords could read and write, but never before had Mark heard of one capable enough to attempt translating—and in not one but two foreign languages.

Pleased by the man's honest admiration, Ida fair glowed while adding, "Aldreth was working on a beautifully illuminated Psalter as a gift for Anne's convent when he died." She continued with a tentative offer, "I have it if you would care to examine his fine work."

"Then Lord Aldreth was unable to finish the Psalter in time for Lady Anne to receive that final gift from her husband?"

Ida mournfully shook her head. "But his death provided Anne with a gift of infinitely more value to her than all the others."

Mark's unhidden curiosity prompted Ida to tell the

rest. "Aldreth's death freed her to take the veil at long last. It was Anne's most fervent prayer that she be allowed that boon before her own life reaches its end."

"They remained wed until death put an end to their union?" In learning of Anne's departure, Mark had wondered about the position of their marriage and by that the status of the maid he'd been offered as bride. Henry, his friend and monarch, was the son of the famous William the Bastard who had conquered all England and thus was not one to hold an unsanctioned birth against anyone. It was a trait Mark had reason to appreciate but one shared by all too few.

"Of a certainty." Ida looked shocked at the notion that he could think otherwise. "They both loved their daughter far too much to see her birth stained and position weakened by an annulment."

Mark's smile was wry, yet it warmed his eyes. Lord Aldreth, by choosing to live a lonely life rather than besmirching his daughter's name, earned more of Mark's respect than most living men would ever hold. Mark was intimately familiar with the consequences of such ill deeds. His own father, for the sake of freeing himself to wed a Norman heiress and sire pure Norman sons, had broken a bond wrought by ancient rites with a Saxon woman. The sundering of that bond had left Mark burdened with the title *bastard-born*.

Aye, in putting consideration of his daughter's future first, Lord Aldreth had acted with an honor few men of Mark's acquaintance could claim. And yet, in Mark's eyes, even that could not excuse the man's mistreatment of his fiefdom. Only did it give Mark a better understanding of Lord Aldreth's character and a hint of why, in spite of his lacks, the people of Wroxton thought so much of him.

Praying she was right in sensing a softening in her companion, Ida added further justification for holding him in honorable esteem. "Aldreth was good to his people and fair in his judgments."

"I've been told much of the good will in which his people held him." Mark nodded, but his face was an expressionless mask. He meant to say no more on this subject. The past lord's habits were of little matter to what must now be done to restore health to the fiefdom. That was a chore to which he must soon return as he intended to personally oversee the reclaiming from Dunstan's chamber of as much as possible of what the man had stolen.

Yet, despite impatience to escape and change into dry garb before taking up the task, Mark chose to tarry a moment longer. He couldn't let pass this opportunity to delve into the curious matter roused with Ida's first words and made more interesting by what he'd learned since.

"Why when Lady Anne returned to Normandy, did you stay at Wroxton?"

Caught unprepared for a question that sensitive emotions heard as a slight on her motives, Ida again straightened and lifted the first of several chins with pride. "To care for Lady Anne's daughter, of course."

Mark slowly nodded. It was a worthy excuse, but after her fervent defense of Lord Aldreth, he believed a deeper purpose lay beyond the easily accepted excuse. "And, good mother, were you never wed?"

"I'm a widow twice over!" Thoroughly affronted by

the unspoken implication, Ida looked even more the irritated hen with feathers ruffled.

Wielding his potent smile to its fullest effect, Mark wordlessly calmed the woman's indignation. He had been told that the boy who'd made a wild attack before throwing himself from a window was her son. It was a leap he'd have sworn must end in death and yet no body had been found. The boy might have been carried out to sea or ... Mark's lips tilted into cynicism. That neither this mother nor Elysia had asked after the results of the search for him, Mark deemed nearly a confirmation of what he'd early supposed.

"Never would I have demanded from your son so high a price for his misdeed as he chose to pay." A steady silver gaze accompanied words whose truth was reinforced by an utter lack of emphasis.

Ida backed up, horrified that the target of Jamie's foolishly gallant assault had learned the boy was her son. Yet an unbidden gleam of desperate hope flickered in her eyes.

"Were the boy to enter the castle now," Mark responded to the woman's obvious wish to believe, "my judgment of him would be shaded by the knowledge that his attempt on me was born of an honorable intent."

With that oblique statement, Mark turned and began climbing the steps to his own chamber.

Mark withdrew a dry tunic from the chest to which his meager supply of clothing had been assigned only hours past. As a warrior and royal champion and even though lord of Valbeau in Normandy, he'd spent most of his life traveling from place to place. Thus he had learned to make do with a few carefully selected items. He shed the tunic Dunstan had soaked and was pulling one of dark crimson on when the door behind opened and then closed with a decided thud. Sensing the fiery presence behind, Mark slowly turned to meet eyes burning bright gold. The tunic settled unfastened against bronzed skin.

"Welcome to my bedchamber ... again." Mark's mocking grin appeared. "It seems your habit to seek the company of men—in their bedchambers and alone."

Elysia had worked herself into a fury beyond bearing with the prospect of this man tricking her out of her patrimony. And that was surely what he intended by drastically reducing Wroxton's income and infuriating the king.

"I would follow you into bed—" Horror froze Elysia's face for an instant. What wicked imp had put that wretched word on her tongue? Quickly she sought to cover the faux pas. "Even into hell I would follow you were that the price demanded for you to recant the wicked decision to slash Wroxton's royal duty and drive Dunstan from his honorable position."

"To my *bed?*" Mark was not so easily diverted and dark laughter underscored his query as with slow grace he settled atop that structure. "Then come." He patted the coverlet to one side of a powerful thigh. "I vow to give your every word my closest attention."

Frustration increased by her own error, Elysia's hands curled into impotent fists that she firmly planted on slender hips. "You can't pretend you failed to hear the purpose I've already clearly stated."

Mark's smile settled into a devastating lure and his voice into an equally tempting purr. "A-a-ah, so I did."

Between potent smile and dark velvet voice, Elysia was overcome by a deep awareness of the man still sitting relaxed on the bed. It knocked her anger askew, forcing a fight to restore its flame.

"I won't permit the dismissal of Dunstan. He has performed his duties well for a decade and more. My father trusted him as I do now."

Black lashes descended until Mark's eyes became narrow slits of silver. "You keep saying I can't do something when it's a deed I've already done."

Frustrated temper came near to pushing Elysia into stomping her foot like some irritated toddling. As self-disgust for the childish urge stoked the fires of her anger higher, vivid spots of color glowed on each cheek.

"You would defend Dunstan?" The ice of Mark's eyes filled the reproachful question. "Are you so heartless that being lady of Wroxton matters only as the source of position and wealth?"

Cherry-bright lips opened to heatedly deny his hateful suggestion, but Mark forestalled Elysia's defense.

"How elsewise can you justify the misery into which Dunstan has driven *your* people?"

"You speak lies!" Elysia wished she could be positive that this was true as uncertainty weakened her claim. "The people of Wroxton are content."

"Are you sure? So sure you would swear an oath on that fact?" Dark brows arched in question while his cynical smile returned. "Have you recently visited their farms? Their hamlets?"

With no answer to give able to do more than lend credence to his argument, Elysia determinedly stood mute a mere two paces from the infuriating, seated man.

"With the morrow's dawn I will take you on a journey through the countryside," Mark flatly stated his intent, silently daring her to refuse. "There we'll both view the extent of the poverty and pain Dunstan's greed has brought upon Wroxton."

Elysia knew herself trapped into spending an uncomfortable, even perilous amount of time in the enticing man's company. Yet how could she allow herself to be seen as shirking the very duties he had accused her of ignoring. Nay, she was well and truly caught in the wolf's snare. Still, there was one task that couldn't be postponed.

"On the morrow," Elysia nodded. "But with the noontide hour, not the dawn."

"Because you prefer to sleep until then?" Mark mocked although fairly certain of the reason behind her proposed delay.

Through gritted teeth, a fuming Elysia tightly responded, "'Nay, because I *am* the lady of Wroxton and have other duties to be met."

When, of a sudden, the dangerous man rose to tower over her, Elysia took a step back. Unfortunately in the haste of that action, one foot caught the hem of her own gown. She would've fallen but for Mark's instinctive reflex in reaching out to catch and sweep her near.

"You're terrified of me." Honestly surprised by the fiery damsel's swift change from fury to apprehension,

Mark gazed down into widened eyes abruptly gone the deep brown of a hunted doe. "I wonder why?"

Elysia struggled to remain immobile within Mark's embrace—neither cringing from nor melting against his impressive strength. Never had her betrothed's nearness inspired such feelings. Indeed, rarely did Gervaise come this close, generally only in greeting or parting. The dark crimson tunic still open at Mark's throat held her gaze while she searched for a fitting rebuttal despite conflicting emotions.

"I swear that never have I taken a woman against her will. Or do you fear I might seduce you?" A stunningly intimate smile appeared. "I give you my oath that I won't."

Wrapped in his arms, Elysia was all too aware of powerful shoulders shrugging with apparent unconcern. Impotent fury nearly drowned the need to stroke fine-grained skin hollowed where throat met shoulders. She licked her lips, desperately fixing her gaze below his chin, willing him not to guess what emotions strove within.

"There's no need," Mark's words were a low rumble. "Not when I can claim you as bride and take you with the blessings of God and man."

The undeniable truth of that statement sent a strong tremor through Elysia.

"Ah, ha! That frightens you most of all." Mark gave a short laugh. Involuntarily one hand drew near her face; one finger slowly traced across the supple line of jaw and down an elegant throat. "Will it calm you to know I am not convinced of my readiness to give up freedom for you—or any woman. Thus, I'm no more certain of the wisdom in an alliance between us than

are you." In contradiction to words, his hand settled
to cradle the nape of her neck.

Elysia didn't know whether to be pleased or affronted. Mark saw her confusion, and it deepened
his amusement.

"No matter my decision on that point, I am determined to return Wroxton to prosperity before I let
you go . . . if I let you go."

With the words, he opened his arms, releasing her.
For an instant as the hand that cupped her neck fell
away, Elysia knew regret and an unbidden urge to
step close to him again. By fanning the embers of
her temper, Elysia struggled to reassemble shreds of
tattered pride and maintain a calm exterior while escaping from the Black Wolf's den.

Chapter 6

$\mathcal{B}$risk air stung bright color into Elysia's cheeks while she moved silently through the ground haze of another dawn. The greenwood's lush vegetation held tendrils of fog low to the ground, but they dissipated once she stepped beyond the last tree and through a barrier of bushes host to summer's abundant leaves.

Once standing two paces within an unexpected grassy glade amidst the woodland, Elysia gave a penitent smile to the dark-cloaked figure striding across the open area toward her. Even though a hood hid bright hair, she easily recognized her betrothed.

"I beg your understanding for being unable to meet you last eve," Elysia hastened to seek forgiveness from her betrothed. "I'd given a promise to Ida that had to be kept."

Jamie and Gervaise bore an unaccountable dislike for one another. For that reason Elysia hesitated to tell of the boy's foolishness and was even less willing to provide a detailed account of her true actions the past night.

Gervaise gave a regal nod as if he were the king and she a peasant come begging for alms. But then his eyes narrowed in disapproval of the glimpse of a bright red gown visible between the edges of her deep-gray cape.

"Leastways keep that gown covered. It stands out like a beacon."

"No matter," Elysia claimed despite the grimace with which she met his rebuke. "None of my people would question my going should they catch sight of me on the path here . . . not so long as I carry these." With an impish grin she lifted the bow in one hand and tilted the other shoulder to draw attention to the quiver slung over it.

Gervaise's frown deepened and it fanned the embers of Elysia's temper that had remained all too near the surface since her conflict with the Wolf.

"Asides"—gold sparks snapped in her eyes—"these are *my* lands and I am free to walk where I will."

"It's not your people we need to fear learning of our time together." Gervaise quietly remonstrated her outburst.

Feeling like a particularly slow-witted child chastised by a parent and recognizing the truth in his words, Elysia suffered pangs of remorse. She certainly ought to have been aware of that fact considering that she'd chosen the cherry dress for the sake of lending courage on the journey that the dark intruder had warned he meant to take her on later this day.

"I am sorry." It seemed woefully inadequate, yet a simple apology was the best response Elysia could find. "And promise to keep it hidden on the return journey."

Then, anxious to think there must be a further excuse for Gervaise's displeasure, Elysia chose to believe his ire roused, leastways in part, by her failure to answer his command. It would mean that although Gervaise often found reason for criticism, still he wanted to be with her. Clinging to that hope, she again repeated her regret for having been forced to postpone their meeting.

Gervaise shrugged. Her inability to meet him hours past had roused in him no emotion deeper than impatience for the delay her action might cause to his plan. That plan rather than any personal interest in the impetuous maid lay at the core of his relationship with her. Thus he immediately brushed aside her concerns to raise matters he deemed of far more import.

"What ill intents has the Black Wolf for Wroxton? Has he warned you of his plans?"

Accustomed to Gervaise's brusque dealings though Elysia was, his apparent indifference to how *she* was faring in the Black Wolf's company was disconcerting.

Seeing a faint frown appear between delicate brows, Gervaise recognized his blunder. As one who prided himself on sharp wits and a keen understanding of human nature, he was annoyed with himself for his misstep on so basic a path. He instantly sought to rectify the error.

"I fear Mark may do something to bring further woe upon *you.*" Gervaise took the bow from Elysia and let it fall, freeing her hands to be taken into his own. "Already Mark has asserted his foul intent to see our betrothal decreed invalid by his king."

As rarely had Gervaise made the first move to touch Elysia, this action went further to pacify her than any spoken word. Her smile nearly glowed. Even did she feel encouraged enough to lean closer, hoping for a kiss able to disprove Mark's claim that Gervaise was incapable of passion.

And a kiss Elysia received—one brief brush of chapped lips across her forehead quickly followed by further impersonal words.

"Although I've heard that the Wolf's men traveled the countryside during the day past, on my way to meet you here I saw no sign of harm done the people or the land."

Her hopes for securing proof of a more intimate concern having come to nothing, Elysia admitted defeat and took a step back. Under that action gleams from a rising sun peeking between drifting clouds rippled over the single thick braid falling from nape to below her waist.

Always she had thought her inability to rouse Gervaise's passions due to the honor in which he held her. Either that or, she feared, it might be a lack of physical appeal. But now the wretched intruder's critical opinion of Gervaise left her to wonder if the fault lay in her betrothed. It was an unpleasant, disloyal thought! And she earnestly attempted to thrust it into some shadowed corner of her mind, never to be considered again.

"I assume, then"—while a distracted Elysia glared at a tuft of harmless grass, Gervaise tentatively went on with matters that for his purposes must be addressed—"that Mark has done nothing to disturb the peace of either you or your fiefdom."

Gervaise's statement was not framed as a question but clearly was one. Though his voice seemed oddly distant, Elysia heard it and realized she had few options but to follow his lead. In truth, she welcomed the call from unpleasant possibilities.

"Radical changes have been made. And Mark has promised more to come." She unthinkingly followed Gervaise's lead in calling the man by his given name. Then, fearing her betrothed's disapproval, quickly bit her tongue only to discover he hadn't noticed.

Under Elysia's response, Gervaise's chin abruptly jerked up as if he'd been landed an unexpected blow. "What has he done?"

Dark head tilting to one side, Elysia curiously watched for Gervaise's reaction while answering. "He has stripped Dunstan of his position as seneschal and, with a declared intent to redistribute his wealth to the people, has reclaimed all the man possesses save for clothing, weapons, and a single horse."

This truly was a blow to Gervaise's scheme. But now better prepared for the worst, he stood unflinching. Although near certain he knew the answer, elsewise the man would surely have already fled to him at Kelby Keep, Gervaise asked a further important question: "Has Mark driven Dunstan from the fiefdom?"

"Nay." Elysia promptly responded. "Ida tells me that Dunstan was given the option to either depart or remain as a mere guardsman subject to the commands of either the new lord or his guard captain."

"And Dunstan chose to remain." With a tight smile, Gervaise nodded his certainty of this fact. Having long viewed Dunstan's greed as a sign of weak will, Gervaise had feared that when presented with a test the man would fail. Thankfully, by this action Dunstan had proven such misdoubts unjustified.

Elysia saw the gleam of a strange satisfaction in Gervaise's eyes. Suffering an inexplicable unease beneath it, she shifted from foot to foot.

Gervaise realized that he'd permitted thoughts of matters far beyond her sphere to dislodge the facade needed in his dealings with Elysia. But while this failure on his part was an unhappy fact, he was pleased that corrective deeds would also lend the opportunity to take a first step in furthering his plan to see Mark's interference undone.

"If we are to marry"—Gervaise forced an expression of deep concern to his stern features—"we must find some method to free ourselves of the barrier Mark would lower between us."

Abruptly the center of Gervaise's full attention, Elysia's brown eyes flew wide. At long last, he had come around to more personal matters. But in his view was their union truly that . . . or merely a business transaction? She had a new and uncomfortable suspicion that he deemed their marriage merely the unpleasant price to be paid for some goal fervently besought.

Elysia gave her head a sharp shake to dislodge traitorous thoughts that she told herself must be part of a false trail laid by the Black Wolf to lead her astray.

To hide surely wrongful doubts from Gervaise, Elysia gave a blindingly bright smile and with overdone earnestness said, "Only tell me what I must do to see it so."

Gratified by her prompt surrender to his logic, Gervaise returned her smile with one of unalloyed approval. "I must think on the problem. But now that I know what has passed at the castle, I'll find a way and as oft as possible will come to this glade at dawn. Meet me whenever you can safely win free of curious eyes."

With that command and another squeeze of the small hands still in his hold, Gervaise strode away, glad for the liberty to shift his thoughts to a message that must immediately be sent. Though he needed to know what plans Mark had laid with his king, Gervaise could see that only time and well-placed spies would tell. But would it come soon enough? And would his implacable leader in the greater scheme be as patient?

Elysia was host to a confusion she found disgusting as she watched Gervaise disappear. She then retrieved the fallen bow and turned down a path leading to the castle and the dangerous man waiting for her there. With each step over the same track of crushed grass and broken twigs she'd laid in coming, the image of the dark man grew more vivid and roused more qualms.

All during the hours of early morn while the two met and talked, neither had been aware of another cloaked figure obscured by forest shadows and mists but closely watching.

Mark sat relaxed in the chair below the window of his bedchamber and rested one arm on the chest beside while gazing up as his young squire told of what he'd learned in twice fulfilling a task given him.

Nearly a decade past Mark had taken with him to Normandy both his half brother, Alan, and the Welsh boy, David. There the boys were fostered in Henry's court. Upon their father's death a year earlier, Alan had returned to Castle Radwell as its lord and taken his friend Sir David home with him.

But that had not been the end of such deeds for Mark. It had become his practice to see that other boys from both Radwell and the neighboring Welsh princedom of Cymer were accepted for fostering under Henry's now royal patronage. It was a much besought boon that provided a fine beginning for any knight. Moreover, Mark had made it his habit to choose one of their number to serve for a time as his squire, most recently a young cousin of the first David who bore the same name.

Mark had offered this David the honor after finding that from childhood to young manhood he'd continued to be reliable, good-hearted, and brave. With those traits to recommend him, a day gone by Mark had even entrusted the sixteen-year-old with a serious and confidential duty, one that the youth had welcomes with pride for having earned such trust from the man he most admired.

"Last eve after following Lady Elysia through a thick twilight fog, I waited in shadows until I heard a door creak shut. And then I waited even longer—for a full, slow count of fifty." With this recounting of his exciting adventure, David's bright blue eyes glowed with all the glee of a childhood only recently left behind.

Mark made appropriate encouraging sounds of interest to gently prod the boy onward.

"Next I followed the damsel's path to the wall through which she disappeared and found the hidden door." David continued with a solemn nod that set many tight black curls bouncing against his forehead.

"It was a puzzle not easily solved, but I figured out how to open the portal . . . and found a fearsome sight! Lady Elysia must have magical powers as a single step beyond the door and any mortal would drop straight into the sea—a *long* way down." Thickly lashed eyes widened with remembered awe. " 'Struth, I swear it!''

"Plainly a magical deed." Mark wryly agreed but in the next instant the ever cheery youth's sudden earnestness won the flash of a white smile.

David was clearly affronted by his master's smile, and Mark rued the instinctive mockery he'd not meant as an assault upon the adolescent's tender pride.

"Nay, do not be offended. I only jest *with* you. And I promise that I, too, wondered what mystical spells the lady might wield when I first caught a glimpse of a similar vision of her slipping through fog and sheer stone—only a few hours earlier than you." Mark's eyes darkened to a solemn gray as they met others of bright blue. "But after time to ponder the matter, I came to suspect the existence of a postern door through the wall."

"A postern door there?" David scowled at what seemed to him a foolish thing. "Of what use is a door that opens to the sea a great distance below?"

Mark steadily met the boy's skeptical gaze. "With a later investigation I think we'll find a path carved into the cliff's face, one able to assure that any members of the lord's family forced into escaping would safely reach the shore."

David stubbornly remained dubious, holding back

the disappointment in hearing so mundane an explanation for his exciting discovery.

"But, David, on entering my chamber, you said you'd two events to report." Mark gently urged David to continue. Little time remained before he must take the subject of their talk on the journey through the demesne that he had promised, though doubtless Elysia had heard it as a threat.

"Aye." Black curls once more danced as David nodded although with considerably less fervor. "As you suggested, this morn before light brightened the eastern horizon I settled myself to wait concealed in a dark corner at the stairwell's bottom. And again Lady Elysia slipped down the steps and out of the castle."

"You followed her?" Mark's words were less a question than a confirmation of trust.

"Aye, from the castle and through the forest to a small hidden glade some distance away that I'd never elsewise have discovered."

"Was there someone there to meet her?"

David instantly nodded. "Awaiting her was the red-haired man who departed this castle with such haste not long after we arrived here." David shifted awkwardly from one foot to another before adding, "But I couldn't get near enough to hear what they said." The youth confessed this much rued inability with the same abject penitence of a sinner guilty of some mortal transgression.

Mark immediately offered absolution. "I never expected that you would."

Chapter 7

$\mathcal{U}$p a dim-lit, spiraling stairway Elysia hastened toward her bedchamber. From one firebrand's pool of light she moved around the corner to the next and then the next. Midday loomed near and with it the moment to fulfill her promise to meet the Black Wolf for that tour of the countryside he'd threatened her with the past night.

Elysia was anxious to tidy herself and remove any betraying hint of her morn's activity before again descending for the meal where *he* would doubtless be waiting. She regretted wasting time dawdling on the return from her visit with Gervaise. Particularly as the solitude won by a lingering pace had taken her no closer toward the goal of resolving troubling issues into neat packages and finding a smooth path through them.

Elysia's way had merely become littered with additional gaping stumble holes. Was Gervaise the instigator of the attack launched as Mark approached Wroxton? It seemed a certainty and one that Elysia accepted. Men ever sought to settle disputes by force. As a warrior accustomed to such realities, the confrontation's victor had plainly expected the assault. What she found more difficult to shrug away was the uncomfortable suspicion that two days earlier Gervaise might've been able to urge her into participating in such violence as a deed necessary to halt a greater evil. And then there was the matter of Gervaise's oblique threat against Mark only hours past. She determinedly closed her mind to the depth of unpleasantness roused by the prospect of such an action meeting with success.

Only since the intruder's arrival had Elysia begun to question Gervaise's motives and actions. Try as she might, Elysia couldn't push them back into silence. Was Mark right in his assessment of Gervaise as a cold man? Were her own unwelcome suspicions correct? Was her betrothal a result of Gervaise's desire not for her but solely for her fiefdom?

Elysia scowled into the darkness beyond a ring of light. She'd returned to the castle with emotions more tangled and host to additional questions without answers—leastways few she wanted to admit.

Annoyance and haste robbed Elysia of her usual grace. She tripped on her own hem, tried to recover her footing but took a bruising fall and twisted her ankle as she landed in an awkward heap.

Saint's tears! It's that wretched man's fault! Elysia repeated it aloud. Yet rather than feeling better, she merely felt more foolish.

With hands palm flat on chill stone, Elysia pushed

herself upright and hobbled the rest of the way to the chamber whose private solace she craved—but didn't get.

"Where have you been?" asked a soft voice full of gentle rebuke. "I came to awaken you this morn only to find an empty bed."

Ida had been waiting for some little time, indeed, since the moment she'd finished making certain that the houseserfs were rightly employed with their daily tasks.

Elysia was no more than momentarily surprised to find her small, plump companion waiting, normally cheerful face full of gentle reproach.

By the dust on one side of Elysia's dark cloak and a multitude of curls escaping from an oddly loosened braid, it was plain to Ida that she was unlikely to approve of whatever had occurred. Since the maid had gone to the sea cave the last eve, it was doubtful that she'd returned to Jamie this morn. But if not that, then what had her impetuous charge been up to?

"I met Gervaise in the glade where my archery range is laid out." Elysia knew this immediate response would do nothing to calm her companion's concern. Ida was as convinced as Jamie of the truth behind that site's reputation as a place of otherworldly dangers, but the golden gleam in brown eyes lifted to a round face silently forbade any mention of it.

"Tch, tch." Ida sailed forward to remove the cloak from slender shoulders. She had a purpose for being here to greet her lambie, one too important for her to easily put aside for the sake of issuing another caution unlikely to be heeded. "Your hair is in a sad state. Come, let me restore it to order."

Elysia realized that Ida was intent on engaging her in a personal chat and saw no option but to yield. Asides, she was curious to know why. Hiding her limp, she promptly moved to settle on a three-legged stool beside the chest atop which sat a basket holding her brush, assorted hair ribbons, and two delicately wrought coronets, one of silver and one of gold. She was glad for this excuse to take the weight off her aching ankle and submitted to deft hands quickly loosening the braid she'd never achieved the skill of plaiting to lie in a smooth black rope down her back.

With quiet skill Ida steadily wove together thick sections of Elysia's glossy hair. During those moments of silence that seemed to stretch to impossible lengths, Ida earnestly searched but found no simple, circuitous way of leading into the topic she wished to raise. Feeling there was no hope for another choice, she took a deep breath and leapt into the subject with both feet.

"After Lord Mark's meeting with village leaders yesterday, I spent quite some time talking with him."

This curious news of a conversation between two who had so little in common drew from Elysia a single-word query: "Why?"

Ida's eyes widened. She was less prepared for Elysia's response than the girl had been for her statement. Having begun flustered by the awkward nature of the mission to be attempted, Ida deemed it fortunate that her position behind Elysia kept hidden an already anxious expression turned desperate. She was not ready to respond to so direct a question. Not when an equally direct answer would lead to talk of matters she'd chosen never to discuss with the maid.

"The *why* is less important than what *he* had to say," Ida gruffly got out at last.

Dark brows met in a faint scowl above brown eyes. Elysia had an uncomfortable suspicion that she knew precisely what it was. And as she wanted to address this subject no more than any one among the muddled morass of issues she'd spent the morning's walk uselessly pondering, she refused to ask the question Ida clearly wanted to hear.

Frustrated on every turn in her attempt to broach the subject indirectly, Ida flatly uttered the information she'd come to impart. "Lord Mark says were Jamie to return today, he'd take into account the honor of the boy's intent when passing judgment upon him."

Elysia would've shaken her head had the hold Ida still had on her hair not been unusually firm. "Did you believe him?"

Ida finished tying off the plait at its bottom end and moved around to face Elysia.

"My heart wants to believe." The words were a plaintive mother's prayer.

Elysia nodded a solemn acknowledgment. She, too, wanted to believe her friend could again be safe and free. But . . .

"Although the man said as much to me, I'm not convinced he is worthy of our trust—leastways not so far as to put Jamie's life at risk on that uncertain possibility."

Ida's hands stilled, and her face went fearfully white. Elysia was right. And she ought to have given a great deal more time in consideration of that danger herself.

"But now I must hurry to the great hall," Elysia

stated, voice going defiant. "Lord Mark"—Elysia hated using that term for the man and nearly spat it through clenched teeth—"will be waiting to meet me at the meal. Once it's done, he means to take me out to survey the countryside."

Ida was confused and showed it. She'd heard nothing of this plan and it was now her turn to ask "Why?"

Elysia's mouth firmed into a tight line while golden fires began to burn in her eyes. "He thinks I've shown too little care for the people of Wroxton and wants me to see how badly Dunstan has mistreated them on my behalf."

I suppose, Elysia told herself, trying not to limp as she stepped from the castle entrance's lowest stair onto the courtyard's rutted surface, *I ought to be grateful that leastways the wretch didn't chide me for lazing abed rather than appearing for the day's first meal.* Mayhap she ought to be, but she wasn't!

Mark's lips tilted into a mocking smile while he watched the dark beauty in a crimson gown and charcoal cloak nearly marching as she rounded the corner to the wooden stable built against a towering stone wall. Elysia seemed intent on keeping one step ahead of him. And he was willing to grant that boon. They had shared the meal just past in near silence, but he'd been aware that she'd spent the time fanning fires of resentment for him and his plan for her afternoon. Blazing indignation lent creamy cheeks a glow near as bright as her gown. All in all she made a lovely sight. The fact that this was assuredly not the response she sought from him deepened Mark's amusement.

With each step closer to their destination, Elysia's

heart thumped harder. It was terribly important that he be at her back when they arrived. In this goal she succeeded but the next promised to be more difficult to achieve.

"Milord," David stepped from the stable's shadows, "as you bade me, I have your steed saddled and ready."

Elysia's hands curled into tight little balls of frustration when the boy, plainly her companion's squire, asked which horse was hers. She could only force a bland expression over her face and pray that the pulse she could feel pounding in her temples couldn't be seen.

"You needn't fetch my mount. Thad will do that deed for me." She turned a speaking gaze full upon the ironworker's son, thankful for the glimpse she'd caught of him mucking out a nearby stall.

Thad froze in place while dumbfounded amazement widened his eyes and dropped his jaw.

"He knows which saddle I prefer." In order to divert the squire's attention from the boy's odd reaction, Elysia forced to her lips a smile she was certain must be sickeningly sweet. Now was certainly not the time to confess that she had never ridden a horse in her life.

Inaudibly muttering about daft gentlewomen who harbored witches and talked of what had never been, Thad disappeared into the shadows at the stable's back. It took some time but at length he reappeared leading a saddled mare.

Elysia viewed the dappled gray beast with an odd combination of trepidation and determination. Sternly Elysia reminded herself that she'd seen others perform this trick oft enough. She could do it. Over and over like a litany Elysia repeated that statement while purposefully moving to the mounting block.

Lifting her skirts, Elysia stepped up with her uninjured foot but came close to tumbling off again upon finding herself practically eye to eye with the curiously watching mare. She must do it! But how to begin? She took a deep breath. To fail in this would be to look even more the spoiled brat that Lord Mark had already condemned her for being.

Watching Elysia hesitate and nearly fall, Mark assumed the damsel had rarely been called to practice the skill of mounting a horse. Doubtless either her father or one of his guardsmen saved her that need by lifting her into the saddle. So be it.

Elysia gasped in earnest when strong hands curled about her waist from behind. In the next instant she found herself deposited sideways atop the amazingly steady mare's back and gazing down into silver eyes gleaming with amusement at her surprise.

"Hook your knee firmly about the pommel. I'm unfamiliar with the path but fear it may involve both steep climbs and descents." With the warning, self-mockery deepened Mark's smile. She must know their path far better than he could. Indeed, he had only Hugh's instructions on which direction to travel and where to stop.

Elysia had seen countless men mount their steeds but rarely a woman her sidesaddle. She blamed this fact for her having forgotten to expect such a thing. Thankfully her head lowered to give full attention to obeying his instruction hid a bright blush caused by her folly.

From that point Elysia found the challenge of riding somewhat easier to meet. She copied Mark's hold on the reins and began to relax as the mare instinctively kept pace with his stallion. For safety's sake, two young guardsmen rode a discreet distance behind.

By the time they'd journeyed a small distance into the cool green shadows of the forest beyond the castle's outlying fields, the tension had begun to ease from Elysia's stiff body. Feeling more confident of her ability to perform this new skill, she permitted her attention to drift back to the same subject that had consumed her thoughts throughout the past meal.

Seemed certain to Elysia that only burning indignation for this man's high-handed ways could help her survive an entire afternoon in his company. It was a goal easily achieved. She had but to consider how, although these were her lands, it was the Black Wolf who directed their path. Why? Was he leading her into some kind of trap? It was a silly thought and she knew it. But leastways it offered distraction from the too attractive man so near.

The distraction Elysia welcomed showed itself to be a dreadful mistake. One moment she was sitting atop her mare with all the grace Ida had worked so hard to instill in her. In the next she was falling backward with skirts immodestly flying. She landed in an inelegant sprawl atop a low-growing bush bordering their path. Its lush greenery softened her landing, but still Elysia was winded and gazed dumbfounded at the horse plainly unconcerned.

Now I've done it! Elysia was mortified. *Now I've given the wretched man all the proof he needs of my ineptness.* Thoroughly humiliated, she immediately struggled to rise from her ignominious position.

The instant the damsel fell Mark had swung down full of concern. But he couldn't hold back a burst of laughter at the sight of the plainly infuriated maid who regained her feet before he could reach her side. She stood with cape twisted sideways and a myriad of curls roughly torn free of her tidy braid to frame a face whose cheeks were temper-bright and eyes were flashing with golden fires.

"I'll help you mount again." Mark offered after mastering the amusement she plainly found offensive.

"Oh, no!" Elysia unsteadily backed away from the mare she eyed with distrust. "Never will I get back on that wicked beast again!"

"Your only option is to ride with me."

With equal disfavor Elysia eyed the dark man whose eyes glittered suspiciously and flatly stated, "I'd much rather walk."

"As you choose." A shaft of sunlight stole out between drifting clouds to pierce the forest's leafy cover and glow on midnight-dark hair as Mark nodded. No point in arguing with the angry maid, not when, considering the distances they'd be traveling, she'd be happy soon enough to once more be ahorse.

Completely forgetting the unobtrusive guardsmen behind, Elysia motioned Mark to lead the way. He looked unwilling, but she mutinously waited for him to go first. At length, he nodded again and complied. She had insisted on the deed to make it possible for her to hide from him the awkward gait she feared would give him an excuse to force her into doing what she'd sworn she would not.

"Riding a horse is plainly not among your talents," Mark called back to the angry maid. "But you must have traveled somewhere ... sometime ..." He twisted around to see her as he asked, "How?"

Beneath a silver gaze Elysia instantly went still. "I traveled atop a horse litter." Her mind filled with the image of the conveyance normally hers. Her father had sworn well-born ladies often went from place to place perched upon the pallet laid atop strong linen stretched over a wooden frame whose either end was carried by a horse.

"Surely ladies in the court where you lived in Normandy have done the same."

"A horse litter?" With a wry smile Mark reined his stallion to a halt. "Aye, I can see you on one, sitting in comfort well above the common rabble and regally dispensing alms."

Although Elysia's temper soared, she stood defiantly mute in the midst of a rutted path. 'Struth, she had dispensed alms from her horse litter but not in a manner so dispassionate, so condescending, as he implied. But to say so would only make matters worse.

When she stubbornly lengthened her silence, Mark shrugged and turned around to continue their journey. However, they'd gone only a short distance before he surreptitiously glanced back over a broad shoulder. He caught the damsel gazing at the ground and grimacing as she limped forward. He instantly dismounted once more.

Elysia heard his saddle creak under the action and glanced up before freezing with a defiantly lifted chin. Mark moved inexorably toward her while Elysia, burning with frustration, inwardly admitted her options were severely limited. She could barely walk and certainly couldn't flee from him.

Mark swept Elysia into his arms and strode forward to plant her firmly on the trunk of a fallen tree before sinking to his knees and lifting her right foot. Elysia tried to pull it away but nearly paid for that action by losing her balance and toppling over again. Fuming, she surrendered with ill grace and turned a defiantly lifted chin as far to the left as possible.

Mark gently probed a badly swollen ankle and frowned. If this was the result of her tumble from the mare, it had puffed up with amazing speed, but he was not such a fool as to think that likely.

"How did this happen?" Silver eyes shifted from the amber gaze drawn by the unexpected question to quickly drop to the injured foot.

"Does it matter?" Elysia put a lofty chill in the words.

Mark shook his head with disgust for her determination to take offense where none was intended. "Nay, but it does mean that you must either mount your mare or share my horse with me."

"Where is that vicious gray beast?" Elysia demanded, making her choice clear while meeting his penetrating gaze unwavering.

Mark's deep laughter echoed through the forest while he fetched the mare. In the short time since they'd met, this woman had made him honestly laugh more often than he had in a good many years. But he restrained it while lifting her again into the saddle although his eyes gleamed with an amusement she probably resented at least as much.

After Mark swung onto his stallion's back, to calm

the maid and atone for his merriment at her expense, he asked a question meant to turn her attention toward a different direction.

"Ida tells me that your father loved to read and write. Did he teach you?"

Elysia stared at the path ahead with such heat that by rights it ought to have burst into flame. With the coals of her temper already glowing, she found a source of further annoyance in what she deemed Ida's betrayal in sharing personal matters with this sardonic stranger. Nonetheless, she gave a single sharp nod and firmly stated, "Aye, I can read several languages and have become quite skilled at writing."

"I'm glad to hear it. Your skill means that while I draw the information from your people, you can write down a complete list of all that they report was demanded from them by Dunstan."

Elysia scowled. Did the mocking man think to test her abilities? Did he think hers an idle boast? Or, worse, that she lied?

While they moved on in silence, Elysia attempted to restore some measure of order to her clothing and hair. She'd just managed to tuck away the last errant tendrils of dark hair when they left the forest's cover.

Their first stop was a tiny cottage in an area of the woodland cleared by the permission that the freeman who worked it had won from his lord. Its fields hosted an abundance of ragged children—all painfully thin and hollow-eyed but busy aiding their parents in tending long furrows of new-sprouted grain.

"What might I do for you, milord?" Filled with anxiety, the question was asked by a man who hesitantly approached his lady and her companion with cap

crushed in dirt-encrusted, gnarled hands. In his experience, this second nobleman come visiting in as many
days surely boded ill for him and his family.

"I am Lord Mark, the new master of Wroxton."
With these words the slightly smiling speaker swung
down from his horse. "And I have come to do something for *you*."

The farmer frowned. This answer roused suspicion
and greater fear. Never, never had any noble done
him a service but that a much larger one was demanded in return. Even the giving of a right to farm
this land cost him three parts out of four of everything grown.

"Tell me your name and give me an accounting of
all that Dunstan Buchard demanded you yield to
him." Mark was aware that the farmer's family had
halted their work and were straining to hear what was
said. In response, he raised his voice while adding, "I
will set his greed aright by returning to you the over-
age wrongly claimed."

The words brought a yelp from one of the younger
boys and grins from the other children, but the adults
remained dubious and looked at the dark stranger
with suspicion. And yet their wariness could not prevent obedience to the new lord's command.

Mark lifted Elysia from her mare and settled her
on a clump of ferns that sprouted beneath a single
tree left standing near the cottage. He gazed down for
an instant into the wide brown eyes of the lovely damsel startled by his action and hoped the vision of these
people's poverty would begin to convince her of the
truth of their ill treatment at Dunstan's hands.

Anxious to calm tremors of pleasure brought by

close proximity with the devastating man, Elysia pulled from his hold. Asides, sore muscles and fresh bruises had taught her the discomforts of riding a horse, leaving her happy to sit on firm ground. She willingly accepted the flat board, parchment, quill, and tightly stoppered ink vial he pulled from a bag attached to his saddle.

As the farmer defensively embarked upon the requested list, she wrote down the information he gave. The pride Elysia felt in demonstrating her skill was soon swamped by compassion for the woe of these people, her people ... and by guilt. Aye, guilt. She felt guilt for the fact that in remaining distant—and she inwardly confessed, self-involved—she had allowed it to happen.

Mark gave the farmer several coins and a white stone bearing a wax impression of his seal. This, he promised, could be exchanged at the castle for a bag of milled grain, salt meat, and a piglet for either raising or eating.

From this first stop they moved on to other sites of equal need. At each Elysia wrote the list of wrongs done and watched Mark. His attitude was never condescending but rather one of honest concern. Although it felt like a betrayal of Gervaise, she couldn't prevent a growing admiration for the dark man.

The sun was hovering over the western horizon long before they could finish visiting all of Wroxton's farms and hamlets. Many would have to wait for another day.

By the time they began their return journey to the castle at the end of an afternoon's work, Elysia was uncomfortably aware of being worthy of Mark's disdain for her many lacks as the lady of Wroxton. She waited for him to pour his scorn over her head, but he did something infinitely worse. He found a far more effective punishment. He ignored her wrong completely. Instead, throughout their journey back to the castle, Mark amicably chatted of those they'd met and the further plans he had for restoring health to her fiefdom and its people.

Chapter 8

Thank the saints! The rain has stopped at last. Along with heartfelt gratitude, Elysia sent upward a quick but appreciative glance while her small party crossed the drawbridge spanning a deep moat. Only soft white clouds drifted lazily across a sky at last free of the ominous storm-darkness that had lingered for days and made her trips to and from Jamie's cave both cold and treacherous.

Elysia once again rode atop the dappled gray mare. However, this time she'd been given a small measure of confidence by Mark's instructions on how to control her mount and perform the deed aright. It was due to his reassurances and reminder that she'd managed the return from their first such jaunt without incident that Elysia risked this second journey.

Torrential rains and the breach they'd caused in the dam diverting a river to feed the castle's moat had forced them to postpone finishing their survey of

Wroxton's people. The dam's repair had daily demanded Mark's presence. Each nightfall he returned dirty and weary.

They'd fallen into the habit of sitting together in the family solar after he'd been provided with a bath and hot meal. With Ida ever in the background as chaperone, their visits included a wide range of topics. They'd talked about everything from progress on the dam to lively discussions of the Greek philosophies presented in various books. In the process each had learned a respect for the other's sharp wits.

Astride his much larger black stallion, Mark kept a careful eye upon the neophyte rider on the fat little mare he took care to remain beside. He willingly admitted that his attention was held as much by Elysia's beauty as by concern for her safety. And, again garbed in the scarlet gown of their first such adventure, she was an alluring sight. Upon meeting the fiery maid, he'd thought to enjoy the battles her spirit promised but had since found himself looking forward to the simple pleasures of quiet time spent in her company.

Mark could almost understand her father's need to see Elysia protected. But it seemed to him that the man had gone much, much too far in denying her the opportunity to learn so basic a skill as riding. In Lord Aldreth's effort to protect Elysia from life's bruises, he might as well have wrapped her in thistledown. And yet, how else when by actions costing the man dearly he'd proven himself an unusually loving sire. Without thinking, Mark said as much to her.

"You are fortunate to have parents who so loved you that they put your well-being above their own happiness."

Confusion darkened the brown eyes Elysia turned to Mark. Apparently he didn't know that her mother bore her so little love that she'd deserted her daughter as a toddling.

" 'Struth, I am fortunate to have had a doting father." With warm memories of lost joys revived, a melancholy smile curled Elysia's berry-bright lips. "Even though I always suspected that, if given his choices, he would've locked me into a comfortable tower to see me cosseted and protected forever."

Having recently viewed the issue in much the same light, Mark absently nodded and found himself speaking of matters rarely shared with another human being. "From my experience I know just how uncommon is such paternal love."

During their evenings together, Elysia had learned that Mark hid his true self behind a sardonic mask and potent smile. Now, from these quiet words and an unwavering silver gaze, Elysia sensed that this private man was opening to her a portion of himself seldom seen by another. She held her breath for fear that any sound might end the moment.

"My father was among William's conquering knights and was rewarded for his military aid with a sizable fief on the Welsh border in exchange for subduing and holding it quiet for his king."

Elysia's eyes remained locked with silver. She'd heard many tales about the Black Wolf but knew few facts for certain and was curious to learn the truth from him.

"To win the bloodless surrender of Radwell, my father agreed to take the Saxon lord's daughter for wife. And by ancient Saxon customs he did." Cynicism robbed Mark's smile of honest humor. "The old lord died while I was a young boy. And not long after that event my father departed with other conquering lords to meet with their king in Normandy. Months later he returned ... with a Norman wife taken by Christian rites."

Elysia gazed into a brooding face from which even the cynical smile had fled. "But that would make you ..."

"The bastard you called me that first day." The statement was flatly issued with only the depth of Mark's voice revealing the pain behind his words. "And again I say you are fortunate to be so beloved of your parents that they did not do the same to you."

"My father, aye. But my mother cared so little for either me or her husband that rather than remain with us she preferred to retreat into a nunnery." The way Elysia said the last word it had as well have been *dungeon.*

Mark slowly shook his head. "Has Ida never talked to you of what actually happened? And why?"

A slight frown drew delicate brows together. It seemed that Ida, Elysia's lifelong companion, had shared more with this stranger than she'd ever told Elysia.

"I see she hasn't." Disgusted with himself for opening subjects that were not his to reveal, Mark turned his attention to the well-worn path bordered by lush green vegetation and overhung by the boughs of towering trees. "Doubtless Ida has reasons ..."

"Whatever Ida's reasons might be," Elysia logically argued, "like Pandora you've opened the box and can't shut it again."

Mark grimaced at Elysia's analogy, but it was true. He'd little choice but to finish what he had begun. Asides, he couldn't see what reason the amiable little woman had for keeping facts from the maid when surely it would be better for her to understand.

"*Both* of your parents showed for you an incredibly selfless love," Mark began.

Intent on his answer, Elysia's hands tightened on the reins. Her attention was so fully held by their conversation that she'd long since forgotten to worry about the challenges of riding.

"Your mother was raised in a convent and living there when *her* father gave his daughter to *your* father as bride to seal a secular bond." Mark could see by Elysia's deepening frown that this was something no one had told her although he'd heard the story from more than Ida alone.

"I'm told your father adored your mother and that she cared for him as well. But your mother had already given her heart to God and wanted more than all else to devote her life in service to Him. And when your father saw the depth of her commitment, he freed his cherished wife to return to the nunnery of St. Marie de Alcun."

"Aye," Elysia nodded, mind whirling with new images. " 'Twas my father's nature to do selfless deeds for those he loved—wife, daughter, or any of his people."

Mark realized Elysia still didn't understand what her mother had done for her, probably not even the full cost of the gift to her father.

"Don't you see that for the sake of your future their marital bond remained unbroken even though it meant that your mother was barred from the one thing she wanted most of all—to take the vows of a nun. And your father lived his life alone."

As he spoke the last phrase, for the first time Mark recognized that this was precisely the end he'd sought for himself by an unwillingness to take a wife. But then, it would be a worse fate to bind himself to most women he'd known. However, Elysia . . .

"Father was not alone," Elysia softly asserted.

"He loved you dearly, but a daughter is not the same as a wife." Gray eyes darkened with intimate meaning.

To escape that intimacy Elysia gazed into the tangled undergrowth on one side, attempting to bring order to equally tangled feelings for the woman who'd given her birth. She had clearly undervalued her father's sacrifice. But had she misjudged her mother for lo these many years?

Jolted from troubled thoughts by the whining whistle and blur of an arrow passing the merest distance before her, Elysia gasped. That sound was lost in the thunder of Mark's voice.

"Valbeau to me!" Mark wheeled his mount toward the direction from whence the arrow had come before spurring the stallion into forging a new path through the trees.

One of the two guardsmen trailing behind urged his steed forward to place himself defensively between Elysia and the green shadows concealing the arrow's source while the other galloped after their lord.

Watching while shaking a glossy dark head to clear her thoughts, Elysia realized that Mark had been the missile's target. And it was meant to end his life. The horror roused by that prospect was deepened by the sudden realization that she very likely had played a part in the deed. Her heart stopped and then pounded furiously. Short of watching his every move, without her, his enemies wouldn't have known of this journey.

That she hadn't knowingly betrayed Mark could never be an excuse for the fact that she undeniably had during the morning meeting with Gervaise at her archery range. When he inquired after her plans for the day, she told him of this journey and its purpose, after which Gervaise had chided her for the admiration of Mark that he claimed to have heard in her voice. In her anxiety to deny it, she'd pushed aside any suspicion for his purpose in asking specifically which farms they were to visit.

Elysia conceded that Gervaise had played the scene as expertly as any professional mummer. Had she not felt the need to soothe his ego, she would've wondered at his concern. Though initially reluctant, she had come to admit that his interest was seldom centered on her. And more telling still, their visit ended for the first time without Gervaise cautioning her that Mark must be removed before they could wed. Elysia confessed to herself that Mark's death was too high a price to pay for a deed she was no longer certain she wanted to happen.

The rustling sound of something large moving in the forest instantly summoned Elysia's attention. She peered into woodland's shadows and saw Mark and his black steed break back through the trees leading a horse across which lay an unconscious man bound at wrists and ankles.

"Gervaise's man?" Mark halted beside Elysia and

reached back to lift his captive's head while silver eyes peered questioningly into brown.

Elysia nodded, wishing she could do more to see Mark safe and at the same time enduring waves of guilt for being the cause of his danger.

"Stephen," Mark spoke to the guardsman who'd remained with Elysia. "Lead this horse and its pitiful burden to the outer edge of the Lord Gervaise's lands, then send him galloping toward Kelby Keep."

"Eve," Hugh called to the young woman constantly disappearing whenever he drew near. Indeed, whenever anyone but her mistress called. For days he had almost haunted the reserve well, site of his rescue of her from the abuse of Thad and his friends. But his multitude of excuses devised to pass by at every opportunity had gone for naught—until now. That fact made it even more important to prevent this too rare moment from slipping away. "Surely, I've proven that you have nothing to fear from me."

Casting a green glance over one shoulder, Eve paused in her habitual flight from personal contact with any human save Elysia. But this was different. This time Eve's hesitation was born of uncertainty about how to respond to the overtures of this man who since their last meeting at this place had occupied too many of her thoughts.

Hugh's lips compressed with frustration. At last he had the timid maid's attention. Unfortunately he'd no notion how to move from this point to the kind of pleasant conversation he sought. For the first time in his life, Hugh envied the skills of a lady-charmer like

Mark. If only he were as able to easily enthrall any member of the fairer sex.

"Please don't run from me again," Hugh gruffly rushed to say when he thought Eve might move to escape. "Never would I hurt you. I only wanted to talk with you. Only to talk and come to know you better."

A shadowy war between hope and doubt darkened Eve's eyes to near the deep hue of the distant forest. Did this bear of a man truly seek only time in her company? Or was there an unwelcome dismal motive behind his request? Though wary still, she turned to fully face him, head instinctively tilting to shield her scarred cheek with a curtain of golden-brown hair.

"Come," Hugh continued although lacking either silky words or honeyed phrases and feeling like an inept blunderer, "sit with me awhile in the afternoon sunshine."

Eve sent a guilty glance toward the castle and the unfinished duties inside. But she bravely returned attention to her protector and gave a shy smile of assent. Halfway between castle wall and well, Hugh doffed his cloak. After spreading the almost full circle of cloth on a patch of ground softened by still damp but thick grasses and clustered ferns, he helped Eve settle atop it and then lowered his bulk to join her there.

"I'm told you lived alone in the forest for years," Hugh haltingly began, knowing of no other subject of any possible interest to a maid. She surely wouldn't care about the rigors of his duties and he knew nothing of hers. Although that first day she'd made it clear that she either couldn't or wouldn't discuss the event that had left her scarred, surely the topic of her life after . . .

Eve caught her breath. This man had asked others in the castle about her? She glanced up at Hugh and then quickly down to a single fern frond tugged from a nearby plant. Doubtless he'd been told of the many ills for which she was blamed. Her shoulders sagged. He could hardly think well of her now.

By the maid's reaction, Hugh recognized his misstep and awkwardly sought to correct it. "I'm impressed that you were able to live on your own. I doubt many grown women could do the same."

A few of Wroxton's older guardsmen had spoken to Hugh of the abandoned ten-year-old girl. By the fear he'd heard in their voices, he should've known that this topic also was too sensitive to be comfortably discussed with Eve, particularly as his informants' anxieties about the maid had plainly been heightened by Eve's ability to survive without the aid of another human.

"They meant for me to die." Eve made the emotionless statement while staring at hands methodically shredding the fern into a pile of delicate green curls.

"They?" Her's was a bleak observation, but Hugh found it leastways a starting point for some manner of communication between them.

"The people who saw the smoke rising from my burning home and discovered where I lay." Her hand unthinkingly covered a scarred cheek. "They were frightened of *me.*"

Hugh frowned at the amazement lingering in her voice for the response of others near a decade past. He could see the scene all too clearly. The blackened, burned-out shell of a house and a misused child surrounded by superstitious fools.

"They wrapped me into a blanket, tied cords about it, and carried the bundle I was deep, deep into the forest." Eve gave Hugh a forlorn smile. "That's where they left me—alone and tightly bound."

Hugh was torn. He wanted both to hug the abandoned child Eve had been and to punish those who had committed the vile act. But the deed was not of itself shocking. Although rarely mentioned, it was an accepted practice to desert unwanted babies, even young children, in the furthermost reaches of the forest. Plainly, that's what frightened people had done to Eve. And since then, they had punished her for surviving.

"But you won free and defeated their deadly intents." Hugh's smile was grim.

Eve slowly nodded. "I won free of the blanket I soon came to treasure. And, thankfully, I'd already learned from my mother both how to cook and which plants aid or harm. From my father's example I had some notion of how to fish and trap small animals. Thus, with a flint I found ..." She ended with a slight shrug.

Hugh's arm laid across an upraised knee and he rested his bearded chin atop it to study the resourceful maid. He now knew how she'd managed food in the wild, but what of shelter? He asked, and she quietly told how—learning from untamed creatures, she'd dug a burrow. Over time she'd reinforced it with fallen branches while enlarging and refining its amenities. Proudly she told how in warm weather it was softly lined with dried grasses, and in cold weather she lit fires within a stone circle to keep it heated and dry.

Eve was warmed by the honest admiration in the

smile Hugh gave in response to her list of accomplishments.

"But," Hugh sought answer to one further question, "what of clothing for the child becoming a woman?"

A gentle grimace came over the face Eve had forgotten to self-consciously hide. "I could do little for myself in that matter. But, thankfully, the very fear that set me apart filled that need."

Dark brows arched in question.

"The aged widow of a woodsman, superstitious and fearful, crossed my path on several occasions." Eve began a difficult explanation. "I think it was as a gift to placate the witch she believed me to be that twice she left a bundle of ragged castoffs where I'd likely find it under a towering oak. I would've thanked her, but I fear she'd have died of fright."

The poorly muffled snickers of children peering around the castle wall shattered the peace. Stricken by fear that others had heard what she had never willingly shared with anyone before, Eve jumped to her feet and fled into the castle's rear entry. Angry with those responsible for the rude interruption, Hugh rose and heavily stomped around the corner. Shrieking children scattered.

"I congratulate you on being shrewd enough to remain at Wroxton Castle." Gervaise nodded to reinforce his approval and the light of his keep's central hearth burned brighter on red hair. Yet, while flattering the portly Dunstan, Gervaise's pleasure came from seeing this man who'd once thought himself superior now reduced to a humble level.

Dunstan stood a little straighter despite the weariness of a full day's work and the late-night furtive journey to this meeting. Asides, the other man's praise was surely his just due after he had chosen to stay in a lowly position at the same place where once he'd been master. That choice, moreover, had forced him to endure all manner of abuse from guardsmen earlier under his admittedly onerous command.

"Your place in such close proximity with Lord Mark," Gervaise silkily added, "may mean the difference between the success or failure of our plans."

Dunstan's face closed into a wariness that made him appear even more like a sly weasel. Though he'd remained at Wroxton Castle with the expectation of being used in just such a way, hearing it baldly stated sent a cold chill over him. But then, Gervaise generally had that effect no matter what he said.

Upon realizing that his cohort meant not to respond, Gervaise gave a slight shrug and offhandedly announced, "Another forest attack was foiled today."

Dunstan was startled. He hadn't slipped free of the castle until the night was well advanced, but during the whole day and evening he'd heard nothing of such a deed.

Gervaise saw the other's surprise and immediately asked, "Was it not reported in the castle?"

Under a negative motion, iron-gray hair brushed thick shoulders.

"Hah," Gervaise gave a sharp hoot of disgust. "The man must fear the truth would weaken his position." He waved one hand as if brushing aside a pesky fly. "No matter. His intents will mean nothing when he is dead. And he soon *will* be."

Dunstan's discomfort increased beneath the steady

look Gervaise turned on him. Aye, it made him more than a little uncomfortable and very much aware that he probably didn't want to know what it portended.

"This afternoon I received a message from Belleme. He'll be here soon. And he stated most firmly that he wants the matter finished before his arrival."

Belleme? Here? This was more than Dunstan had bargained for in allying himself with Gervaise. He would never willingly have put himself so close to that evil man. And the thought that Belleme might have expectations of him was terrifying! Many were the ghastly tales of vicious punishments wreaked upon those who failed him.

Gervaise watched, amused by the desperate expressions chasing over the once proud man's face while plainly casting wildly about for some plan to meet Belleme's demand. Dunstan was afraid of Belleme and rightly so. Gervaise was wary of the man himself even though they'd been friends for decades.

Feeling trapped after long, silent moments passed, Dunstan raised his hands palm up to indicate defeat. Dunstan knew he'd rue the action for his companion had assuredly already devised a scheme—one certain to cause him infinitely more distress.

"As two attacks launched beyond castle walls have failed, 'tis clear that success can be achieved only by the actions of someone inside."

Dunstan was too aware of being Gervaise's only remaining ally within the castle. And that meant that he would be expected to do the deed. But as a master, not a minion, he had never killed any man. It wasn't the concept of killing that appalled Dunstan but the danger that most certainly accompanied such a deed that set him to searching for some argument to block the demand. The only defense he found was the story of an action others said had taken place the night he'd spent in hiding.

"A futile attack *has* been made inside Wroxton."

Gervaise scowled, suspecting a lie. He felt certain Elysia would have told him of something so momentous had it actually happened.

"'Struth!" Dunstan could see his cohort's disbelief. "I swear it."

"Were you present?" Gervaise dubiously inquired.

"Nay," Dunstan promptly answered. But, affronted by the other's hesitancy to accept his words, he immediately added, "I heard the same tale from many who were there . . . too many for it to be false."

"Then tell me the name of this hero to our cause." Sarcasm laid a thick layer of frost over Gervaise's question.

"Jamie." The answer was a defiant statement of fact. "It was Jamie, the son of Elysia's companion."

Gervaise's hands came together, fingertips meeting at the top to press against pursed lips. This was a possibility. The foolish boy had long been Elysia's shadow and had suffered from an adolescent crush on the beauty for several years. Aye, this was just the sort of feat the youngster might think able to both impress his ladylove and win her favor by ridding her of her unwanted suitor. Indeed. A frightening smile appeared on Gervaise's lips. He would've thanked the boy himself.

"Plainly Jamie failed. Where is he now? In the dungeon keeping company with all the others thwarted in attempting the same task?"

"Nay," Dunstan shook his head mournfully but with no honest regret. "The boy leaped out the window of the lord's bedchamber."

"Leaped from the window? Poor little bastard. I daresay the lad had adequate time to repent during the long fall between window and the rocks so far, far below."

"No body was found that night." Dunstan ominously stated. He enjoyed the repeating of an eerie tale as much as ever had any gossiping old biddy. "Nor did it later wash ashore."

"Hmmmm ..." Gervaise absently returned joined fingertips to brush against the point of his chin.

Chapter 9

$\mathcal{A}$s her arrow sailed uselessly between two trees, Elysia scowled. She had completely missed the bale of hay that served as target. Clearly her skills were fading for lack of regular practice. And that unpleasant fact, atop Gervaise's failure to appear this morn, was enough to deepen an already irritable mood.

"God's blood!" Gervaise's shrill curse rang from the shadowy forest brief moments before he burst through its cover. "You could've killed me!"

"How could I be expected to know that you had come at last . . . and from the wrong direction?" Elysia instinctively defended herself from his unjust condemnation. The dimensions and directions of her archery range had been established long ago. Gervaise knew its layout and usually entered the glade from behind. That he hadn't this time was *his* mistake, not hers. Asides, he was late, late, late. She hadn't begun to take aim at the target until she'd every reason to believe he wasn't coming.

Annoyed with Elysia for the action that had shaken him from his habitual calm, Gervaise returned her words with a burning glare. Then, standing stiffly erect, he coolly readjusted clothing disarranged by the mad dash through undergrowth to escape her unintended assault.

Watching while Gervaise regained his normal chilly serenity, Elysia felt a guilty fool. But then an inner voice that sounded remarkably like Mark's mockingly told her that doubtless Gervaise deemed this the appropriate response for her to host. The last thought left Elysia feeling even more blameworthy.

"The near miss lends credence to what I've said many times." Gervaise unknowingly reinforced what Elysia had been thinking. "Archery is a crude skill appropriate only for low-bred soldiers. *Never* for well-born ladies!"

It proved no such thing! Eyes darkened near to black remained determinedly downcast while Elysia struggled to stifle the retort burning on her tongue. Noble huntsmen often used the skills of an archer when stalking their prey. And what's more, she told herself again, archery or no, by coming late and from the wrong direction, *he* was at fault, not she!

Gervaise frowned at the clearly unrepentant maid. Their relationship had begun subtly shifting since the Black Wolf's arrival at Wroxton. He must speak to Elysia about the man and in terms that would allow him to reassert his own influence over her.

"The Black Wolf . . ." Gervaise began while taking a step closer to the damsel who instantly interrupted.

"Aye." Elysia's dark head came up at the mention

of Mark. " 'Tis because I deem it important to talk with you about him that I came this morn."

"Indeed?" Gervaise's eyes narrowed against an unexpected development, one that he much doubted would meet his approval.

"I was with Mark yesterday when an arrow was shot far closer to me than mine of moments past could possibly have come to you." Ebony tendrils clustered around an ivory face host to a slight frown. Elysia bit at her lips, realizing that in her anxiety to make a case for Mark's safety, she'd found the purely wrong words to lead where she wanted to go, particularly as her goal was unlikely to be welcomed by Gervaise.

Ah, she was concerned for her own safety. A faint smile curled Gervaise's thin lips, and as his chin lifted to an arrogant angle, the morning sun burned the brighter over dark red hair for the deep greens of the forest behind. He expected such womanly fears and well understood such self-interest.

"There will never be another such attack," Gervaise smoothly assured the dark beauty still clutching her bow.

"I pray not," Elysia nodded, a smile of relief warming lips nibbled to rosy brightness. Though she'd failed to get the plea out, it seemed Gervaise had understood and granted the boon she sought. "Never could I accept happiness purchased at the cost of Mark's life."

Gervaise's fierce scowl returned to top a sneer of disgust. "By your defense of him I gather that you—like so many, many women before—have been caught by the famous lady-charmer's wiles."

Elysia straightened against words that felt like an unforeseen assault.

"Oh, aye." Gervaise's voice fair dripped with the acid of disdain. "Mark cut a wide swathe through the multitude of feminine hearts in every court of which he's been a part for any length of time. Not"—Gervaise shrugged—"that Mark requires much time to accomplish his goal. Only see how quickly you succumbed."

"He hasn't seduced me!" Elysia instantly denied the implication.

"Yet . . ." Gervaise coldly examined Elysia from the dark curls escaped from her marginally proper braid to the tips of dainty toes peeking beneath the hem of a gown as green as their surroundings.

"You do both me and Ida a grave injustice to believe that I was so poorly reared," Elysia defended herself against this unjust condemnation while hoping Gervaise would think the vivid color flooding her cheeks with the memory of heated kisses merely a sign of temper.

" 'Tis not *your* training at fault but *his* well-practiced charms." Gervaise knew that now was the time to convince the maid that blame for all wrongs lay with Mark.

Elysia's stubborn nature would not easily yield the argument, but inwardly she began to question her own responses to Mark. In their rides and evening talks had Mark, in truth, merely played over her emotions as expertly as some master musician his harp?

"Has Mark convinced you that he means only good to Wroxton . . . and you?" Gervaise's voice sank into gentle tones that held a silky inducement to believe.

Confused, Elysia refused to respond, leaving Gervaise to continue.

" 'Tis the first bait the wily Wolf would use to lure you into his snare."

Although the maid remained mute, Gervaise saw the faint uncertainty in brown eyes and struck again at this area of vulnerability. "For proof of how successful are his charms, only think of your fervent rejection of Mark when first he appeared and next of your desire to protect him now."

Gervaise reached out and took the maid's free hand in apparent concern. "Take care elsewise you'll wake one morn to find yourself thoroughly trapped."

Having no answer to give, Elysia stood her ground, glaring at the man she'd idolized for so long, the man who ever left her feeling childish and full of self-doubts.

"Take care," Gervaise repeated, caressing her cheek in a more personal show of affection than ever he had before. "Elsewise the Black Wolf will see our marriage plans come to naught and you tangled within the inflexible bonds of his power while he seizes all that is yours."

Deeming it best to leave her in solitude, the better to ponder the issues he'd raised, Gervaise calmly turned and departed from the quiet glade warmed by a morning sun peeking through hazy clouds.

The fading glow of twilight flowing through the sea cave's entrance was of a sudden blocked, and in that same instant Jamie gasped. Heart beating an erratic pace, Elysia spun around to find a cloaked man silhouetted in the opening.

"You followed me." Elysia's voice held both shock and disgust.

As Mark nodded, his mocking smile appeared. Yet, rather than speak to the damsel, his attention turned to the boy pressing himself tighter against the wall at his back. From those who had long lived within Wroxton's borders, Mark had made an effort to secure information to help him better understand this boy.

"Jamie, repeatedly have I sought to convince your mother and your friend, Elysia, of the right in coaxing you back home to the castle."

Jamie dubiously watched the intimidating man he'd attempted to kill. Willingly return to the castle and lose his head or leastways his hands? Not likely!

"After learning of your close friendship with Lady Elysia, I realized that from your perspective the action you took against me was done with an honorable intent. And though I cannot let it pass unpunished, I doubt you will find working with my squire too unpleasant a duty."

Jamie brightened. When Lord Aldreth was alive, he had begun as page to train for knighthood. But after their lord's death, the boys sent from elsewhere to foster at Wroxton had been returned to their families while Jamie's training had ended. Thus this lord's "punishment" came much closer to being a gift.

Though still mocking, genuine warmth entered Mark's half smile. "Mayhap understandably, the gentlewomen to whom I appealed were too concerned for your safety to trust my word. But I hope you will."

Jamie looked warily between the man about whom he knew almost nothing and his friend Elysia. No matter the lure in the new lord's pretty promise of a much desired goal, if she didn't trust this stranger, how could he?

"I hope that by the good I've done for Lady Elysia's people I've proven to her that whatever oaths I give, I keep."

Elysia reluctantly nodded, torn between Gervaise's arguments of the morn and this man's twilight reasoning.

"There you have it, Jamie." Mark turned a penetrating silver gaze to the boy. "Proof that my word I keep, and I give you my oath that you will come to no harm at my hand."

Still Jamie cast a questioning glance to the maid who hesitantly nodded before looking back to the man extending a strong arm toward him.

"Come, stand and shake on our agreement." When the boy lifted his hand, Mark pulled to his feet the awkward youth growing too fast for grace of movement to keep pace with sprouting height. Then, gripping a thin arm just below the elbow, he joined their forearms together in confirmation of an honorable alliance made man to man.

The hint of a shy smile tilted Jamie's mouth upward. This was the first time any adult had treated him with equal respect. Elysia saw the boy's response and couldn't help but feel warmed by the man's consideration of an adolescent's tender pride. However, her next thought was to question the sincerity of the action. Had Mark merely wielded against Jamie the same charm Gervaise had warned her about?

"Dinner has doubtless been delayed by my absence." Mark gave a rueful grimace. "And we three must all hasten back."

Elysia knew it was true that the evening meal would not be served until the lord took his place at the high table. It was true, too, that Mark was unlikely to leave without both her and Jamie in his company. Thus, hoping for the best but fearing the worst, an absently frowning Elysia led the way from the cave. With her in the lead, Jamie following, and Mark at the back they climbed a path made slick by the mists of twilight.

Elysia sat beside Mark at the high table for a meal that seemed to last forever. Mark had casually talked while a fine selection of food was served and eaten but she had taken hardly a bite and spoken not at all. Elysia was far, far too aware of being caught in the snare of the Black Wolf's attraction. She glanced sidelong only to be pierced by an intense silver gaze abruptly turned her way. Unable to pull free, the impact trembled through her and her heart thumped wildly.

Mark's jaw went rigid. He could feel the fiery maid's tension. And in rightly reading its source to his mouth came a stunning smile, absent of cynicism and filled with warm invitation.

Drawing a deep, ragged gasp, Elysia purposefully bent her head and glared down at the trencher they shared, determined to focus her attention safely away from the powerful man. Her wise intent was foiled by the houseserf who removed the now empty platter, leaving her to study diligently the table's bare planks like a witless moonling until her attention was reclaimed by unexpected words.

"Jamie," Mark softly called to the boy sitting between Elysia and the woman glowing with joy for her son's return, "a young man ought not be dependent upon his mother to cut his meat and bread."

A faint blush stained the boy's cheeks. Although he shared his mother's platter, for years he'd had his own dagger—the same dagger he'd tried to drive into Mark's heart.

Elysia was appalled that the Black Wolf would tease Jamie about the very implement used in the misdeed at the root of his woes. It threatened to destroy what good opinion he'd won in wooing Jamie back to the castle. Mark's next action robbed his words of their sting.

From behind his own wide belt, Mark pulled the blade he'd retrieved from the floor of his bedchamber after a failed attempt to take his life. This he handed to Elysia who in turn passed it to Jamie.

The boy's hand closed about the bone hilt of his knife while a grateful smile bloomed.

"I give you my oath that never will you have reason to regret your forgiveness of me." Jamie gave the fervent promise while leaning forward to steadily meet a silver gaze.

"Of that I have no doubt." Mark nodded, shifting a potent smile to the maid for some reason grown wary of him once more. In resentment of his tracking her to the sea cave? "Elsewise, I'd not have given it back to you."

For the most part, it was with approval that the people at tables stretched out below in two long lines at right angles to the dais watched this exchange. Only Dunstan's eyes narrowed with particular interest on the errant youth and the dagger returned.

Dunstan had spent the days since his meeting with Gervaise hunting for some method to do the deed demanded and safely escape. The reappearance of an erstwhile assassin opened whole new avenues for his consideration. Moreover, he could now see leastwise one fortunate result to his demotion: Not one of his fellow guardsmen would bother wasting a moment's attention on him. Thus they failed to see either the grin of satisfaction spreading thick lips or the hands folding complacently atop the shelf of his well-fed belly.

Elysia feared that by this action Mark might be wielding the enticement of a famed warrior's approval against Jamie just as he'd all too effectively worked a lady-charmer's magic on her. Soon her thoughts were fully occupied with worry that Gervaise was right in claiming she'd been led astray by the Black Wolf's wiles. A likelihood that would make her a fool indeed! But then hadn't she recognized the danger of such a handsome man the very moment she first laid eyes on him? Yet, even forewarned, still he'd overcome her suspicions. It meant she must reinforce her defenses fourfold and stay as far from Mark as possible!

That decision brought to mind a dangerous fact. Their meal was over and soon Mark would expect her to retreat with him to the solar where it had become habit for them to meet and quietly talk each evening. She must find an excuse to avoid such close contact now and in future.

"Pray forgive me ..." Fearing that her inability to easily feign false emotions might permit Mark to read the truth in her gaze, Elysia refused to look up. Instead she rubbed fingertips gently over her temples. "My head is pounding and I would seek my bed."

"I will miss our visit," Mark replied, concern adding a dark velvet thread to his deep voice.

Elysia gave an honest grimace but one born of her discomfort in lying rather than pain. Her chair scraped over the dais's plank surface as she pushed it back and rose to depart. Attention firmly downcast, Elysia made her way to the corner stairwell aware of Mark's eyes on her back and fearing he had recognized her deceit.

Once in her bedchamber, troubled thoughts were not lessened but increased, setting Elysia to pacing from one side of the room to the other. As she had stated her intent to go to bed, go to bed she would although sleep was unlikely to soon come. Knowing the chill of a cold floor and prickly rushes beneath bare feet would drive her into the comfort of warm bedclothes when nothing else could, Elysia bent to remove dainty slippers. After placing her shoes neatly below a row of wooden pegs driven into the wall beside the door Elysia stripped off her kirtle and added it to the array of garments hanging there.

Dressed only in a fine linen undergown of pale blue, Elysia began loosening her braided hair while turning to gingerly make her way toward a bedside chest. Atop its smooth surface sat a brightly glazed ewer and basin beckoning with sweet promise. Elysia was intent on cooling tension's heat by rinsing hands and face before retiring when she lifted the pitcher. But as she moved a step closer to pour fresh spring water into the basin, her heel came down hard on a sharp twig.

Elysia jerked the injured foot back and the heavy

vessel slipped from her hold. It smashed against the floor. Pottery shattered into a thousand pieces while water sprayed in a wide arc.

"God's blood!" Venting this most unladylike but heartfelt oath, Elysia glared down at soaked feet. The heel of one already felt as if a nasty thorn were buried deep inside and both were certain to be lacerated by any attempt to move across the shards of pottery spread all around.

"Elysia!" The door crashed open under a concerned Mark's forceful shove. "What happened? Is the pain in your head too great?"

Doe-brown eyes wide, Elysia spun toward the door with hands instinctively joined to press against the base of an elegant throat. She saw that any answer to his questions, even could she regain her composure so far as to give them, were rendered useless by a silver gaze dropping to the jagged disorder at her feet.

Recognizing her predicament, Mark took two long strides forward, reaching out to lift her into gentle arms and carry her safely over the danger.

The unbidden thrill of being wrapped in the tender cradle of a strong embrace left Elysia all the more certain of what danger lay behind such frightening pleasure. With unshielded apprehension she studied the male face too perfect to be trusted. To her shame the emotion inspired by the sight was not disgust. Of a sudden Elysia was aware of having melted against him and pulled back while inwardly cursing the body's ability to play traitor to the mind.

Mark had been entranced by the feel of this alluring damsel light as thistledown and surrounded by the faint scent of wildflowers. But as Elysia went rigid in his hold, Mark realized that he was standing as motionless as any dumbstruck oaf. His jaw went tight, and he moved to set her atop the bed. But he fell to temptation and gazed down into unwavering brown eyes in whose depths golden temper flickered. The vision paradoxically restored his good humor.

Elysia couldn't break the visual bond with Mark. And that inability confirmed her growing belief in the accuracy of Gervaise's admonition to be wary of the devastating man towering above. She leaned away from him, speaking without pausing for wise forethought.

"You *are* the wicked danger I've been warned to fear."

"Me?" Black brows arched with wry humor. "Do you mean as a skilled warrior meeting armed foes?" His smile took on an intimacy that sent a potent shock to her toes and his voice dropped to a deep purr. "Or as a lover?"

"Both." Elysia's chin lifted in defiance of Mark's undeniable appeal. She had no intention of telling him precisely what had been said or by whom. Asides, the Black Wolf was renowned as a warrior. And likely the only reason she'd not earlier heard of his reputation as a lady-charmer was because few men dared share such talk with any wellborn woman.

"Don't confuse me with your betrothed's dear friend Robert of Belleme. I am proud to be known as a fierce warrior in battle but I take up arms only when summoned by my liege or in defense of my own."

"Belleme?" Elysia had heard many whisper the name with dread but never had she heard it spoken by Gervaise. How could that be if in truth he were Gervaise's *dear friend*?

Mark saw Elysia's confusion. Misunderstanding its source, he stated the difference between himself and the cruel Belleme more clearly. "I have harmed others only when both just and necessary while Belleme maims and kills for pleasure."

Elysia nodded, this much she'd learned from overheard talk amongst guardsmen at their leisure.

"Best Gervaise guard his actions carefully," Mark added with a mockery unhidden. "Belleme has been known to demand high prices for so much as a hint of disloyalty or suggestion of ineffectiveness.

"Thus, I am a danger to my foes but as a lover ..." Mark's tone dipped into a velvet enticement while his attention fell to an inadequate shield for tempting curves before rising to a piquant face. "Already I've told you that never would I force myself on any woman. To that I add that neither would I seduce a virgin like you."

Though blushing at such intimate talk, Elysia could not look away from the power of silver eyes sending thrilling bolts of lightning through her. A slight whimper escaped her tight throat while a satisfied smile curled male lips slowly descending.

Mark moved his mouth gently, enticingly across smooth cheeks to nibble at the corner of her beguiling lips before searing them with the tender heat of joining. With the action he once again sampled the intoxicating taste of an innocent passion able to set his blood afire. And when small hands lifted to clutch at powerful shoulders as if the seated maid felt in danger of losing her balance, Mark sank to his knees and urged her more fully into his embrace.

Melting against the formidable wall of his chest, wild sensations throbbed within Elysia. Her heartbeat took on an erratic pace while she felt herself lost in the black haze of hungry need. Fighting for a last shred of sanity as his mouth made a fiery path from lips, down a throat arched beneath the touch, Elysia's lashes fluttered open.

"Ida . . ."

Elysia's single word was a soft, horrified sigh but spoken near enough to Mark's ear to earn his attention. He cast a quick glance over his shoulder to find the plump woman hovering in the doorway, looking more pleased than upset by what she'd come upon. That, leastwise, was reassuring when by looking back to the blushing woman in his arms he found a confused mixture of shame and lingering passion.

Even while struggling from clinging mists of desire, Elysia acknowledged their heated exchange as proof that she'd been truly snared by the Black Wolf's lure. Her head bent and eyes clenched shut but only for a moment. Rarely had she failed to meet any challenge face to face. To fail in this instance and before this man would bring her greatest humiliation.

Mark viewed Elysia's proud action as further proof of her strength and wished only that he could do more to lessen her discomfort at another's discovery of their embrace. But, knowing what she was most certain to welcome, he granted her the boon of his departure.

Elysia watched as with masculine power and grace, Mark stepped around the block Ida made in his path to disappear from her chamber. His absence released Elysia's determined will. Her heated face dropped into cupped hands.

Chapter 10

Elysia hadn't meant to eavesdrop on a friend. Yet she couldn't help but hear Jamie when, after quietly taking a single step into the shadows beside the open stable door, she paused to allow sunlight-accustomed eyes to adjust to new surroundings.

"I've lost it." With grooming brush in hand, Jamie stood on one side of Mark's destrier while David worked on the other.

"Lost it?" The voice of an adolescent struggling toward manhood broke on the doubtful query. "How in sweet heaven did you do that?"

Elysia identified the voice of Mark's squire. In the brief span of the few days that had passed since Jamie was given the *punishment* of joining in the other lad's training, the pair had become fast friends. She was not surprised. At Wroxton there'd been no boys of an age with Jamie since Lord Aldreth's death and the return of fostered lads to their families.

"Would that I knew." Jamie's dejected spirit dragged the words down into a sigh of doom. "It disappeared in the night while we slept."

Elysia was loath to interrupt a plainly private talk but just as uncomfortable with spying. Uncertain what action to take, she hesitated for several moments while the two boys worked in silence. Although Jamie had shared his mother's small bedchamber near every night of his life before the failed assault on Mark, two evenings earlier he'd begun staying in this stable's loft with David. It was Ida's difficulty in adjusting to this change that had brought Elysia here in time to catch the odd conversation.

"Waste no thought on the circumstances." Quiet desperation filled Jamie's voice. "Only help me devise some plan for what to do until I can find it again."

"First, don't panic." David's answer was immediate. "Then tell Lord Mark. He's an understanding man and never ready to level unjust blame upon anyone in haste. 'Tis a quality that you of all people ought know by now."

"Don't you see it's for that very reason I cannot—"

"Nay," David interrupted. "For that *very reason* you should be better able to simply explain." Seeing Jamie's dubious expression, he fervently added, "I give you my oath that there is good reason for the honor and respect with which our master is held in three countries."

"Three countries?" Jamie was temporarily diverted from personal troubles.

Despite the stable's dim light, David's broad grin flashed white while he lifted one finger of his free hand for each point made. "In his father's English fiefdom, the Welsh princedom of his sister's husband, and on his own Norman lands. Moreover, it seems to me he's gone a fair way toward proving his worth here in Wroxton as well."

" 'Struth, it required naught but an amazingly short time for Lord Mark to begin winning the people's loyalty. Yet it is a fact that makes me only more certain that I daren't confess my loss without an acceptable explanation ... not *this* loss."

"What loss?" Elysia moved forward, no longer willing to even inadvertently spy on a friend.

Jaw dropping in shocked distress, Jamie whirled toward a slender figure nearly lost in shadows deepened by the block of bright sunlight falling through an open door. Unable to find a believable lie, least of all one able to fool this woman who knew him so well, he was thankful when David promptly spoke in his stead.

"The key that opens the chest containing Lord Mark's favorite gauntlets has been misplaced." Seeing his new friend's panic, to divert the lady's attention without speaking a falsehood, David immediately substituted the confession of a recent wrong of his own. His ploy won a grateful glance from Jamie.

Knowing the value of mail gloves, a relieved Elysia accepted the explanation. "That being so, Jamie, I also counsel you to confess your wrong to the man whose loss it actually is."

"Were you looking for me?" Jamie quickly shifted the subject of their talk, anxious to avoid being forced into confirming a half-truth or agreeing to an unnecessary deed.

Elysia nodded and moved until the sunlight falling from behind lent her figure a golden outline. "Since you began training for knighthood in earnest, your mother has missed your company. She wanted to seek you out, but the pain in her joints was worsened by the damp of recent storms. And since the nasty ailment makes any sustained movement difficult, I offered to fetch you instead."

"I'll go to her now." Welcoming an opportunity to escape an uncomfortable scene, Jamie was half out the door before these words left his mouth.

Perched atop the bright scarlet of her draped bed's coverlet and facing a long evening of boredom, Elysia drew up and wrapped arms about her legs before resting cheek atop knees. In the several days since Ida had found her in Mark's embrace, she'd fallen ever deeper into concern for his power to sway her sane intents. To escape the man's potent company, she'd gone so far as to skip evening meals rather than be forced to invent further excuses for retiring early to avoid joining him in the solar.

Long hours of boredom were the price of her choice but, happily, not hunger. Under the firm belief that good food was the key to recovery from every ailment, a concerned Ida hovered near any patient with nourishing meals. And the plump woman, thinking her charge the victim of recurring evening headaches, had supplied simple but abundant repasts.

Had Ida, despite personal pain, attempted to deliver them herself Elysia would've confessed her deceit rather than have discomfort increased on her behalf. But the woman's aching joints caused her to assign the chore to houseserfs. That they'd done Ida's bidding was testified to by the platter balanced on one corner of a bedside chest although it now supported only a few breadcrumbs and an apple core.

Elysia had meant to retrieve one of her father's precious books from the bedchamber across the hall before Mark returned from his day's chores. In that intent she'd failed. And with nothing to occupy her thoughts, they returned to the morn's overhead conversation between Jamie and Mark's squire.

Though at the time Elysia had accepted the latter's hasty response to a question addressed to the former, on closer thought she found it curious. The answer provided by another had been no answer at all while, in truth, the playmate become admirer had given no response.

What possible explanation could there be for Jamie's reluctance to share any fact with a trusted friend such as she was? Were the two young men conspiring in some misdeed? Surely David would not be a part of any plot to harm the man he'd so warmly defended as a just lord? The lord respected in three lands.

Blocked by a tangle of unsettled emotions, Elysia's thoughts wandered down a smooth pathway into all too pleasant visions of the darkly handsome man with potent smile and glittering silver eyes. Elysia brought herself up short. Having gone to such lengths to avoid the Black Wolf's company, she would *not* allow him to sneak into her mind. Sleep. Sleep was the answer.

Quickly disrobing, Elysia doused the bedside candle and climbed into bed, determined to block with sweet slumber the self-betrayal found in these thoughts. Unfortunately that welcome oblivion was not so easily summoned. She lay awake, alternately tossing restlessly or staring blindly into the darkness for what seemed an eternity.

A firebrand had gone dark. Mark idly noted that fact as he climbed the stairway's tight spiral. Arching and then rotating his shoulders, he vainly attempted to lessen the discomfort of an aching back. He'd spent evening hours hunched over the closely scrawled records of the castle's accounts. That depressing task, added to Elysia's all too obvious decision to stay as far distant from him as possible, had increased his stress.

As Mark took another step up, he acknowledged the glimmer of hope it perversely afforded. Though at first he'd worried over Elysia's possible complicity in treacherous deeds, Mark realized that if that concern were justified, she'd never have taken such obvious steps to avoid him. Rather, she would surely have made herself both available and amenable to his company.

Even amidst a darkness alleviated only by the faint glow of the next firebrand some distance around the corner, a dagger's honed edge flashed. Slashing from behind in a deadly arc, it sliced toward a bared neck. Mark's hand instantly came up to grip the gauntleted fist wielding the weapon. Even so, his breath hissed out as he suffered a stinging sensation followed by the welling dampness of blood.

Halted short of success, in a matter of seconds, the silent assailant pulled free, leaving Mark holding an empty gauntlet while the loosed knife clattered down stone steps. Spinning about, Mark set off in pursuit of the unseen foe whose fleeing footsteps could be heard in rapid retreat. Mark was so intent on his goal that he failed to see the purposefully discarded cloak. With his second stride, two stairsteps in length, entangling cloth caught at Mark's feet. It tripped and sent him crashing down.

A single vicious curse demanded and won the full attention of the maid dozing in a chamber not far distant. Elysia leaped from the bed, wound its scarlet coverlet haphazardly about her nude form, and rushed toward the stairwell opening.

Mark's curse was aimed equally at the black-hearted foe and his waylaying ploy. While impatiently fighting free of impeding material still wrapped about his feet, he discovered the garment was made of a velvet as fine as that which formed his own best cape.

By the time Mark regained his feet, he was certain that to follow and capture the wretch responsible for the attack and his fall would be a wasted effort. It was too late to achieve that much desired end. This was a disgusting fact but no matter ... Mark's face closed into a harsh mask. He had in his possession clues to his assailant's identity—the cloak at his feet and glove still in his hold.

Mark glanced down at the abandoned gauntlet. By the light of a torch on the stairwell's next landing, he found a sinister reality. The armor-plated leather glove was a single one from his own favorite pair. Gold detailed and a gift from Henry—once prince and now sovereign. Mark wore them only while acting as champion for his patron. Because of their great value, he had long kept them safely locked inside a small chest.

In a foul humor Mark turned to reclimb the steps responsible for already aching bruises. A short distance above where he'd landed, Mark's attention was caught by another unpleasant discovery. It was the dagger that had been wielded against him ... again. The same dagger he had returned to Jamie. Before Mark could bend to retrieve it, he sensed another's presence. Glancing up, silver eyes took in a vision framed in the arched opening of the corridor leading to his chamber.

The firebrand held by an iron ring driven into a stone wall lent an alabaster sheen to flesh rising from bright cloth and highlights to a soft cloud of ebony tresses. Elysia was a tempting sight.

Elysia stood uncertainly as focus of the Black Wolf's penetrating eyes. For someone who wanted safe distance between herself and this man, such a late-night action was incredibly foolish. Even that self-derisive thought was driven from her mind by the discovery of a bright gash angling across Mark's throat with blood dripping from its lowest point.

"Is that why you cried out?" While Elysia gripped the red coverlet closed with one hand, the other flew up to press against her own throat.

Elysia's alarm sounded sincere. But, having just survived yet another attack while this woman was near, Mark's distrust was roused. Though almost had Mark forgotten the surely negligible injury, he solemnly nodded while a half smile tilted his lips. Had the alluringly disheveled damsel come to this stairwell in the off chance that it might be necessary for her to distract him until the deadly feat was performed?

"Should we summon your guard to find your assailant and prevent another assault?" Elysia asked.

"Nay." Mark slowly shook his dark head. "I much

doubt a craven fool so easily put to flight possesses courage enough to dare another attempt this night."

Unconvinced and still fearing for him, Elysia made an awkward attempt to move back when Mark climbed to stand on a level with her. He towered above, but her desperate action was hampered by the unwieldy folds of cloth designed for beauty and holding cold at bay—not for wearing. Despite the risks of once again being caught inadequately garbed and alone with the Black Wolf, she was more fearful of the greater peril in leaving so dangerous a wound untended.

"Come ..." Elysia reached out to lightly clasp Mark's arm. "Let me care for your wound."

In her gentle touch and the doe-brown softness of her eyes, Mark recognized a concern whose sincerity he could no longer doubt ... leastwise not in so far as her honest desire to treat his injury. When cynicism fled his smile, it became more intimate. And its potency increased as his gaze slowly drifted over the innocent's expanse of creamy skin not meant for any man to see yet bared by haphazardly wrapped cloth.

The smile without mockery mesmerized Elysia and her legs nearly gave out under the intensity of his gaze. Her toes curled against the use-smoothed floor until, self-conscious, her hand dropped away as quickly as if he'd transformed into red-hot steel. Upon turning with the intention of leading the way to her chamber, she made a disconcerting discovery. Beneath the weight of Mark's full attention, it was no easy thing to walk while swaddled in heavy material that dragged like a riptide behind.

With one hand Elysia tugged the front edge of her makeshift garment higher and with the other desperately attempted to jerk trailing folds into submission. Bending her head, she sent a rich array of curls flowing forward. With that dusky curtain Elysia sought leastways to hide the tide of color rising from the vulnerable curve of her neck to warm satin cheeks with a shade near as bright as her improvised garb.

After quietly laying his misused gauntlet on the landing, Mark willingly followed Elysia. Though appreciatively watching, intrigued by the gentle sway of her hips, he wisely thought to take the firebrand from its iron ring. The tapers in the damsel's chamber had doubtless been extinguished long past.

While the man relit her darkened bedside candle, Elysia inwardly chastised herself for not taking that sensible action on her own. Doubtless her lack would further convince Mark either that she hosted thoughtless expectations of others or that she possessed naught but the simple wits of a moonling.

During the moments required for her visitor to step back into the corridor and return the torch to its holder, Elysia hastily rewound and tucked the coverlet more firmly about herself. After Mark again entered her chamber and this time closed the door, she motioned him to sit on the same three-legged stool where she daily perched while Ida braided ebony hair.

After casting the barely adequate seat a dubious glance, Mark simultaneously stripped off his tunic and gingerly lowered his huge frame. Despite an ominous creak, the stool held steady while he settled as comfortably as possible. He restrained the threat of a renewed grin with a carefully bland expression maintained only with difficulty.

"Milady," Mark spoke in a tone equally bland, "I

daresay you'll appreciate a clear field for your ministrations." In truth, he thought no such thing but couldn't resist the opportunity to bait her fiery spirit.

Between words so flat they were a taunt in themselves and the sparkle of humor Elysia saw in Mark's eyes, she wanted to stomp her foot in a temper. Instead, although thick lashes descended to narrow her gaze, she forced a bright smile. Then she presented him with her slender back and moved to fetch the basket of bandages and salves brought back from the sea cave.

Mark's voice dropped into a deep velvet caress as he quietly added, "I find it difficult to rue such misbegot attacks as have been launched against me within castle walls when their result is my winning of your tender attentions."

Fighting the strength of his charm, Elysia paused to take a deep breath and bolster her defenses before again facing the dangerously handsome man. As with the first wound of Mark's that she'd tended, the blood of this one had already dried. Never had Elysia dealt with an injury of this sort, leaving her to fervently rue the offer of care. She made her way to Mark's side with eyes downcast and wondering if it were even possible to bandage such a wound without strangling him.

Nearly could Elysia do that very deed with glee after glancing up to find herself still subjected to the poorly hidden amusement in a silver gaze. Curled fingers threatened to snap in twain a tightly clutched wicker handle.

"I assume you mean to cleanse my wound?" In breaking the long silence fair crackling with her ire, Mark made a valiant attempt to keep mockery from his voice but could nowise tame the laughter in his eyes.

Elysia gave a curt nod and stiffly moved to dip a clean cloth into water she'd earlier poured from ewer into basin. Struggling to prevent further betrayal of her emotional turmoil by acting with unnecessary or even harmful force, she returned to gently dab at the brown edges of the gash across a strong throat.

Too soon her attention dipped to the texture of sun-bronzed skin below. Mindlessly wishing she could trace the dusting of dark curls across the broad expanse of his chest, her eyes were drawn uncontrollably down its dark V to where it was blocked by the cloth impediment of his chausses. Shocked by the sudden awareness of a wrongful fascination, Elysia forced her gaze back to the task at hand.

A few droplets of fresh blood had appeared, leaving Elysia to fear her ministering actions anything but helpful. Temper cooled by errant thoughts and alarm over what harm her insufficient skill might have wrought, she concentrated on the goal of curbing the minor flow and failed to realize her scarlet covering was slipping perilously low.

With the delicious damsel bending near, Mark could hardly keep from catching tantalizing glimpses of far more of alluring curves than her modesty would knowingly permit. His pulse pounded under the dangerous awareness that generous breasts were so near to freedom the smallest tug would liberate them. By clenching his eyes shut against her unknowing enticements, Mark fought an ill-conceived compulsion to loosen that barrier and view the bounty of ivory flesh draped only in a luxurious cloud of dusky curls.

"Have I hurt you?" Elysia misread her patient's action as a wince of pain.

Dark lashes slowly lifted to reveal a silver lure that drew Elysia helplessly into the net of his incredible attraction. Pulled deeper by her own longing for an unknown but surely inevitable end, she barely felt the hand sliding beneath her wealth of hair, cupping the back of her neck, and bringing her lips to his.

Although Mark fought the compulsion to immediately taste her full measure, to swallow her into his embrace, the melding of their mouths seemed to drain strength from the damsel's limbs.

Elysia sank gratefully into the powerful circle of arms gathering her nearer and easing her down across the hard muscles of his thighs. Releasing the damp cloth to slip unnoticed from her hand, she was lost to logical thought. Tumbling ever deeper into the welcome heat of passion's hungry flames, Elysia failed to realize that while yielding to Mark's hold the scarlet covering had fallen into a soft bunch about her small waist.

Mark was all too well aware of full, sweet-silk curves unexpectedly melting against the broad plains of his bare chest. Beneath that fiery sensation a low groan rumbled from his chest. He swept the hand still at her nape down a satin back to urge her hips nearer to the center of his need even while holding her close with his other arm and gradually increasing the slow, delicious torment of their kiss.

Although temporarily lost amongst a host of delicious new experiences, Elysia suddenly became aware of the shocking feel of his powerful torso against her breasts. Shuddering with wild excitement, she instinctively responded by arching deeper into his embrace.

Surrendering to the devastating man whose intimate caress burned, Elysia willingly fell prey to an earlier temptation. She slowly stroked over broad shoulders, learning their strength by touch before tangling her fingers into the cool strands of a mane as black as her own.

While luscious flesh helplessly trembling with desire melded with the hard muscle of his own, Mark struggled to control the urgent need to immediately merge their forms in passion. Inwardly he cursed himself as a fool for having permitted the fires of this inflaming embrace to flare so strongly they threatened to incinerate the bonds of even his famed restraint. Breaking the seal of their too tempting kiss, he pulled back to draw deep, ragged breaths but made the mistake of looking down at the full measure of rare beauty softly yielding in his arms.

Elysia was unable to remain motionless beneath the demands of an aching hunger she hadn't the experience to control. Despite the slight distance Mark attempted to enforce between them, she writhed against him, dragging the sensitive tips of her breasts back and forth across the wiry curls covering his chest.

Though groaning in one moment with the anguish behind his attempt to regain command over passionate fires threatening to burst free, in the next Mark suddenly pulled Elysia tight. By that abrupt action he unknowingly brought an immediate end to their embrace. The stool called to bear far too great a weight collapsed.

Following the crash of splintering wood and thud of

falling bodies, silence fell but only for brief moments. Soon, while laying on his back amidst broken pieces and overwhelmed by the situation's absurdity, Mark's deep, rich laughter softly filled the chamber.

Disoriented by lingering fires of passion rudely dashed by the frigid water of cold reality, Elysia struggled to pull from the man across whose chest she'd come to lie pillowed. Sitting up, horrified by mental images of her own ungovernable response in the scene just past, she belatedly attempted to arrange the red cloth too long ignored and reestablish a modicum of modesty.

"You've been rescued," Mark wryly stated. "You should be thankful to our rickety perch." He, too, sat up. Then, climbing to his feet, he shook a dark head as much to clear it of desire's mists as to shake into place the senses disordered by their fall.

While he rose, Elysia gazed up at the man so recently ardent lover now abruptly returned to mocking stranger.

Mark saw the anger in her glare but also the golden sparks still burning at the back of brown eyes. In their fire he recognized a lingering danger. He could take Elysia—seduce the unintentional temptress into yielding if he chose. Aye, he undeniably possessed that capability—but not the right. He had sworn that he never seduced innocents and had even given Elysia his oath that he wouldn't take her virtue. But either he leave *now* or see himself forsworn.

"Thank you for cleaning my wound." Mark motioned toward the dark line across his throat. "I've no doubt it will mend of its own."

With those final words Mark strode toward the door

and departed. No need to excuse his leave-taking by confessing how near he'd come to breaking his oath. The hour was late, and he had items to retrieve and tasks that must be done before the sun rose on another day.

As Elysia watched the door quietly close behind a broad back, she was confused—not by his abrupt departure but by her own unpredictable responses to unforeseen events. How had it come to be when she'd tried so hard to avoid the Black Wolf's company?

Thinking back, Elysia acknowledged that it was her loud curse that had brought Mark to her chamber a few nights before and that his rude expletive had drawn her out to invite him in tonight. Plainly the priests were right. Curses were the devil's invitation to sin. She made a firm decision to never, ever under any circumstances repeat or respond to such wrongful words again.

Her conscience was only temporarily eased by that oath. Far too much had occurred for so simple a penance. Indeed, nearly had she surrendered her chastity to the man who'd sworn he would never seduce her. Nearly ... Only the stool unable to hold them both had saved her. Mark had the right of it. She should be thankful for the stool's inadequacy. She should be! But, to her own disgust, Elysia found a troubling lack of fervent gratitude.

Chapter 11

*E*yes determinedly lowered, Elysia took her seat on
a high-back chair at the dais while striving to look
utterly unaware of the powerful man too near. This
was the first evening in near a sennight that she'd
come to the great hall for the day's last meal. Although avoiding dinners and thus the Black Wolf's
company had been her purpose in feigning a lingering
illness, it was perversely their previous night's passionate encounter that drove her to return this eve. Their
heated embrace in the dead of night had proven how
useless was such a tactic for evading him.

Indeed, yestereve's scene had left Elysia ashamed
of herself for having taken the coward's path in the
first instance. No longer was she willing to play the
fainthearted maiden. Rousing a rebellious spirit, she
purposefully stoked a fiery temper with thoughts of
the man's mocking smile and cynical words. She intended, moreover, to prove herself capable of with-

standing his charms by turning a cold shoulder though sitting at his side. And with Ida for company, she meant even to dare joining him in the solar after the meal's conclusion.

The room was awash with the noise of arriving guardsmen, rowdy and jostling each other in taking their places, while with hooded eyes Mark watched the beauty settle a mere handsbreadth away. He was host to diametrically opposed emotions—warm pleasure for Elysia's unexpected return to the hall clashed with a chilling suspicion that her presence this night would vastly complicate delicate matters. It would've been far better had she waited a single day more. No matter. What was done was done.

"Welcome, milady." Mark's deep voice was so low only Elysia clearly heard the words while his strong bronze hand came into her downcast view and lifted her chin.

To her own disgust, Elysia felt cheeks heat with a rosy hue as she looked up. Despite her best intentions, she found herself tumbling into gray depths where silver lightning flashed with elemental power.

Captured by the graceful woman's allure, Mark experienced much the same sensation while gazing into brown eyes wherein golden sparks appeared. Beneath his steady attention they took fire, a fact that summoned a wry smile full of masculine satisfaction.

Breath caught in Elysia's throat for this devastating man's sheer male beauty and the potent excitement he so easily wielded. The warmth of Mark's body reached out to envelope her. She felt the net of his attraction wrapping its gentle tendrils around her and struggled to break the bond with silver eyes.

Elysia, once freed, became horribly aware of being the center of attention for a great many curious onlookers and strived to focus her attention elsewhere and on anything but Mark. Gripping a pottery goblet so hard it was a wonder the vessel failed to snap in twain, she gazed blindly at a nebulous spot on the rush-strewn floor between two lower tables.

Elysia's intent scrutiny roused Mark's curiosity. He couldn't be certain at what or whom she stared but suspected it was the man she'd heatedly defended after he'd demanded the greedy toad forfeit a price for his wrongs.

Were Elysia and Dunstan laying plots against him? Mark tried to banish that bleak prospect. However, her quick arrival at the site of the past night's assault had roused too many unpleasant possibilities for him to easily dismiss the likelihood of this one. He told himself the sharp pain of what felt like betrayal was merely a result of the certainty that any interference by her would make what was soon to follow more difficult. But the same well-honed perceptions that kept him from being misled by others prevented him from accepting the comfort of his own lie.

The plain but filling meal including both fowl and fish was accompanied by lively conversation at tables below but near silence on the dais. By the time it was done Elysia's certainty of her wisdom in returning to the great hall was badly shaken. Mark's closeness was unnerving. She must—and, Elysia firmly told herself, would—find some better method for controlling too wayward responses.

But before the matter could be pondered further, her attention was diverted when Mark leaned forward to send a pointed silver glance down the table to the young man sitting beside his mother.

After Elysia had fetched Jamie for Ida the past day, mother and son had come to an agreement. He would spend his days in training and nights in the stable's loft with David. In return for agreeing to the plan, Ida won Jamie's pledge to continue joining her at the high table for evening meals. This, Ida had asserted, would allow her the opportunity to see her son each day and share his excitement by hearing about all that he learned.

"Jamie," Mark called clearly enough to be heard by those at tables below, "I have something that belongs to you, the same that already once I've restored to your hand."

A puzzled Elysia watched Jamie freeze and bite his lower lip in apparent apprehension. She saw, too, when Mark pulled a dagger from behind his belt, just as he had the first night after their return from the sea cave.

"Again this was wielded with the same deadly intent as before." The blade's edge glittered while Mark motioned toward the line across his throat. Many had seen the thin, ominous mark, but amongst the men of the garrison only Hugh knew him well enough to ask its source. And thus, beyond Elysia and the perpetrator, only Hugh knew the truth.

"Know you how your dagger came to be used in a further attempt to take my life?"

Crying out, Jamie jumped up. His chair tipped backward to land with a resounding crash as he leaped from the dais and dashed from the hall.

Elysia gasped. It couldn't be true! Was this what

she'd overheard him telling David had disappeared in the night? It must be so! And were that true, then he was innocent of the implied wrong. Heart pounding, Elysia abruptly rose. And, although with more grace than her childhood friend, she raced after Jamie, determined to find the truth and see him absolved.

Restraining his first instinct to immediately pursue the fleeing pair, Mark remained motionless long enough to observe the actions of those at lower tables. Following Jamie's flight came the immediate clamor of many voices attempting to be heard above all the others. Then, after the lady's hasty departure and despite the practice of remaining seated until their lord left the dais, his supporters rose and gathered in clusters. But Mark did not stand until one particular man slipped quietly from the hall.

"You've dithered too long." The acid in this ominously quiet rebuke struck fear into the hearts of two listeners already in dread of the speaker standing silhouetted against the orange glow of Kelby Keep's central hearth. "Duke Robert is even now working out the final details of his plan to set sail for these shores."

"So soon?" Gervaise's voice faltered as did the arrogance normally his. Only Robert of Belleme could do this to him, only this *friend* of many years. Aye, he was a friend but one who must never be crossed. It was a fact well proven by too many others counting themselves friends of Belleme only to have ghastly penalties exacted for deeds that he deemed traitorous.

"Soon?" Dark brows whose outer edges naturally angled upward met in a fierce frown. Belleme enjoyed his ability to frighten people. Even did he cultivate that talent by adopting the appearance of a godless infidel. Ever black garbed in clothing that shared the style of those worn by the Moorish inhabitants of southern lands bordering the Mediterranean Sea, he took pleasure in terrifying his Christian peers.

Belleme's next question, nearly a hiss, was accompanied by an eerie, penetrating stare. "Would you have the Duke of Normandy idly waste his time and our advantage until autumn storms turn a simple channel crossing into the first lethal trap to hinder our goals?"

"Nay." As Gervaise shook his head, russet hair caught and reflected the fire's brightness. "But we've barely entered the month of July, and much time remains before such woe is likely to befall us."

"Are you then refusing the duke's command?" Belleme's frown deepened, lending his brows an even more truly devilish slant.

"Nay." Again Gervaise firmly denied Belleme's accusation. "I would refuse neither the duke nor you, but ..."

In vicious undertones an earl and a lord debated the issue while an uneasy Dunston entertained desperate wishes. If only there was some way for him to completely escape the reach of the terrifying earl. Or leastways that he could slink into some dark corner of this great hall and cower unseen. Knowing too well that neither was possible, he sought the only escape available. He attempted to concentrate on anything but the topic of quiet, yet heated words passing between the other two men.

Hosting qualms enough about allying himself with Gervaise, never had Dunstan possessed the slightest desire to have truck with the fearsome Belleme. But, here he was in the same room with that dark-souled man, trembling with apprehension and anxious to do nothing to draw always dangerous and often deadly attention. So numerous were the tales whispered of Robert the Devil that they'd come to be commonly if caustically known as the Wonders of Belleme. Wonders? Hah! Terrors more like.

"Three failures?" The daunting disapproval in Belleme's soft snarl demanded even the resistant Dunstan's full attention. "Three times your hirelings have tried to slay the Black Wolf and failed?"

Gervaise's chin lifted against this scornful condemnation, but he did not speak.

"Plainly the minions you've recruited are inept." A sneer curled Belleme's thin lips. "Mayhap the failure was yours in not giving them effective inspiration?" His sneer became a cruel grin when he added, "Those I choose either succeed or wish for so simple and sweet a punishment as quick death."

As the one who had most recently failed at the chore, Dunstan went white. Pray God the earl would not call the same price forfeit for prior thwarted attempts. Of a sudden, as if the thought had been spoken aloud, Belleme turned toward Dunstan who went so weak he nearly fainted.

"What say you?" Belleme passed a long, measuring look over the portly man with his many chins. "Are you ready to do battle on Duke Robert's behalf?"

Dunstan, unwilling to risk revealing the depth of his terror by squeaking out a verbal answer, contented himself with a vigorous nod.

" 'Tis a task for the success of which you would be well rewarded." Belleme waved an open hand that with his next words abruptly closed into a powerful fist. "Or for its defeat be equally justly punished." The unholy glee in Belleme's eye as he spoke the last word made it clear that he would most enjoy meting out the latter.

Gervaise was frustrated by contemptuous rebukes and threats that got them no nearer their goal. " 'Tis true that attempts to put an end to the Black Wolf made both amidst the forest and inside castle walls have not accomplished their goal." Ill-hidden disgust infused Gervaise's voice as he asked, "Possess you some better plan?"

"I have." Belleme's distaste for the question's dubious tone was obvious. He paused, waiting for Gervaise to acknowledge his subservient position by meekly seeking details from his master.

Gervaise refused to yield and thus feed the other man's pride at the cost of his own. However, Dunstan was easily overwhelmed by the implicit danger in a lengthening silence. The once haughty master of Wroxton revealed the true cowardice of his nature by humbling himself to the earl with a quiet appeal.

"Pray tell us your plan, and we'll put it into motion afore another dawn arrives."

"You've failed by approaching our prey directly, a ploy doomed to futility when worked against one with abundant experience in defeating such actions." Though answering Dunstan, Belleme's piercing gaze remained upon his red-haired ally. "More than simple strength and forthright assaults are required. Only cunning will outwit the wily Wolf."

"Cunning?" Affronted, Gervaise's hands clenched while his shoulders straightened. "You think I employed no shrewdness in learning the man's path and sending an arrow winging through the forest? Or in plotting the late-night knife assault in a dark stairwell?"

"Shrewdness, aye. But not subtlety, not cunning." Belleme slowly shook a head of gray-streaked dark hair. "And only subtle cunning will succeed. Cunning entwined with the witless superstitions of many."

Gervaise's eyes narrowed. Witless superstitions? It was a phrase that could have many meanings when spoken by this irreligious man. 'Struth, could mean anything from a pious man's belief in God to a common alewife's fear of ghosts and goblins.

"I believe you have a witch lingering hereabouts?" Belleme directed this seemingly idle question at the easily intimidated Dunstan.

"You mean the young witch Lady Elysia brought to live in Wroxton Castle?" Dunstan tentatively responded.

Although his face betrayed nothing, Belleme was surprised. This bit of gossip hadn't earlier reached his ear. That in itself was rare for he employed spies in every corner of most French duchies and throughout all of the British Isles.

"Makes no matter where the woman is harbored," Belleme shrugged. "Not so long as she is feared by the common folk of Wroxton's farms, villages, and castle."

"Oh, indeed," Dunstan answered promptly. "Eve is so greatly feared that each time she appears adults ward off her evil by signing the cross while their children have attempted to stone her."

"Good," Belleme's cruel grin held no warmth, only vicious glee. "We'll use her mere existence for the benefit of our scheme to first discredit and then slay our foe." Belleme assuredly found no fault in the fact that by this action he would also settle an old score. He would wreak his retribution upon one of the few amongst his myriad prey to escape his toils.

"Subtlety requires time but, though our goal will not be won so quickly as you suggested, friend Dunstan"—the full weight of Belleme's attention rested heavily upon the stout and satisfyingly frightened man—"by the end of the coming sennight it will be a done deed. And it will be completed in time for Duke Robert's intended arrival.

"Come." As if the hall were his own, the dark-clad speaker motioned the eyes of both of his companions toward the dais. "Join me at the high table and give me a clear picture of Wroxton's borders along with the farms and villages contained within."

Chapter 12

*G*od's blood!"

Elysia, frustrated and alone in the dark woodland, did nothing to muffle the loud curse. Gasping for air and exhausted by her futile pursuit, she sank down on a soft patch of ferns underlaid with thick grasses.

From atop steps leading out from the great hall on the castle's second level and thence down to the court-yard, Elysia had caught a glimpse of Jamie disappearing into the dark line of forest bordering Wroxton's demesne fields. She'd followed with all possible haste, heartened by the fact that even in a panic Jamie knew better than to again seek haven in their sea cave. It was doubtless the first place Mark would look—a welcome fact providing the gift of a precious head start.

Only after restoring a measure of easy breathing did Elysia guiltily admit that she ought to be ashamed of having recently become so fond of the wicked expletive. She ought to be, but the rebellious spirit roused by unrelieved worry and a frustrating end to her mad dash forbade it. After all, the curse was a result of her fruitless chase after Jamie who'd fled from the Black Wolf's unspoken threat. This meant that both her thwarted quest and its profane verbal aftermath were Mark's fault. It was he who should carry the blame.

"Who would've thought that I would twice be summoned by such an indelicate oath from a lady-born?"

Startled brown eyes flew up, and while golden sparks flared in their depths, the breathing so recently calmed became unsteady once more. The man Elysia had just blamed as that wrongful imprecation's source stood half hidden in shadows, leaning against the trunk of a massive tree while his lips curled in a wry, one-sided smile.

Elysia was torn between jumping up to lessen the intimidating effect of the powerful man looming above and remaining where she was the better to conceal his sudden arrival's daunting effect. Disgusted to find no immediate answer, she settled for glaring at Mark although nervously nibbling a full lower lip to brightness.

Mark purposefully misread her dilemma. "You need entertain no fears on Jamie's behalf."

Elysia's gaze narrowed dubiously on the man straightening to move toward her with dangerous grace.

"It was not Jamie who assaulted me yestereve." With that direct reassurance, Mark lowered himself to sit beside the maid whose increasing tension he found amusingly clear.

Though more annoyed than comforted by his state-

ment, Elysia was drawn to this too close source of
alarm. Valiantly fighting the Black Wolf's wiles, she
demanded, "If you knew that, why—"

"I suspected then"—Mark lifted a hand to signal an
end to her challenge—"but I am certain now."

The man spoke in riddles. And Elysia was irritated
the more by this further puzzle on an evening already
bestrewn with questions lacking answers. Was Jamie's
dagger—the one responsible for yet another attack—
the same item she'd heard him claim had disappeared
in the night? Seemed certain he'd run in dread of the
Black Wolf's punishment. But why when the man's
willingness to listen and bestow mercy had already
been proven to him? Elysia didn't pause to consider
the sincere admiration revealed by this unintentional
praise. Rather, her thoughts raced onward to the most
important question: If Jamie was not responsible for
the attack on Mark, *who* was?

Even in the limited light of the ominously warm
night laboring beneath a heavy layer of storm-threat-
ening clouds, Mark saw the myriad emotions chasing
across the passionate damsel's piquant face. Despite
her possible role in the recent assault, he couldn't bear
to increase a distress he'd the power to lessen.

"After I left your chamber last eve, I made a visit
to the stable's loft."

"Why?" Elysia frowned while asking the obvious.

Mark's answering scowl was far fiercer. Elysia's immediate question seemed to prove her innocent of col-
lusion in the action taken against him. And were that
so, even though he was the one who had opened the
subject, Mark was loath to reveal all that he'd learned
from the boys' misdeeds.

"Both Jamie and David owed explanations to me." A once gentle breeze had grown strong enough to near toss Mark's words into a wailing oblivion.

Elysia ignored the rising wind lashing her face with tendrils of black hair pulled free from a once tidy braid. She slowly nodded, but delicate brows remained furrowed in a silent demand for further information.

"The gauntlet worn by the attacker was mine." Mark leaned forward and spoke directly into a small ear to prevent his response being lost in the approaching storm's roar. "It was one from a pair given me by King Henry and so valuable they were kept in a locked chest, a lock for which only I and David possess keys."

Refusing to allow her attention to be diverted by the weather's growing fury, Elysia leaned away from the man while again nodding although her questioning expression did not change. The existence of such a locked chest was not news to her. David had spoken of both it and the loss of his key only the day past.

Mark's own rarely released temper simmered beneath the stubborn damsel's wordless demand for more than he wanted to reveal. One additional fact and only one would he share.

"I demanded and won explanation for how my foe came to be in possession of that key and the dagger that left this mark on me." Mark idly motioned toward the dark memento of a deadly attack on his throat.

"They knew who had taken these items?" The query startled from Elysia was easily heard amidst a sudden lull in the tempest's descent. She'd heard no such certainty from boys unaware of their listener.

"They didn't know *who*, but now I do."

"Who?" Elysia asked instinctively and then wished she could call back the foolish question doomed to win nothing but his contemptuous dismissal.

Mark shrugged, cynical half smile returning. This he assuredly would not tell to one who could still conceivably be a secret partner in plots against him. He'd assured her that both boys were safe from retribution, but he neither owed nor was willing to give more.

Her search for Jamie stymied, Elysia was unwilling to linger as prey for the Black Wolf's amusement. But even as she rose to begin her return to Wroxton Castle, a bolt of lightning pierced the storm's menacing pause. With a loud crack, it shattered the tree Mark had earlier leaned against. And the thunderous roll that instantly followed knocked Elysia off balance. She fell in a graceless heap. Just as she managed to take firm hold of nerves badly rattled by the first traumatic jolt, another jagged streak ripped open the sky and set loose a drenching downpour.

Under the sudden cloudburst Mark moved to sweep Elysia into his arms. Toward a haven absently noticed during his search for her he quickly carried this damsel who'd remained amazingly calm in the face of dangers that would've driven other females of his acquaintance into hysterics.

Almost hidden in the center of a grove of ancient trees rose a massive stone monolith half again Mark's height. On dry ground at the base of its lee side, protected from both rain and wind, he sank to his knees. Mark knew the wisdom of remaining low to the ground when caught in a lightning storm and lowered Elysia to lie with back pressed against their rock shield. Then he stretched out alongside the tempting form too clearly revealed by soaked clothing.

Dealing with the thunderbolt's effects had been Elysia's first challenge, the abrupt descent of torrential rains another. These she'd met with relative equanimity, but the devastating man's rescue followed by his overwhelming nearness in this refuge was too much too fast. Thus, although holding her body stiffly unyielding, it was in vain that she struggled to stave off the dangerous thrill of Mark's too close proximity.

"Thank you," Elysia whispered. She was flustered by the unsteadiness of the words even though the sound of her voice was likely lost to the howling wind. Despite the fervent hope that he couldn't hear, still she went on. "It was unexpected . . ." Abruptly realizing this might be misunderstood, Elysia stumbled over her own tongue to correct the error. "The fall . . . not your . . ." Further flustered, knowing she was on the verge of babbling, which was less than no help at all, a frowning Elysia stubbornly added, "It took my breath and I couldn't move."

Clearly hearing the damsel a mere whisper away, Mark recognized her plight. Elysia's distress revealed a welcome awareness of him that earned a smile without mockery. Twice as potent for that lack, his smile held her in thrall while the fingertips of one hand tested the texture of a cheek soft and delicate with the fresh fragrance of wildflowers. He wanted desperately to trace a reckless path down her arched throat to the bounty . . .

The gentleness of this utterly unanticipated caress trapped breath in Elysia's throat and drove from her mind sane thoughts of all that had passed before, even of the gale howling through the forest. From the point where Mark's fingertips lightly touched her flesh a current of wild pleasure trembled through Elysia's body with the heat of an intimate bolt of lightning. Feeling as if she'd been turned to molten ore, Elysia's once rigid body melted into the amazingly tender cradle of powerful arms.

With lush curves full against him and a burning temptation near beyond bearing, Mark went still and clenched his eyes shut while attempting to rouse sufficient will to honor the oath he'd given to leave this sweet virgin pure. But the hunger of desire argued with the small voice of cool reason. For a moment, only a moment, he would savor the luscious morsel she was and then pull back to leave the spirited damsel unsullied.

Mark's mouth brushed across the velvety petals of Elysia's yielding lips before returning to nudge them apart and ease his tongue inside like a bee after nectar—delicious and addicting. While drinking a full measure of that heady ambrosia, he loosened her single thick braid and combed his fingers through the wealth of ebony satin thus freed.

The exciting, enticing kiss quickly carried Elysia into a steamy haze of passion that muffled the admonishments of her conscience. So firmly caught by the Black Wolf's seductive wiles was she that when his lips moved to trail liquid fire down her throat and nuzzle in the dip at its base, the action earned only a desperate sigh of longing for pleasures yet unknown.

Sparing a brief thought of gratitude for the front closure of both bright kirtle and gossamer undergown, Mark began loosening her laces with far less deftness than was his wont. His fumbling haste was born of unconscious fear that despite raging need a single moment's hesitation might end in cool sanity's demand for a halt to such wrongful actions.

Mark spread unlaced edges wide to bare tender flesh to the searing touch of his silver gaze. Beneath its power Elysia shivered. His fingertips then embarked on the journey he'd earlier longed to take. They lightly traced a tantalizing path from the tip of her chin, down an elegant throat to the dip at its base and then onward through the deep valley between generous breasts.

Gasping, Elysia felt her heart pause and then thump erratically while masculine fingers next burrowed beneath cloth she immediately resented. As they explored the tiny indentation of her navel and a burning hunger built, desire-weighted lashes descended to shield eyes gone to golden flames.

Sensing that his sweet, yielding temptation found the barrier between them no more welcome than he, with sensual motions meant to stoke the fire of Elysia's desire to greater heights Mark rid her of damp garments. Then Mark's maddening, caressing touch began another tormentingly slow journey.

Mark's outspread hands glided over the sensitive skin of a slim waist and tender midriff only to hesitate below the first swell of aching breasts. Elysia's breath caught in an agony of waiting. Motionless seconds stretched into an eternity. At last her lashes rose, and she met an undreamt of hunger in the charcoal depths at the center of a flashing silver gaze.

For additional long, breathless moments Mark held back to study the perfection of Elysia's body—an enticing vision of luscious cream and sweet rose framed by a black satin mane. Hers was a heart-stopping loveliness unmatched in his considerable experience by any other woman.

Once fearful of the powerful man's looming presence, Elysia was now impatient to lure him still nearer. Shifting restlessly, she reached up to wrap her arms about his neck and twine fingers into thick black strands in an attempt to pull his mouth back to hers.

Mark was drawn to the beguiling damsel as much by her wildflower scent and soft warmth as by enticing arms. Gladly yielding to her irresistible temptations, his mouth descended to again drink in the intoxicating essence of hers. Determined to see her as thoroughly caught in the ravenous flames of insatiable need as he was, Mark deepened the kiss with a devastating slowness that sent shudders of delight rippling through her body.

Elysia welcomed the scorching winds of the intimate tempest sweeping over her, loved the feel of this powerful man, the taste of him. Heart beating madly, she sought a measure of the same pleasure he'd taken from her. Although the bond of their mouths remained unbroken, small hands urged his body a whisper away and then took advantage of that slight distance to unfasten the laces of his tunic and spear through wiry black curls. Far too lost in the hungry firestorm to hear the once quite voice of conscience now screaming warnings of future regret, Elysia found only unthinking annoyance in the restrictions of his wool tunic. She tugged at it to no avail.

Mark knew the seductive danger of skin against skin. But ignoring that peril, he pulled free of her arms to strip off the offending shirt in one quick motion that set muscles rippling. Mesmerized by the view of his strength, Elysia's exquisite face went tense with increasing desire. That tantalizing fact pushed any hope of stopping completely beyond Mark's reach despite his bitter certainty that this was purely the wrong time and wrong place.

Elysia gasped with pleasure when Mark suddenly buried his mouth against her breasts. Overwhelmed by incredible sensations as he applied a sweet suction to their tips, her hands instinctively moved in silent praise over the breadth of wide shoulders. Every feeling centered on teasing caresses doing impossibly exciting things to her, she ached with delicious pleasures she'd never known existed.

Mark fought through the disorienting smoke of his own burning hunger seeking the last vestiges of his control. He was determined to see that the innocent Elysia's final surrender and initiation into the sphere of passion's satisfaction would be accompanied by as little pain as possible. While reining in his own unmanageable needs, he carried her with potent kisses and tantalizing caresses ever deeper into searing flames.

The blazing tempest raging in Elysia's quaking body was fiercer than the furious gale wailing through the woodland around them. She writhed desperately against the source of her torment, incoherently crying out for surcease. But when Mark broke from her clinging embrace, she moaned with the painful anguish of loss.

Mark sent a sensuous smile of promise to the delicate beauty he meant to claim while hastily winning free of the last impediment to their joining. Once his chausses had been tossed aside, Mark's hands swept down the hot satin flesh of her slender back to cup a firm derriere and pull the passionate maiden's softness tight against his own powerful contours.

Burning with unimaginable heat, Elysia twisted nearer. Mark began rocking her hips against his in a primitive rhythm matched by the thrust of his tongue in the warm cavern of her mouth. But not until the wildly passionate beauty's body instinctively echoed his movements did Mark shift her to lie on her back while he rose above. Sliding one heavily muscled leg between shapely thighs, he moved to lie full atop her slender length.

Elysia cried out with pleasure under this shattering intimacy. Caressing the smooth planes of his back, she felt every line and curve burn beneath her touch, reveled in the tension changing and building in powerful muscles. Welcoming this closeness, still she yearned to be nearer, wanted more.

Mark tilted her hips to aid their slow merging. The violence of passion's tempest swept Elysia so far into its turbulent depths that she barely felt the inevitable moment of a pain quickly overwhelmed by the ever-increasing intensity of feverish need. Twining and moving together, Elysia clung desperately to Mark, her firm anchor amidst the whirling firestorm while thinking she must surely perish in its scorching heat.

Of a sudden Mark went motionless and Elysia found herself in the stillness at the eye of the storm, breathlessly caught in a dangerous vortex of fire. Certain she could bear the intensity of need no longer, Elysia surged upward. Her cry of sweet anguish was matched by Mark's harsh growl as walls of flame burst into glittering sparks of mindless ecstasy. Pleasure washed over them in towering waves. Only slowly did that tide ebb into a gentle lapping of warmth. It lulled Elysia into satisfaction's sleep after Mark rolled to one side and cradled her near.

Mark gently held the exquisite creature dozing with cheek pillowed on his shoulder and nuzzled the ebony silk atop her head. Drinking in her alluring scent and the vision of her loveliness, he reaffirmed the fact acknowledged earlier—she was unlike any woman he'd ever known. With that admission came the certainty of another infinitely more disturbing truth. Was it the tide of a growing tender emotion he feared impossible to stem that made her so unique, so precious in his view? Had the famed Black Wolf fallen prey to a virgin's innocent wiles?

Innocent? Guilt darkened Mark's eyes to smoke. Though he'd once deemed her selfish, Elysia had proven herself blameless by both her care for a woman others would reject and loyal defense of Jamie, even of Dunstan. Truly, Elysia was deserving of a mate far worthier than the man she'd claimed as her betrothed. Who? An inner voice mocked, *You?* Self-disgust roused by the wrong he'd just committed against her warned Mark that Elysia was assuredly deserving of someone more honorable than the man who'd broken his oath to steal her virtue.

Chapter 13

$\mathcal{S}$ilver eyes glared into the shadows of the stairwell's arched entry. The evening meal's first course had been served but still no one appeared. Had the uneven path of their relationship looped back to that once more? Would Elysia stubbornly remain in her chamber rather than join him at the high table? And if true, was it shame or anger that kept her there? Even while Mark pondered the damsel's likely resentment of him for the fiery pleasures they'd shared when last together, her again scarlet-clad figure came into view.

Fanning the embers of her temper as a support to courage, Elysia had briskly descended spiraling steps but paused in their opening to the great hall. She was about to face a man not seen since their parting in the wee hours of morn. Flushed with tension, she rested one palm on the stone door frame and welcomed the chill of blocks laid to join in a curve overhead.

Determined to look no higher, Elysia gazed down long lines of trestle tables flanked by guardsmen devouring chunks of bread soaked in pea and lentil soup. Then, as if drawn by a power stronger than her own will, Elysia's attention rose to be snared by the Black Wolf's silver gaze. Yet, lured to meet what she had rather not, Elysia closed her eyes to break the unwanted bond with this man whose dangers she now knew all too intimately.

Uncomfortably aware that a late arrival left her the center of attention, Elysia crossed the hall and stepped up on the dais. As she made to slip into her seat on Mark's right, she'd the misfortune to catch an utterly unexpected glimpse of Dunstan's positively poisonous glare.

Startled and uncertain what wrong had earned such animosity, the normally graceful maid stumbled. Elysia would've taken an awkward fall but for Mark's quick, bracing hand on her arm. Though doubtless she ought appreciate his action, it only deepened a much deplored embarrassment in her seducer's presence.

"Welcome, milady," Mark murmured while helping the damsel settle into her chair. "I feared you might intend to hide in your chamber again." With a wry smile of self-mockery, the famed lady-charmer rued this poor choice of words even as they left his tongue.

Hide? Elysia sent the speaker a pointed glare and pulled sharply away the instant she was safely seated. What a wretchedly inauspicious beginning to an evening dreaded at the outset. Finding herself hopelessly tangled in a morass of such conflicting emotions as resentment and admiration, she went motionless. Elysia stared down at the morsels of soaked bread remaining on the trencher she was meant to share with the source of her discomfort.

The dark man was so close that—as too oft before—the aura of his attraction wrapped its gentle but inexorable tendrils about Elysia. Intensified by hot memories of events mere hours past, that proximity stole not only steady breath but hunger enough to swallow even so little as a single bite. She toyed with their food, surreptitiously nudging it to his side of the platter with a crust of the fine wheaten bread quickly provided by the hovering Eve ever assigned to serve those at the high table.

Although Mark made several valiant attempts to draw Elysia into conversation, she remained silent while a parade of savory dishes was presented. She gazed at the woman seated beyond Mark and tried to concentrate on the fact that though Jamie was still absent, Ida seemed unconcerned. Here was proof that Mark must have reassured the mother with the news he'd given to her during the dark hours ...

Elysia clamped down on wayward thoughts reviving heated memories. She focused on the question of how the man failed to see that the plump woman's unaffected appetite and lack of lingering grief would betray awareness of no imminent danger to her son to any curious enough to wonder.

Then while from a small, steaming pot Eve ladled spicy wine sauce over braised trout, the attention of all was demanded by the noise of a loud scuffle. It echoed down the tunneled entry through the castle's thick stone wall in an advance warning of the two men who shortly tumbled into its opening to the hall.

"Lord Mark!" The desperate call came from a ragged peasant struggling to escape a husky guardsman's restraining grip.

"Cedric, release our friend Udell." Mark gave the firm command that saw one of the farmers recently visited set free to move forward.

"Pray pardon my comin' amidst your meal." Udell gulped and twisted a knit hat between gnarled hands. Now physically unrestrained, he was flustered yet tentatively approached this new lord. Lord Mark was too recently come into power over Wroxton for Udell to be certain of the man's temperament, particularly when met with such unpleasant news as he'd arrived to share.

"You are forgiven, Udell." Mark's smile was crooked yet reassuring. "So long as you waste no time in telling me why you've done the deed."

"Aye, milord." Udell gulped again before attempting a haste-garbled explanation. "Milbury Farm's been burned ta the ground."

"Was anyone harmed?" Mark immediately asked, assuming a plea for help to be the purpose behind this desperate man's arrival.

"Nay." Udell shook a head of dull brown hair. "Even the weest babe was saved ... but all the buildins is gone an' the pigs were roasted in their sty."

"An unfortunate loss. Was it a result of sparks rising from the hearth to catch a thatched roof on fire?" Mark frowned. If there had been no human price, what reason was there for Udell's rude demand of his lord's immediate attention? "Are guardsmen needed to help extinguish the flames?"

Another loud gulp preceded Udell's answer. "Fire burned out as the sun rose this morn."

Dark brows arched over piercing silver eyes that silently demanded explanation for why the man had interrupted his lord's meal to report an event apparently over and done.

" 'Twere a warnin' plain as plain kin ever be . . ." Udell shifted uneasily from foot to foot. "Given with an omen of evil dug inta the ashes." The speaker's attention shifted to where Eve stood just behind Hugh's shoulder with the handle of a pot full of steaming sauce tightly clutched in both hands.

"What omen?" Mark demanded, growing impatient with the man forcing him to waste time extracting each fact with the same care required to remove deeply imbedded slivers.

"Saw it drawn in ashes once afore . . ." Udell's voice sank to the depths of a bell tolling doom. " 'Twas a star inside a circle like as what's on her cheek." The man slowly pointed a crooked forefinger directly at Eve.

Eve cried out. She dropped the bowl of bubbling liquid into Hugh's lap in an action that increased her horror. The room had gone unnaturally silent, but to Eve it seemed the entire hall shouted accusations at her. Clapping both hands over her mouth, she leaped from the dais and dashed into the outgoing tunnel.

After the first instant of shock, Hugh jumped to his feet. He paid no heed to the thick liquid running down his thighs while rushing after the ever elusive maid who too oft fled from him.

In the babble that broke out on the heels of the fleeing maidserf and her pursuer, Elysia sought to rise and rush after an unjustly abused friend. Mark wrapped a gentle but inflexible hand about a slender arm and held Elysia in place.

"Leave Eve to Hugh."

Elysia glared directly into Mark's solemn face. "I'll never abandon her to the rough care of others."

"Are you so blind that you think Hugh might mean Eve harm?" Mark's mocking smile returned but with it a potent intimacy near able to melt Elysia's bones.

Even while blinking rapidly against his steady gaze, through Elysia's mind flashed barely noted scenes of Hugh's tender attentions for Eve. Yet even as they came into focus, she refused to accept them as just excuse for being prevented from aiding a friend.

While the couple still at the high table were thus preoccupied, Dunstan watched closely, with hands resting atop the shelf of a belly in some small part diminished by recent hard labors.

Hugh was thankful for the pale gray of Eve's homespun gown. Only catching glimpses of its light hue offered possible success to his tireless pursuit. He followed the willowy figure into dense reaches of the forest where tightly packed trees and undergrowth intertwined to trap wisps of fog and appear nearly impenetrable.

When Eve completely disappeared, Hugh felt certain her burrow home lay near. In the last glimmers of lingering twilight, he continued until her trail of footprints and broken twigs abruptly ended. Sinking to his knees on dew-damp earth, he began a slow, methodical search.

Fruitless time dragged. But though growing discouraged Hugh refused to admit defeat. Then of a sudden, while patting the seemingly solid surface of a short, steep hillside, one section the size of a table top slid away to reveal a faintly lit haven behind. Rather than investigating the mechanics of that peculiar event, Hugh's attention was captured by a mist-green gaze.

"Keep you pushing on the door to my abode, you'll break it in." Though delivering an accusation, Eve's tone held gentle welcome. Accustomed to painful rejection, she'd feared to believe this man truly sincere in his stated desire to stand as her friend. But his continued pursuit—despite the most recent damning tidings—went a fair way in convincing her it was so, and a shy smile bloomed beneath the warmth of new hope.

"And so I would've done had you not opened it to me." Grinning, a relieved Hugh was unrepentant.

"Then 'tis best I bid you enter." Eve motioned the big bear of a man to literally drop into her burrow.

Eve had constructed an abode of amazing proportions although one never intended to comfortably house a man of Hugh's size for any great length of time. This fact was proven once he lowered himself into the subterranean vault and the slender maid shifted the false hillside back into place.

Hugh took quick stock of Eve's home. Deep and reinforced by thick branches with a packed-dirt floor covered by the same type of rushes spread throughout the castle, it provided a snug haven. Moreover, he realized that part of the ground mists seen above rose from an oil-fed brazier. The unpolished copper fixture hosted a weak flame able to lend only inadequate light but sufficient heat for a midsummer night.

Idly motioning toward the lamp, Hugh asked, "A

gift from the same fearful widow who left you cast-off clothing?"

Eve shook her head. "Nay, 'twas among the few things I was able to salvage from my own home." Seeing the dull and battered object through Hugh's eyes, she twisted nervous fingers together while hastily giving an apologetic explanation for such limitations. "I haven't lived here for some little time and thus have no store of animal tallow from which to form candles . . . but I will again soon."

Hugh captured wringing hands and calmly tugged Eve down to sit beside him on a crude pallet formed of rags sewn together and stuffed with grasses. "You can't hide forever from those who are terrified by what they've refused to understand."

"I hid for more than a decade." Eve resisted the temptation to beg this unexpectedly gentle bear to share his strength and shoulder her troubles. "And I can do that and more again."

Regretting reality on her behalf, Hugh slowly shook his head. "This time the villagers and castle folk believe you have directly harmed one of *their* number. Thus, they'll mercilessly hunt you down."

Eve recognized the truth in these words. One silent tear rolled down a flushed cheek and over the scar branding her for life with another's wickedness. Hugh was certain this sight was enough to wring blood from a stone. It was more than enough to pierce his loving heart.

"Ah, sweeting." Hugh tenderly pulled the disconsolate maiden near. "I would extend to you my protection but 'tis a gift I cannot give when you constantly flee from the shield I wish to provide."

Freely offered the very gift she'd hesitated to request, still Eve was too apprehensive to accept. Not in fear for herself but for Hugh. And when she spoke, the words ached with concern for him.

"If you help me, they'll think you also are in league with the devil."

Hugh lifted Eve's chin and gazed down into eyes sparkling with unshed tears. "My strength is battle tested, and I am capable of proving them wrong by fighting both my foes and yours."

Hugh's confidence overwhelmed Eve's trepidations. In truth, it was pleasure at the thought of this valiant warrior standing as her champion that flooded through Eve. For that response Eve believed she ought to feel guilty and buried a winsome face gone rosy between the curls of her beloved's chin and his broad shoulder.

With his heart's desire so temptingly near, Hugh fell to brushing his lips over the silky tresses on Eve's head and then down to the abused cheek. From there he found welcome on soft, untutored lips.

A passionate fire, stoked to blue-white heights by love, carried the pair into its blazing, swirling storm. And by the time they at last dozed on the billowing smoke of contentment, all doubts had been reduced to unimportant cinders.

After Mark prevented Elysia from joining Hugh's chase, the evening meal in Wroxton Castle's great hall continued although amidst a stilted atmosphere of tense silence. Elysia didn't pretend to partake of the meal's final course of cheese and freshly picked strawberries.

"These berries are sweet." Mark's deep voice

sought to tempt. "Leastways try one." With a single luscious berry, he gently nudged lips near as bright.

Elysia's mouth firmed into a tightly clamped line. To this man's sin of seduction she added the crime of thwarting her attempt to aid a friend. These were two wrongs for which she felt he must rightly be blamed.

"I pray you will feel no guilt for what passed between us yestereve."

Intending comfort, Mark spoke in a tone so low only Elysia could clearly discern the words. However, she heard not comfort but accusation. And it rankled the more for having just assigned him the blame for luring her into that sin.

Mark saw golden sparks take fire in her eyes and took an unbelievable misstep for a man with his reputation as a renowned lady-charmer. He compounded his error by quickly adding, "I will gladly put right your wrong by wedding you with all possible haste."

"Right *my* wrong? Hah!" Elysia hissed. "You do me no honor in claiming my fiefdom for yourself."

Mark's face immediately closed into cold lines as if he'd abruptly turned to pure granite. "You are wrong. I need not wed you to continue holding what is already *mine* by King Henry's command."

Elysia's hands slapped palm down on the table. Despite the surface's several layers of white cloth, the sound resounded against stone walls and drew the attention of every person in the hall. They watched as she stiffly rose to her feet.

"As I stated on your arrival"—no longer restrained, Elysia's each word was clearly enunciated—"I am already betrothed and have *no* wish to marry you!"

When Elysia proudly turned, stepped down from

the dais, and stalked from the hall, silver eyes narrowed in anger and followed her gently swaying figure. This unpredictable woman had spurned what he had never offered another. He wished he could shrug and truthfully claim he'd no care for her deed ... but he couldn't. Her action felt like a well-honed blade painfully driven dead-to-point in his heart.

Chapter 14

"Take! Just take?"

The quarrelsome words disturbed Eve's rest. Her lashes slowly lifted to the unfamiliar but welcome sight of a muscular chest. Warm visions of the past night's delights joined with sweet emotion to further open the tender blossom of hope in her soul ... until another voice was heard.

"Of course, just take."

This voice held echoes from Eve's past that struck with a terror threatening to uproot tentatively unfurling petals even while jerking her attention to men talking somewhere beyond the walls of her secret haven.

Eve immediately moved to peer out from a crack between the snugly woven reeds of a false wall. Despite the purple mists of predawn, she could clearly see that the ever somber-clad Gervaise had drawn his horse to a halt not far distant while quietly arguing with another mounted man.

"But the king will—"

"The king will know nothing of a matter quickly over and done."

Eve gave a soft gasp. Though this second speaker's back was turned to her, the timber of his voice revived the image of a flame-lit face forever emblazoned in her memory.

When the frowning visitor swung toward the noise, Eve pressed both palms over her mouth to prevent any further betraying sound. As if struck to stone, she remained motionless even when Hugh leaned over from behind to peer from her viewpoint through the small cleft in the false hillside. Warrior-trained to sleep light, he had awakened the moment Eve first stirred.

"Why are we traveling such a difficult path to a site you claim to visit near every dawn?" Gervaise's companion demanded while an unseen Eve trembled with fear.

"You claimed a wish to arrive firstly, the better to conceal yourself," Gervaise stated. "And this is the most direct path to see your ends achieved."

"Just as a simple taking would be the most direct method to achieve *our* ends." With these words, the man turned to cast his red-haired cohort a mirthless smile.

Concealed in the hidden shelter, Hugh's eyes narrowed on the unpleasant sight as his mouth soundlessly formed a single word: "Belleme."

Not until the mounted men rode some distance beyond Eve's burrow home did her stress abruptly drain away, leaving her to limply sag against Hugh's strength.

"Do you know who that was, sweeting?" Hugh quietly asked. He was himself all too familiar with the vicious man who was the largest landholder and most powerful individual lacking royal blood in either England or Normandy. That Belleme ruthlessly wielded his power only for selfish gain and cruel pleasures made him the more despicable.

The unnatural pallor of a solemn face heightened the green of Eve's eyes as she straightened to answer, " 'Twas the devil who laid his curse on me." Eve tilted her face upward to bare the scar she normally tried to hide.

Hugh scowled. That Belleme was truly a devil he'd no doubt, but how was it that the man had come to these lands today and by what wretched quirk of fate had he been led across Eve's path so long ago?

To Eve her beloved's frown seemed proof that admitted contact with the human demon had turned even Hugh against her. Shoulders forlornly sagging, she dropped her face into cupped hands.

Realizing the sensitive maid had misunderstood the source of his disgust, Hugh gently drew Eve into his embrace.

"Ah, sweeting," Hugh murmured into the smooth hair atop Eve's head. "My ire is for the wicked fiend who wreaked his villainy upon you. That I don't understand how Belleme's attention came to center upon an innocent child does nothing to lessen my disgust for his appalling abuse of you."

"My mother was beautiful." Eve gazed up at her protector. As Hugh looked to be startled by what he must think an inapt comment, she quickly added more. "On a visit to Kelby Keep that demon saw Mother and thought to use her for his pleasure."

Hugh grimaced at Eve's matter-of-fact statement. To most wellborn people, a serf was merely an animal to be used, and even simple knights thought nothing of taking physical satisfaction from the body of any serf, willing or no.

"My father objected." Eve flatly revealed a fact she knew to be the cause behind all the vile actions that had followed.

For Hugh no further explanation was necessary. He could plainly see what had happened. The resistance of any serf would end in a lord's retribution. But a lord as proud and vicious as Belleme assuredly was would enjoy wringing the cruelest of punishments from his victims.

"Our farm was put to flame and my father killed." Eve's words were choked with anguish. "Even while dying Mother called out my name, screaming for me to flee into the forest ... to run as fast as I could." Silent tears flowed. "I tried to obey but that devil caught me. He said that as I bore the name of the first sinner, I ought also to share her shame." As if the wound were fresh, Eve pressed both hands to the scar. "He laughed while carving my cheek."

Hugh gently moved Eve's fingers aside and brushed a tender kiss of healing across wrongly marred flesh.

Knowing Belleme's cruel nature, Hugh was not surprised that the man had not been content to simply kill both husband and wife and destroy their belongings. Doubtless that human demon had taken perverse pleasure in allowing their small daughter to live but bearing the dreaded mark of the devil and thereby ensuring she'd forever remain a feared outcast from humankind.

Leastways, Elysia righteously told herself, Gervaise couldn't fault her choice of garb today. She was clad in a green kirtle and russet undergown that blended with her surroundings as she moved through dawn-gilded mists trapped by densely grown trees.

While absently keeping her bow from tangling with either bushes or low-hanging branches, Elysia was filled with curiously opposing emotions. Although on her way to meet the cold man she'd once been pleased to claim as her betrothed, Elysia couldn't rid her thoughts of a dark and passionate man. And no matter how heatedly she might rue the fact, neither could Elysia deny a sincere wish that she'd been able to accept the Black Wolf's offer of marriage without destroying her pride. But then, was pride worth the cost of a lifetime without Mark?

As Elysia stepped beyond the last barrier and entered the glade of her archery range, she privately admitted herself lacking courage enough to honestly answer that question.

"You're late."

Elysia scowled. Gervaise's unfriendly greeting was startling, particularly as they'd agreed she would come only when the journey could be safely made. She hadn't come every morn in the past and now wished she'd stayed abed today.

Gervaise realized that his words had stirred the coals of the spirited maid's quick temper to life. And, uncomfortably aware of their hidden observer, he immediately sought to placate her.

"I thought I heard a voice cry out and feared some ill might have befallen you." Gervaise removed the bow from Elysia's hold and let it drop before taking her small hands into his own.

Elysia studied the man with narrowed eyes that all too clearly saw his age and complete lack of human warmth. What witless imp had led her to believe Gervaise merited admiration, even less understandable, to think him worthy of her love? Now with experience of Mark's heated wiles to compare against, the reluctance and wintery cold in this man's touch was unmistakable.

Shocked by the unexpected golden gleams of distaste in a brown gaze, Gervaise began to think it might be necessary to do as Belleme suggested and simply seize Elysia.

Uneasy beneath the frost coating Gervaise's expression of a sudden, Elysia shifted the full weight of her attention to a willowy bush covered with delicate flowers undeserving of such abuse.

"I have nothing new to report of matters at Wroxton Castle." Wanting to be quit of this uncomfortable visit with all possible haste, Elysia invented an excuse. "And I must needs return immediately to meet with a delegation from the village."

" 'Tis unfortunate but this morn the villagers will have to make do without their lady's presence."

Alarmed by an unfamiliar and chillingly quiet voice coming from behind, Elysia would've whirled toward its source had her arms not been jerked back and held in a tight grip. Despite a valiant struggle against restraining hands—one that succeeded only in wrenching her shoulder—Elysia's wrists were quickly tied together at the base of her spine.

"Who are you?" Elysia demanded of the culprit as yet unseen.

"A friend of your betrothed's." The answer came as the speaker thrust his captive into an unprepared Gervaise's embrace.

Fighting for freedom while her ankles were joined one to the other with stout rope that would severely hobble her ability to walk, Elysia recognized in the words an unpleasant sarcasm far more acidic than any she'd ever heard in Mark's oft-mocking voice.

"Smile, milady," the unknown man sneered as Gervaise turned the plainly furious and now securely bound woman to face him. "Your deepest desire, long postponed, will soon be granted."

Elysia glared at the black-clad stranger whose mere appearance was first startling and then fearsome. Dressed in strange layered garb and with black brows that winged upward at outer edges, he looked like a demon.

"Not curious?" The question was addressed to Elysia although the stranger immediately glanced briefly into the eyes of the man holding her. "You've found a rare woman for yourself, Gervaise." His full attention shifted back to their captive, and a too silky voice was ominous as he gave the explanation for which she'd refused to ask. "You and your betrothed will be wed on the morrow."

"Who are you?" Elysia ignored the no longer welcome statement and steadily demanded the answer not earlier given.

"I am Robert of Belleme"—the newcomer's smile

was a sneer of contempt—"duke of Shrewsbury, lord of Arundel and Chichester, Montgomery in Normandy and in Wales, and of Seez, Alecon, and numerous other castles and landholdings in England, Maine, and Normandy.

Elysia said nothing in response to this litany. What was there to say when presented with the most infamous and supercilious man in several countries?

"I trust you are duly impressed that I mean to personally oversee your marriage to Gervaise," Belleme prodded the captive for a response.

Still a determined Elysia remained mute before the condescending man. Though presented with what she'd once thought to be her heart's desire, Elysia admitted that she most definitely did not want to wed Gervaise. The further bright light of another undeniable truth drove into shadow the obscuring tangle of too many emotions from useless pride to unworthy fears. It was Mark she loved, and it was he who held the single key to her happiness.

Inwardly Gervaise gasped at the maid's continued willful silence before a man it was dangerous to annoy. In the next instant he was relieved to see that Belleme apparently found amusement in her stubbornness. It could so easily have ended in a brutal price being demanded.

Belleme recognized Gervaise's concern, and it deepened his entertainment at the pair's expense. He could be charitable now that the lady of Wroxton was firmly secured; he could be merciful—leastways until after the wedding with its transfer of her inheritance into Gervaise's control and thus into his.

Elysia watched as the man renowned for his malevolence moved to place a parchment bearing a few elegantly shaped words on the bale of hay that served as target for her practice with bow and arrows. She was not such a fool as to be unaware of the peril she courted with her silence, yet refused to yield.

Belleme returned to the man holding a dark beauty with a reluctance painfully clear.

"Knowing how repellant you find women, Gervaise," Belleme announced as he reached out to take control of their bound captive, "I'll keep the Lady Elysia restrained atop my own stallion."

Although Gervaise glared in response to the insult, he dared not dispute the words of this dangerous ally throwing Elysia over his shoulder before striding through a wall of greenery to where two horses waited.

Loathsome laughter sent a hollow echo through the dense forest before Belleme glanced again toward Gervaise while requesting an answer he'd no honest expectation of receiving. "Give me the solution to a puzzle I've long wondered about: Is your distaste only for feminine flesh or for *all* human contact?"

Despite his years of observing the delight Belleme took in making people squirm, Gervaise's face went so pale his bright hair seemed to burn brighter. He had to force clenched fists to open, enabling him to swing up onto his steed's back.

Belleme's humorless laughter continued as he tossed Elysia roughly across his horse and mounted. But silence reigned as the small party retraced a narrow path.

A sun partly obscured by drifting clouds lingered just above the western horizon as Mark stepped into

Wroxton Castle. He was surprised to find Hugh impatiently waiting a pace within the gloomy entrance tunnel although not surprised at seeing Eve firmly clasped against the burly man's side.

"We must speak to you privately." Hugh restrained his usual booming voice to a whisper.

"Can it wait until I've bathed away the grime of a day's labors?" Mark was weary from long hours of toil and weighted down by even more time spent in bleak worry over Elysia's unwelcoming response to his previous night's sincerely intended proposal.

"Nay." Hugh's immediate answer was unnecessarily loud and he tamed the volume while continuing. "Once you've heard and seen what we've come to share, you'll agree we were right to insist on avoiding delay."

Despite surrounding darkness, Mark's nod could be seen. "Then come with me to my chamber. I fear 'tis the only place where we can be certain of securing complete privacy."

Mark led the way from the tunnel and across a great hall that went instantly quiet when the three appeared. By that peculiar reaction it was plain to Mark that something truly was afoot. And while he and his allies climbed spiraling steps, his nerves went taut in preparation for what was almost certain to be an unpleasant report.

Once inside the lord's bedchamber with thick door firmly shut, questioning silver eyes turned to Hugh.

"We saw Gervaise in the forest just before dawn," Hugh began, curling gentle hands over the shoulders of the much smaller woman he stood behind.

Mark's dark brows arched with warm amusement.

Evidently the pair hadn't returned until after that time from their flight into the forest near a full day past. The likelihood that his friend had fallen prey to the same kind of tender emotion that had so recently triumphed over him seemed only just.

Donning a long-suffering expression, Hugh responded to the teasing man's silent laughter with a speaking glance even while hurrying on with important news. "Gervaise was not alone."

Mark's face closed into a blank mask. That the lord of Kelby Keep traveled with another was in itself nothing of great note. However, Hugh's ominous tone suggested an unspoken threat skulking behind that simple fact. Mark immediately suspected the identity of that companion.

It was a suspicion promptly confirmed by Hugh, who simply said, "Belleme."

Mind racing with all the implications raised by this fact, Mark absently glanced around looking for a seat and focused on the one below his window. Yet remembering how easily a similar stool had shattered beneath the combined weight of himself and Elysia, Mark refused to trust its questionable strength.

"You were right to loose no time in reporting this unwelcome reality." Without hesitation Mark gave the couple the recognition of a wise deed that they were assuredly owed. However, he was wrong in assuming that so simple an end could be put to their dutiful report.

Hugh recognized Mark's intent and responded with a smile nearer to a grimace. "But that's only the beginning of what we've discovered."

Uncertain how much time would be necessary to see this account finished but anxious for a few moments' ease, Mark signaled the other man to pause in the telling.

Though reluctant to yield so much as an instant of possibly precious time, Hugh obeyed the command of a man not merely friend, but lord. Asides, while Mark busied himself clearing the surface of the chest resting beside a disdained stool, the bearded man had another matter to cover.

Hugh provided Mark with a brief but comprehensive outline of Eve's first meeting with Belleme and its cost to her.

Mark straightened from shifting an empty ewer and basin to the floor to send Eve a grim smile of sympathy for the inexcusable pain caused her by a vile man. He then motioned the couple to settle atop his bed while he sat on one corner of the chest he'd cleared. Once all were seated, he nodded to signal that Hugh should continue his initial report.

"During our return to the castle, we found this." Frowning, Hugh reached into his rumpled tunic and pulled out a carefully folded parchment. This he leaned forward to place in Mark's outstretched hand.

The room's unnatural quiet seemed to thicken the very air they breathed while Mark opened the document and soundlessly read its contents:

> The witch in Wroxton's midst bears the blame
> for every ill that has and will continue to befall
> its good folk ... harm descending even upon the
> lady who wrongly befriends the evil one.

When Mark looked up, silver warnings flashed from his eyes.

"No villager or castle inhabitant has seen what you hold—" Hugh motioned toward the message, speaking in an utterly flat voice—"Nor could they have heard its words. And yet by the time you met us in the entry, the whole of the demesne was whispering of Lady Elysia's disappearance. And with one voice they blamed Eve."

"Elysia is missing?" Mark immediately focused on the dangerous possibility most important to him.

"Aye." Hugh's answer was brief. By long experience of Mark's habits, he knew enough to then go motionless and quiet, thus permitting the man uninterrupted time in thought.

To block visual distractions, Mark dropped thick lashes and forced calm reason upon himself. Had Elysia merely gone out to visit the people he'd once accused her of failing? Nay, considering her limited skills at horsemanship, she surely wouldn't risk going alone.

Another potential reason for Elysia's absence fought to be acknowledged by a mind that wanted to bury its unpleasant image in indistinct shadows. Mark clenched his jaw. If he were to see his love safe, he must examine all possibilities, no matter how distasteful.

With a strength that had met and defeated many bleak realities, Mark forced himself to honestly ask: Could it be that his proposal of marriage had driven Elysia into a desperate attempt to escape his company? It was not only likely, but more painful than any battle wound he'd ever sustained.

"How long has she been missing?" Mark finally

asked in a voice so lacking in emotion that the friend who knew him better than any other recognized the depth of his distress.

Still unmoving, Hugh answered with equal calm. "Ida says Elysia was not in the bedchamber when, as is her daily habit, she arrived to awaken the damsel this morn."

Mark's eyes closed again while the paper tightly gripped forced upon him an even more likely and less acceptable explanation. The same sinister fiend who'd both written this document and burned Milbury Farm was almost certainly responsible for Elysia's abduction—if abduction it was. The culprit? With the alliance of Gervaise and his friend Belleme so near, there could be little doubt save for the question of whether or not Elysia had willingly fled into the arms of her erstwhile betrothed.

"And where did you find this parchment?" Mark asked the question of Hugh. However, despite the fact that the bearded man had done all the speaking for the pair thus far, it was Eve who answered.

"It was lying in the glade where Elysia often practices her skills as an archer."

Because soon after their arrival at Wroxton his squire, David, had followed the damsel to such a place and there watched her meeting with Gervaise, Mark heard this fact as confirmation of his worst fears. And yet, whether Elysia had entered Gervaise's control by choice or by force, he would retrieve the damsel if only to give the people of these lands proof of Eve's innocence and his foes' wicked intents.

Mark could not fool himself that his intentions were

so pure. Oh, he meant to attain both claimed goals, but he wanted far more. He wanted Elysia for himself.

Rising to his feet, Mark strode from the chamber without a word of explanation. Twilight was falling and he preferred avoiding the need to navigate the cliff face in total darkness. Since descend it he must, that deed could not be delayed.

Chapter 15

"Don't worry, milady." Relaxing on the most comfortable chair in Kelby Keep's near deserted hall, Belleme spoke to the captive still bound at day's end and awkwardly perched atop the stone ledge of the room's central hearth. "After our goal is won, Gervaise will appear with a bride miraculously rescued from the slain cur known as the Black Wolf. So you see, I've plotted a happy ending for us all."

Hiding the horror his words inspired behind a blank expression, Elysia continued the established pattern of remaining mute. This demon meant to kill her love! Moreover, from her viewpoint, the future Belleme painted would not be a happy ending but rather a miserable beginning for the rest of her life.

Wary of being alone with the earl, to Elysia the opening of the wooden structure's door was a welcome interruption. She gladly watched Gervaise enter, clutching a neatly folded and sealed parchment. Her attention was held firm by the rare sight of the russet-haired man's agitation.

"A messenger arrived bringing this for you." Gervaise handed the missive to a frowning earl.

After glancing at the duke of Normandy's seal, Belleme was irritated that the man sent to deliver so important a communication had dared place it into anyone's hands but his own. Though under any other circumstances he would've demanded a high penance for that misdeed, he wasted no moment in breaking the flattened lump of wax that closed folded edges. He reviewed its contents once in silence before reading Duke Robert's words aloud to answer Gervaise's nervous curiosity.

"I intend to reach your shores twelve nights before Lammas. With daybreak's low tide my men will land on the castle's beach while from the boat I will loose my black hawk as the harbinger of my coming.

"Stand ready for our victory."

The two men exchanged a telling glance, proof of how unnecessary it was for Belleme to risk speaking the author's name aloud. However, only a short time later Gervaise uneasily broke the silence to hesitantly voice an apprehensive concern.

"The date proposed is a mere three days hence!"

" 'Tis not a deed *proposed*," Belleme sneered. "It is our leader's firm commitment to act and one for which we must be prepared."

While plowing the fingers of one hand through silver-streaked red hair, Gervaise earned Elysia's surprise. Prior to the past few hours in these two men's company, she wouldn't have believed it possible for Gervaise to ever become flustered and less to be so thoroughly disconcerted as he now seemed.

Of a sudden, the arrival of an utterly unexpected visitor shattered the hall's growing tension.

"Lord Gervaise," Jamie cried out as he sank to his knees before the man, "I've come to beseech your protection from the Black Wolf's rage."

Both men looked to be as shocked by the plea as Elysia felt although surely she'd more reason to feel the emotion. After all, Mark had explained that her childhood friend's flight from their dinner table had been planned with him. Her first instinct was to question the truth of Mark's claim but one quickly followed by the decision to trust most the man she loved. With that choice came the possibility that Jamie's appearance here was also by Mark's design. It was a reassuring thought.

Although initially too stunned by Jamie's arrival to call out, Elysia was glad for her silence. Any overt action he might take on her behalf could only make already difficult matters worse.

"What has Lord Mark done to threaten you?" Gervaise asked with a chill serenity restored. He knew, of course, about Dunstan's failed attempt upon the Black Wolf and about this boy's dash for freedom after being presented with the implicit accusation of his own dagger. But that had happened the night before last, and it therefore seemed unlikely the boy had only now arrived. But still Gervaise listened to Jamie's account of these events.

"During his first night in Wroxton Castle I tried to

kill the bastard and failed. And yet, though he blames me, I was not responsible for the second such attempt." Jamie's voice broke on a piteous note. "I'd no option but to flee and have remained hidden for two days ... until this eve when Lord Mark near discovered my shelter." While joined hands pressed against the smooth curve of a young throat, an abject plea was repeated. "You are now my only hope."

"What a fine development, Gervaise," Belleme responded for the man who was in reality his minion. "Now you've a guest from Wroxton to witness your exchange of marital vows with Lady Elysia at the morrow's noontide hour."

Accustomed to inspiring fear, Belleme saw nothing untoward in the horrified look Jamie turned to him. Indeed, it pleased him.

But because Jamie refused to glance her way even under this great provocation, Elysia had reason to question uncomfortably the accuracy of her hope that Mark had sent him. Nonetheless, she continued steadily staring at him.

Gervaise noted the damsel's pointed gaze with simple curiosity until he realized that Belleme was just as interested. Uncertain what fearsome action it might inspire from the other man, Gervaise promptly moved to see that bond broken.

"Come, Jamie. You must be weary ... and hungry." Gervaise motioned the still kneeling boy to rise. "I'll lead you to a chamber where you may rest after you've eaten the platter of food I'll command be delivered to you there."

After Gervaise led Jamie away, Belleme again threw Elysia over his shoulder. Already bruised by earlier such handling, Elysia bit back a moan and kept her eyes clenched shut. She refused even to open them for some little time after being roughly dropped onto the severely limited padding of a lumpy pallet.

Only after hearing a bolt shot home followed by the sound of retreating footsteps fading into silence did Elysia's lashes rise to the discovery of an unpleasant view. Still firmly bound, she'd been deposited in an utterly black void of unknown dimensions and no amount of intent peering changed that fact. But soon the darkness seemed to fill with the formless foes of the day's unpleasant memories and images from the disturbing future her brutal captors intended for her.

Unwilling to submit to this mental assault, Elysia drove it into submission beneath a wry humor she deemed doubtless learned from Mark.

This bed of rough homespun stuffed with moldering straw made a strange yet appropriate resting place for her bridal eve.

Seated at the high table of Wroxton Castle, Mark was aware of the wide variety of unsavory sentiments swirling around him. The great hall's usual cheery banter was absent. In truth, no one spoke aloud although the indistinct hiss of many whispers spread an unpleasant fog throughout while sidelong glares pierced the shadows where an apprehensive Eve sought shelter.

Ida sat glumly silent on Mark's left while a scowling Hugh had taken Elysia's seat on his right. Neither of Mark's table companions was willing to chat with the man they mistakenly thought had failed to take action toward righting wrongs each clearly saw. Their error put a faint, wry smile on Mark's lips, one certain to be misinterpreted by critical onlookers.

The shroud of false peace was abruptly torn away by the shrill voice of a village woman bursting from the entrance tunnel's gloom.

"That witch put a hex on my son." A bony finger pointed to Eve. "And now Thad lies near death!"

Within the span of a few moments the hall erupted into a pandemonium focused upon a single terrified woman.

Hugh instantly forced his way through the crowd to place himself as a substantial block between the threatening mob and tender maid. But, though Mark took no such dramatic action, it was the deep roll of his thunderous demand for attention that subdued the uproar.

Once every eye was trained on him, Mark implacably stated, "None of you possesses the power to stand in judgment over one of Wroxton's serfs." Now it was his audience who cowered. "That right is mine alone. Take care else it may be you who stands accused in my court."

The disorganized crowd would've fallen back had each member not been too fearful of drawing the silver ice of Lord Mark's attention.

"Put the boy on a litter and bring him to me," Mark commanded.

Although a wave of muttered resentment was heard, a hastily formed collection of guardsmen and servants promptly set out to do their lord's biding.

The tension of a painful silence settled over the hall and steadily increased until broken by the thudding sound of returning booted feet. The makeshift litter formed of a straw pallet placed across four wooden slats and carried by eight men was carefully lowered to the rush-strewn floor below the high table.

Stepping down from the dais and sinking to his knees, Mark peered closely at a white-faced boy. Was it illness or fear that robbed Thad's cheeks of color? He brushed a thatch of dust-brown hair from a cool brow, caught a guilty gleam beneath a flutter of thick lashes, and grimly smiled.

Rising to his feet, Mark turned toward the lad's mother, silently wondering how sincerely she believed the poorly feigned illness. "Is it solely by your son's word that you think him cursed by a witch?"

"Aye!" The gaunt mother defensively straightened as if the lord's stern question were an insult. "Said as the witch hexed him after he led village lads in an attempt ta rid us of her presence with a rain of stones, and he would'a done the deed but for the interference of the guardsman what's been seduced by her evil wiles."

Rather than meeting her lord's penetrating gaze, the woman glanced into the faces of one after another of the people who'd earlier joined her unruly attempt to wreak vengeance on the devil-marked woman. "For Thad's ailment the witch deserves to pay."

"Nay, good woman." Mark slowly shook a black mane. "Your son is as healthy or more so than you." He carefully enunciated each revealing word as he exposed the sham. "For Thad's attempt to trick me, I could justly demand a high cost from him—and from you."

Onlookers closely gathered about the unfolding

drama shifted uneasily at the undeniable truth in Lord Mark's claim.

"However, I am a merciful man." Mark's half smile appeared and deepened when he caught another glimpse of the lad peeking up at him. "And I extend to you both the opportunity to earn my pardon, but only if you and your son are willing to pay the price."

The woman gazed anxiously down to the son still stretched out at her feet and then, with an audible gulp, looked back up to meet the waiting lord's unblinking gray eyes.

"What must we do?" Her naturally thready voice was so faint it could barely be heard.

"Only two tasks simple and easily done." Mark paused until the woman nodded while the boy reluctantly sat up. "First, make a confession to me." Again Mark paused and this time did not continue until *both* had nodded agreement. "Next, give your apologies to Eve."

The latter demand brought a gasp from the throats of many listeners, yet the woman made haste to comply with each duty. However, for the obstinate boy these requirements proved to be more difficult to face and time-consuming to perform.

Even after these deeds were finished, the crowd remained. Mark decided not to waste this opportunity but took advantage of their full attention. He stepped up on the dais again. From that higher point, Mark assured the people from castle, village, and farm that he would soon bring their lady home. He did not stop with that welcome oath. He went on to warn them that a human danger hiding behind false rumors of devilish powers was hovering near, a peril that likely would require the joined might of all Wroxton to defeat.

Mark dispersed the crowd with these serious words to consider before motioning for two friends to accompany him as he slipped from the castle. Now was the time to share with them a plan already in motion.

Amidst the darkest hours of night a nervous adolescent strode across Elysia's archery glade from a bale of hay often riddled with arrows to where the forest began on the opposite edge. Across and then back again and again. Jamie gave no thought to the path he'd worn in the grass, so intent was he upon a danger past and another to come. His stealthy escape from Kelby Keep had been difficult to achieve but likely less so than the unseen return he must attempt before dawn.

Jamie could only hope he'd not erred and by a poor choice made even before setting out undone the good won since.

Although Eve was the reason Jamie had long avoided this site, it was by his suggestion that he and Lord Mark were to meet here on the border between Kelby and Wroxton. It had also been his suggestion that Eve was the person most able to quickly lead her master here. And it was this choice to involve the witch that Jamie feared might've already led to the foiling of otherwise well-laid plans.

Jamie's pace doubled to match an increasing strain. Thus, it was a relief when a deep voice interrupted the apprehensive tenor of his thoughts.

"Jamie," Mark softly called to the lad whose presence proved him resourceful. "How were you received and what have you learned?"

The one summoned hurried to where Mark stood with Hugh and Eve at his side. Jamie ignored the first part of the question in his haste to answer the second.

"I'm to witness a marriage on the morrow."

"Whose?" Hugh immediately asked the most obvious question while a wary Mark remained silent.

Proud to have secured the information by his own courageous actions and confident that his quick report would aid in seeing the deed forestalled, Jamie responded without realizing that Lord Mark had gone still. "They plan to see Elysia wed with Gervaise."

Mark wanted to know if the intended bride was a willing participant or if the rite were to be a bond forged solely by might. And yet, fearing to know the answer, he had to force himself to ask the question.

"Is Elysia pleased with their plan?"

Jamie cast the speaker a look of such scathing disgust that no verbal reply was necessary.

Doubts abated, Mark's wry humor returned. "Did your hosts happen to mention at what time this auspicious event is to take place?"

Jamie promptly nodded and matched his lord's teasing tone. "The earl of Shrewsbury told Lord Gervaise he should rightly be pleased to have someone from Wroxton Castle witness the exchange of vows at the noontide hour."

"You've done very well, Jamie." Mark congratulated the young man worthy of praise. "The information you've provided will help ensure that their plans come to naught."

Even in the faint light of a cloudy night, Jamie's beaming smile could be seen.

Chapter 16

When Elysia awakened, her windowless chamber was as completely dark as the moment before she'd at last been granted the comfort of a dreamless sleep. Without natural light there was no way to tell whether only minutes or unmarked hours had passed—a jarringly disorienting fact. If only . . .

As if some unnatural presence had read Elysia's thoughts, a door swung wide. She blinked rapidly but as much against that disagreeable notion as the assault of unexpected light. While her eyes adjusted, Elysia fought to focus on the dark silhouette of a hunched figure framed in the portal oddly sited halfway up a wall. Plainly this captive bride's unpleasant chamber was a part of the keep's cellars.

"Been sent to see to your mornin' needs." The obviously aged woman's voice was raspy, and with a bony hand she motioned the lady visitor in Kelby Keep to climb a flight of rickety stairs and follow her lead.

Much to her surprise, Elysia discovered her sleep must have been considerably sounder than she'd thought as at some point during the night her restraints had been cut. Free to stand, the damsel stiff and sore from the previous day's cruel bonds and rough handling found the action of rising more difficult than it ought to have been. Yet once on her feet and moving to join her guide, a clear view of the elderly woman bent low beneath the weight of many years and slowed by an awkward gait pricked Elysia with shame for having rued petty discomforts.

Elysia paused one step before entering the ground level chamber plainly a storeroom with access to kitchens for safety's sake located in a separate building. Very nearly did she yield to a mad urge to thrust caution aside and recklessly attempt an escape from the prison Gervaise and the alarming earl had made of Kelby Keep. However, a single quick glance through the doorway revealed that impulse's folly. Like pillars of doom armed and steadily watching men were stationed on either side of the opening.

With silent disgust Elysia acknowledged herself well and truly trapped. Then, once inside the storeroom, she saw another fact even more daunting. By the angle of sunlight slanting through an oddly unshuttered window Elysia could tell that the morn was almost over and the appointed hour for a deeply resented deed looming near.

There must be a way to forestall the event, and she must find it. That desperate hope became a determined litany during time quickly passing while she prepared to meet the unwelcome day and its dreaded rite.

Elysia's deep green kirtle and russet undergown were woefully creased. But leastways her raspy-voiced companion provided fresh water with which to wash and a borrowed comb to smooth tangles from silky hair. Though a task difficult to perform for herself, she fumbled to tame the dusky cloud by replaiting it into one simple thick braid.

When came the demand for Elysia to join her captors and their guests where they'd gathered in the great hall, her knees shook and hands went cold. Yet, with each step over a winding path through stacked baskets and sacks of provision toward a joyless wedding, Elysia soundlessly repeated her valiant resolution: She *must* and she *would* find some method to prevent this unwanted union.

Once standing framed by the hall's rear doorway, Elysia froze. Amidst the cluster of people waiting below the dais at the far end of the room she recognized and mentally dismissed several of Gervaise's guardsmen and more important vassals. But golden sparks flashed in brown eyes while she critically scrutinized several others.

Elysia deemed Jamie's grin a travesty of the friendship they had shared. However, Belleme's sneer seemed the most natural part of his face. And although a similar expression rode uneasily upon the nervous Dunstan's lips, she was not surprised to see it. And yet it was for Gervaise that Elysia reserved by far the strongest glare of disdain.

"Come, sweet bride." Belleme had already grown tired of waiting for the unwilling woman to comply with an unavoidable reality and impatiently strode toward her. "I'll escort you to meet your groom."

Rather than gallantly offering his arm to her, the earl seized Elysia with a bruising grip just above the elbow and marched her forward.

Rudely thrust into the tight knot of waiting people, Elysia for the first time noticed the abbot of a neighboring monastery. With the sight of his cowled figure fearfully cringing in her unwanted betrothed's long shadow, the faint gleam of a weak but plausible plan flickered to life.

"Now let's have done with getting vows exchanged and this bond blessed." Belleme again reached out to shove the reluctant bride, this time to stand beside the man he knew to be an equally reluctant groom. Continuing to exert his rough control, the earl jerked the startled Abbot Simeon around to face a frowning couple.

Certain at this point that she must either act now or not at all, Elysia promptly spoke.

"Good Father, as an innocent lamb in our Heavenly Shepherd's flock, I pray you to hear my plea."

Rather than meeting the steady gaze of the hall's only damsel, the abbot nervously glanced between the infamous earl with devilish brows and the red-haired holder of lands nearest to his monastery. Either of these men held sufficient power to demand a stiff penalty were he to refuse their commands. Yet, as a man of God, what choice had he? He must listen. Surely there was no wrong in listening?

"Remember, Abbot Simeon"—despite the cowled man's obvious distress, Elysia rushed onward with the one argument she felt was sure to overwhelm all others—"along with my hand in marriage goes a fiefdom of worthy size. And it is my position as the heiress of

Wroxton that places me in the king's ward." A triumphant smile curled her lips. "I cannot be wed but by his royal leave."

Shocked, the abbot instantly assumed an attitude of prayer—flat palms coming together while he pressed the tips of joined fingers against a bowed forehead. Here was a dangerous temporal quandary far beyond the judgment of someone such as himself whose experience was severely limited to religious matters.

Anxious to loose no momentum, Elysia immediately stated, "Lord Gervaise possesses no writ from King Henry granting him permission to claim me as wife."

" 'Struth!" A new voice firmly agreed. The attention of all shifted to the raven-haired man blocking the keep's outgoing door and holding the effortless threat of a bared blade angled across his broad chest. "Gervaise does not, but I do."

While the name Black Wolf could be heard whispered by several onlookers with awe, a brilliant smile warmed the suddenly rosy face of a dark beauty. A welcoming Elysia hastened toward where her savior, her beloved, unexpectedly stood, backed by the full force of his garrison.

Caught unprepared and armed with naught but pretty daggers meant solely for show, neither Gervaise nor Belleme was in a position to challenge the newcomer. Though each knew the time for deadly battle drew near, very near, in this moment they could only watch all that followed with a stifling frustration.

Mark pulled the document in question from a pouch attached to his belt, glad that he'd had the foresight to carry it here against such a hoped-for need.

Elysia barely glanced at the writ whose existence

she'd once resented but now treasured—and not merely for its rescue from an unwanted marriage but as the physical symbol of the bond she fervently desired. When dark brows arched questioningly over silver eyes, she recognized the action as an unspoken second proposal. This time, no matter the strange circumstances or scowling witnesses, Elysia was not so foolish as to reject what she'd come to recognize as truly her heart's desire.

Presenting the neatly folded parchment to the abbot, Mark made a serious request. "With royal approval, Lady Elysia and I ask that you oversee the solemnization and blessing of our union."

Seeing the unmistakable royal seal, Abbot Simeon nodded his relief. Were Wroxton's heiress rightly wed, he'd be freed of any duty to their king to see her protected from Kelby Keep's lord and the fiendish earl he feared too much to deny. And, protected by what seemed the whole of the Black Wolf's fully armed garrison, he would be pleased to personally see the deed done.

In a hall initially intended to host the marriage of its lord yet utterly unprepared for an occasion so festive as a wedding, Abbot Simeon directed this recast bridal couple through their exchange of vows.

Elysia cared nothing for her surroundings' lack of such touches of beauty as candles and flowers. Beyond the priest, only Mark's presence was necessary to fill her cup of happiness to overflowing.

Certain that a life without Elysia would be filled not with peace, but loneliness, Mark gazed down into the golden glow in brown eyes and gladly surrendered a bachelor's once solitary future into this gentle lady's hand.

After vows were spoken, considering the circumstances and company, Abbot Simeon offered over the beaming bride and pleased groom the briefest wedding blessing he'd ever given, yet one of the most heartfelt.

Once the rite was complete, Mark turned toward his unintentional host. And on Gervaise's face he caught an odd expression containing a curious combination of hatred and relief.

"Thank you for actions that hastened this event which I greatly desired." The wry amusement in Mark's initial words was completely absent in the statement flatly added, "Of course, had I somehow failed to arrive in time to halt the marriage you intended, I would have killed you."

As if the assertion rendered more powerful by its utter lack of emotion had been a physical blow, Gervaise's chin jerked upward before he made a belated attempt to blunt the impact by striking back. "As I assuredly will slay you."

An obstinate Elysia refused to permit her happiness in the admittedly odd-timed union to be dulled by the cold neighbor who had turned her fondness for him into scorn. And yet she was all too aware of the growing tension of open enmity.

"Pray take me back to Wroxton, back to *our* home." Elysia anxiously sought to lure her new husband to the safety of his own den before prey became predator and snarling battle broke out.

For the sake of protecting this beloved damsel already subjected to too much danger, Mark willingly yielded to her plea. He wrapped the reassurance of a strong arm about Elysia's shoulders, but before he could lead her from the keep another voice was heard.

"Soon a bride ... but as quickly a widow." The sibilant poison of Belleme's threat was unhidden.

"Ah." Mark turned to face the foreboding man in the black garb of another land. "But how oft have you and your cohorts failed to secure the goal of my death?"

"Me?" Scorn dripped from Belleme's response. "Never have I made the attempt. Nor will I fail when comes the hour in which I choose to take your life."

"Never?" Mark ignored the other man's last phrase. "Then was it not *your* plan to see me slain and my murder blamed upon the valiant maid you long ago ensured would be named witch? The woman who grew from the innocent child you scared with the undeserved mark of Satan?"

"Eve?" Belleme asked in feigned amazement. "Has she been lending her aid to my cause? I'll have to think of some worthy reward to give her." These words of mocking gratitude were yet another barely veiled threat.

Hugh lunged toward the evil speaker, earning Elysia's attention for the first time that day. And in that instant she thought the bearded giant certain to finish his vicious foe's wrongdoings for all time.

But with swift grace Mark thrust his body between the two men and restrained his friend's attack by manacling Hugh's wrists with his own powerful hands.

"Think on it, Hugh." Because of the strength required to tame a fury-driven man, it was through gritted teeth that Mark reasoned with his angry knight.

"I'd be pleased as you to see this fiendish traitor dead. But by killing Belleme amidst a time of even uneasy peace, you break the king's law. And Henry would have little choice but to see you pay the price set by his father."

Hugh's eyes clenched shut against the verity in a rationale he'd far sooner deny and yet could not. 'Struth, the Conqueror had laid down a law demanding that any royal vassal breaking the king's peace by wreaking mayhem upon another would in disgrace forfeit all he had—his liberty if he possessed nothing of greater value.

Seeing that his reasoning had begun to take hold, Mark ended by delivering an argument certain to be the most effective. "If you were imprisoned or dead, then what would become of Eve? She needs your protection."

Arms going lax and shoulders slumping, Hugh gave in to his friend but not the man to whom he sent a glare brimming with hate. Hugh still wanted to see Belleme pay an ultimate penalty.

As Mark directed the departure of Wroxton's armed force from Kelby Keep, his piercing silver gaze turned to a plump man cowering behind the much taller Gervaise. "Dunstan!"

Rather than stepping forward, the one called nervously fell a pace back and trembled while Lord Mark issued a warning.

"I suggest you remain here where, even amongst your treacherous friends, you're less likely to meet with the same peril you turned upon me—a sharp dagger in the night."

* * *

As if storing up warm memories to later wield as a protective amulet against all the trials yet to be overcome, Elysia unabashedly reveled in the simple pleasure of riding home wrapped within Mark's strong arms. She closed her eyes and her thoughts to the large company of armed men riding behind and their unintentional reminder of the confrontation just past. Instead Elysia pressed nearer to a broad chest and soaked in the warmth of her husband, her lover . . .

When the bride in his embrace shifted, Mark glanced down in concern for her comfort only to be snared by the beguiling temptation she embodied. The golden sparks in the depths of brown eyes ignited a flame in his blood. Mark bent a dark head, intent on joining his mouth to enticingly parted lips.

"Ahummm." Hugh's soft growl earned Mark's immediate attention.

Despite the grimace of feigned irritation that Mark sent his friend, in reality he appreciated the interruption preventing an action inappropriate for either this time or place.

Hugh frowned but immediately embarked on what he'd come to say. "Suspecting you'll wish an early night and possibly a late rising, I thought it best to arrange with you now the hour for the start of our morrow's duties."

Considering the shield of a thick beard, Elysia couldn't be certain but suspected that a blush actually accompanied the gruff knight's words. She wisely restrained a grin that could only deepen his embarrassment.

Mark sensed Elysia's amusement and its cause. That she had sufficient tact to hide it earned his admiration.

It was a talent possessed by few of the women he'd known.

After Mark provided his guard captain's query with answer, a period of well-earned peace settled its gentle blanket over the party making a late afternoon return to Wroxton Castle.

"Elly." The soft call of a worried voice eventually slipped through that silence.

Elysia peered around a broad shoulder to find her near lifelong companion riding pillion behind one of Mark's guardsmen.

"It was all planned, you ken?" Since entering Kelby Keep the night past, Jamie had grown ever more anxious to be certain his friend would understand that he hadn't truly sought the despicable Gervaise's help.

"Planned, I mean, by Lord Mark." The youth faltered, fearing Wroxton's new lord might think him claiming more credit than he justly could.

"Planned by us both," Mark corrected. "But for your advice I wouldn't have known about the close proximity of the archery glade so useful for our all-important late-night meeting."

"Late night?" Elysia questioned the timing of this meeting, certain she knew where Jamie had spent the previous one.

"*Last* night," Mark murmured with a mocking grin while Jamie gleefully laughed and Elysia's brow puckered with confusion.

" 'Tis true!" Jamie took joy in proudly stating that fact and even more in explaining how he'd initially tricked Gervaise, who like many priding themselves on sharp wits did not recognize the wiles behind a youth's actions. He told, too, of compounding that feat next by successfully sneaking out from a storeroom window in Kelby Keep and later quietly slipping back inside.

Elysia sent Jamie a warm smile to accentuate her sincere praise of his amazing success with a difficult task.

The first purple haze of twilight had risen to obscure their mount's hooves by the time a weary but triumphant band approached Wroxton Castle. Once the drawbridge was lowered over the fast-flowing waters of a deep moat, they urged steeds to a quicker gait and clattered across.

Elysia was met by a surprising sight, yet one she was happy to see. Waiting a step outside an open door on the castle's second level, Ida and Eve stood side by side in apparent harmony—or leastways in grudging tolerance.

The darkly handsome man now officially lord of Wroxton was the first to rein his destrier to a halt at the bottom of the stairway rising to the fortress's entry. Mark wordlessly swung down and immediately lifted Elysia into his arms. But though both she and those watching expected Mark to set his burden on her feet, he cradled Elysia nearer and marched up the steps past a startled welcoming party.

Elysia was laughing in delight by the time Mark stopped a pace inside the lord's chamber where someone had thankfully possessed the good sense to light at least a single candle. As Mark kicked shut the thick oak door and carried Elysia to the bed, she rained quick kisses on his cheeks, chin, and throat.

"I hope you are not ravenously hungry." Mark's whisper was more a tender growl as he lowered delicious prey for a wolf to lie atop the lush softness of a white bedfur. He'd brought the rare pelt from his home in Normandy but first spread over the coverlet only the day past.

In answer to Mark's question, Elysia slowly shook her head and lifted inviting arms toward the man already stretching out at her side.

"I am . . . for you . . ." Mark punctuated the deep purr of his words with teasing kisses over the cream silk of her throat.

After rising above the yielding temptress whose ivory skin was framed by the sharp contrast of a dark mane against white fur, Mark lightly tugged at a single ebony ringlet. Once released, as if possessed of a will of its own, the curl bounced back against the smooth curve of her cheek. Mark's lips descended to brush the tendril aside before trailing fire across satin skin to fully claim the berry nectar of her mouth.

This savoring of one remembered delight increased Mark's desire to again taste others, to touch every texture, to swallow her into the possession of his arms. And as he gazed down into eyes gone to molten honey, need became father to the deed.

Despite the limited experience of their single fiery night amidst a forest's storm, Elysia unhesitatingly welcomed the sweet, wordless promises offered by the gentle hands freeing her body of every annoying barrier to exquisite pleasures.

Mark meant to earn the greater delight of rousing within this innocent damsel a potent hunger to match his own aching desire. Only then would he reward them both with love's most brilliant explosion of an ecstasy that was certain to end in purest satisfaction.

While fighting for sufficient self-control to achieve these goals, Mark spread burning excitement with caressing hands. He laid a slow, searing path up the shivering damsel's sides to the sensitive flesh beneath arms clinging to his shoulders. But the same stroking motions over incredibly soft curves that flooded Elysia with fiery sensations roused in Mark a desperate, burning hunger.

Mark pulled away and quickly stripped off his own clothing before turning back to find wide gold eyes intently studying him.

Stunned anew by the magnificent sight of his powerful torso, Elysia's breath caught in her throat. She helplessly reached out to touch the awesome power of bronzed muscles highlighted by candlelight and shadow. Taking sweet retribution for her devastating play, Mark came down to trail over her flesh the delicious torment of his caresses and wicked enticements of his lips.

Mark then took Elysia's hands into his own and gently pinned them to the bed beside her head while shifting to hover over her. Only at an agonizingly slow pace did he ease his body closer. The anguish of pleasures withheld heightened Elysia's senses until she felt it impossible to bear more. A smile of triumph barely tilted the corners of Mark's passion-tight mouth when his beloved moaned with need and he at last brushed a wide chest across sensitive tips. She gasped and arched upward, trembling wildly.

Mark could hold back no longer and lowered his burning strength completely to merge with her utterly pliant body. With freed hands, Elysia stroked across wide shoulders and down a powerful back to desperately curl her fingertips into his hips. Then, entwined by soft limbs, Mark again rocked Elysia with him into a rhythm as old as time and as fresh as new life.

Although feeling buffeted by a wild and contrary tide, Elysia exalted in Mark's strength. She arched into him while the remembered gale of passion returned and waves of unruly sensation carried them both higher and deeper. Gasping as a sea of burning delights broke over them again and again, Elysia clung to the firm anchor of Mark. He was the tempest's source and also her guide to safe harbor.

When Mark suddenly went still, caught at the crest of a towering wave, with a cry of feverish yearning Elysia writhed against him. Groaning incoherently into Elysia's ear, Mark held her still tighter against his tense form while together they dropped over an invisible edge to sink through the unfathomable pleasures in a sea of burning delights.

At length the gentle lapping of a peaceful tide on an ocean of foam washed the satisfied couple onto the shore of a piercingly sweet lassitude.

While the bride who'd been through a morass of tangled events and emotions in the past few weeks drifted into a well-deserved slumber, Mark watched and marveled at his unmerited good fortune in winning her for his own.

In a keep purposely emptied of all save three conspirators, the gloom was barely lessened by the fading flames of a dying hearthfire.

"Now that the Black Wolf has claimed the heiress for his wife, what hope have we?" Dunstan muttered his doubts aloud, frustration having overcome even his fear of provoking the dangerous earl.

Gervaise silently glared at the irritating speaker from across the single trestle table left standing in the deserted space below the dais. This night was far advanced and only one more remained, which meant that the hours before an all-important event were both too few and too rapidly dwindling.

"You are fools." Glancing between his two worthless fellow conspirators, Belleme's never sweet temper went so sour it curdled into bitter scorn. "At this late hour the heiress could be of little use to our cause."

"But then today why ..." The question Gervaise began melted into nothing beneath the heat of the earl's fierce gaze.

"An alliance formed today might have saved us sufficient time or provided our cause with warriors enough to make it worth the effort to secure. However, by the time the morrow dawns inadequate hours will remain to see the bond become more a value than a hindrance."

"But without control of the castle's beach"—Gervaise tentatively asked a further question too important to leave unspoken—"how can we obey Duke Robert's command and stand ready with the aid he expects?"

Belleme's sly grin was sinister. "By keeping the Black Wolf and his supporters thoroughly occupied in defending themselves against our attack on the west, we'll see the eastern beach left inadequately guarded and thus provide all the aid the duke requires of us."

"And between our army and the duke's invading force we'll crush the Black Wolf."

"His army you are welcome to destroy," Belleme hissed. "Even the friend who assaulted me you may have ... but the Wolf himself is *mine.*" Belleme's viciously pointed gaze dared his far weaker companions to fight his claim. "I will dispatch Mark of Valbeau with my own hand."

Chapter 17

*G*ently awakened by the first sounds of a castle stirring to greet a fresh day, Elysia smiled with enjoyment of a new pleasure—the warm cocoon of a bed shared in love. When she drowsily snuggled closer to the firm pillow of a masculine chest's hard muscle and smooth skin, welcoming arms momentarily crushed her even nearer.

"Ooof ..." With a gasp of pretended pain, Elysia pulled back and rose on one elbow to gaze indignantly down at her stunningly handsome husband.

Mark was not so easily misled by the expression in brown eyes more sultry than offended. With a forefinger he smoothed the furrow between delicate brows and responded to his tender bride's feigned injury with a slow, potent smile.

That smoldering enticement kindled in Elysia intimate visions of recent fiery scenes, which in turn heated her blood and robbed her of sane thought.

Mark intently studied the loveliness of a delicate face overwhelmed by an ebony cloud of curls before threading his fingers through that silk and urging her mouth to his for a teasing series of brief and unsatisfying kisses.

When at length Mark withdrew, Elysia boldly followed until he kissed her again and more thoroughly while she melded silken curves tightly to the hard angles of his body. The burning winds of passion steadily built anew, sweeping them both into the whirling eye of its hungry tempest before drowning willing victims in the liquid fires of love's searing pleasures.

An uncounted time later Elysia drifted with Mark through the sweet haze of unthinking contentment. Suddenly a horrible memory intruded, scattering gentle mists with the cold reality of fear.

"I forgot!" Elysia wailed and in self-disgust impotently thumped a fist against the badly disarranged white fur covering their bed's feather mattress.

"What did you forget, sweeting?" Mark rolled to his side to face the lovely bride lying so close.

Though Mark's brows arched in an echo of his question, Elysia saw by his mocking smile that he hadn't taken her honest desperation seriously.

Golden sparks flared in the depths of brown eyes as Elysia twisted to face him and with a blunt answer promptly proved the importance of what she'd remembered. "The message that came from Duke Robert for Belleme."

The warmth of humor instantly fled Mark's face, leaving it a mask of ice that hid all natural emotion.

Gazing at the man abruptly gone solemn, Elysia

knew what he was silently waiting to hear what he needed to know and what she ought to have told him the moment they rode from the keep. As Elysia hurried to correct that wretched error, her voice was choked with guilt for the dangerous mistake of then allowing both relief for a rescue and joy for a bond unexpectedly solemnized to end in such a wrongful failure.

"Duke Robert's message stated that with the dawn in three day's time he would sail to Wroxton's shore and that his supporters should stand ready."

"Three days' time?" The question was not a question but rather Mark thinking aloud. After a brief pause, his usual sardonic half smile appeared. "Counting from the hour you say Belleme received this message, the 'dawn in three day's time' would mean not the morn of the day we wed nor yet the dawn now breaking but rather the one that will follow on the next morrow."

Elysia felt struck by the horror of that impending peril so near. It was her fault that hours for preparing a defense had been lost. She bit at her lower lip, caught between terrified tears and useless frustration over her own lack—one that might have made the difference between success and defeat. Or worse, her wrong might cost her beloved his life.

"Nay, sweeting," Mark instantly denied the blame he could see she'd taken fully upon herself. "I am a warrior trained with years of experience as a tactician. It's I who should have asked you for any possible pieces of useful information learned." Voice dropping into a deep, comforting velvet, Mark attempted to shift the burden of wrong upon his own broad shoulders. " 'Tis my fault, not yours."

Elysia remained unconvinced. After all, not only was she the one who had been present to learn of the proposed invasion but at the moment of hearing had recognized the grave importance of the plans revealed.

A grim expression darkened Elysia's winsome face and she slowly turned her head from side to side in a negative motion.

"The opportunity was mine and it was I who failed to act while there was still a chance to see looming dangers blocked."

It appeared Mark could neither force nor cajole Elysia into accepting his comfort for the deed already done. But he was determined that she be made to realize no justification existed for her to assume the struggle for their cause lost before it was fought.

"We still have every chance to devise successful strategies and secure our victory."

Elysia saw that the strong warrior she'd wed was affronted by her suggestion that he might fail. Though biting her lip in remorse, she couldn't help but question the reasoning behind his confidence.

"But how?" Elysia was not trained to battle but possessed sharp wits and a talent for logic that enabled her to see the extreme difficulty of winning any conflict when cursed with the inherent confusion of troops divided at the outset. "With the duke and his men arriving by sea on one side while Gervaise and Belleme attack from the opposite direction, it would be necessary to maintain a successful defense on two sides simultaneously."

Mark's gray eyes widened. He was impressed this

woman had so succinctly outlined a difficult military challenge, but a challenge he believed could be met with a simple response.

"Neither the duke's force nor those issuing from Kelby Keep can hope to succeed without the aid of the other." Mark brushed a forefinger over Elysia's cheek and down her throat to the dip at its base while with a tempting grin he added, "Therefore, by halting either one, **we** stop the other."

Mark had **wanted** to calm Elysia's apprehension but was convinced by her lingering frown that he'd succeeded only in deepening her concern. Cuddling her nearer in an instinctive effort to leastwise provide physical comfort, he prayed his failure to ease her tension would not be mirrored by defeat in the attempt to thwart an imminent assault upon Wroxton.

Unable to so easily accept defeat on either score, Mark made another fervent attempt to sway Elysia's mood. "There is every reason to believe in our ability to win success!" The dark man pulled back to turn the full power of his silver gaze upon the tender damsel in his arms even as the inherent honesty of his nature forced him to acknowledge a limiting factor.

"Aye, success we can win . . . although 'tis true that with but a single day to lay our plans, there is no time to be lost. We must all labor to see necessary preparations complete in good time." To Mark's amazement it was this admission that won Elysia's warmest smile.

Elysia saw Mark's surprise that this was true and mentally shook her head in bewilderment over the strange inability of men to understand a woman's logical mind. How could Mark not see that the prospect of doing something, anything, provided more reason for lifted spirits and raised hopes than all the platitudes men ever mistakenly deemed appropriate to calm females they chose to believe irrational.

In truth, Elysia and most women of her acquaintance were both infinitely more practical and more capable of improvising to overcome adverse challenges. Elysia knew herself able to bravely face danger if allowed something productive to do. Conversely, if forced to sit safely huddled but useless in a chapel, she'd soon be buried in despair.

"Come, milady, we must dress," Mark murmured into Elysia's ear the moment before abruptly bounding to his feet and formally offering an arm to help his lady-wife rise. "With much to be done, it's past time to begin."

As the pair later descended spiraling steps they were intercepted by the agitated guardsman who'd been posted to watch Kelby Keep from forest shadows. He'd hastened back to the castle to give his lord an ominous report of the arrival of increasing danger. Mark's eyes went to ice as he motioned Elysia to continue leading the way downward.

The bridal couple's early appearance for the day's first meal surprised everyone in the hall but Hugh most of all. It was to his guard captain that Mark had named a much later hour for them to meet. However, once Mark began to speak, the people's concern for the early health of the newlyweds' relationship was immediately overshadowed by distress for troubles infinitely more dangerous.

"I've received undeniable proof that Duke Robert's invasion of England is imminent. And even more ominous for we of Wroxton is the fact that he intends to land with the morrow's dawn and on the shore below our castle."

Mark paused, waiting for the roar of many shocked voices speaking at once to subside. "To foil that threat, I am calling a meeting of the warriors in my garrison and the men of the demesne."

A silver gaze moved steadily over watching men gone still. "I ask that you immediately depart to carry my summons for others to join me here as soon as possible after this message is received. Go, see this errand done with all the haste your fleetest steeds can provide."

Guardsmen grabbed hunks of rye bread and cheese even as they rushed from the castle to do their lord's bidding.

The hall soon emptied of all save houseserfs laboring to clear the large room in preparation for the soon arriving crowd. Mark commanded that writing implements be fetched before joining his wife who still sat patiently at the high table.

Elysia had closely watched Mark set the wheels of Wroxton's defense in motion. The further demonstration of his ability to command obedience with respect rather than with threats like Belleme or even Gervaise increased her admiration of the core of this man she loved for more than his stunning looks and charming manner. She enjoyed observing her husband yet had patiently remained for another purpose.

Mark blindly glared at a stain on the table's white covering. He was impatient to see matters well in hand and found it difficult to wait on others to deliver messages or bring necessary items.

To distract himself from the growing tension of waiting, Mark began to mentally compose the message he would dispatch to the royal court with all the speed at his disposal. He must warn King Henry of his brother's planned invasion and Belleme's part in that treason. In addition to that most important information, Mark intended to assure his king that he would do everything in his power to ensure that the duke's ship would find no welcome harbor at Wroxton.

Mark knew there was no need for him to point out that were he to fail and the duke to succeed in landing here, the invaders would win the ability to spread out unchallenged, gathering supporters and momentum as they continued onward. Nay, he needn't emphasize that too clear danger. Rather, he would remind Henry of a more welcome prospect. By preventing the duke from landing at Wroxton, they would force him to continue sailing further along the coast to the unwelcoming town of Portsmouth.

Elysia counted herself fortunate for the gift of a private moment with her husband provided by the wait for his requested blank sheet of parchment, quill, and ink. Though realizing his thoughts were rightly occupied by weighty matters, still she broached a subject important to her that he seemed to have forgotten.

"Mark, what tasks would you have me undertake to aid our fight to preserve the peace of Wroxton and the kingdom?"

Mark didn't answer, but by his startled expression, Elysia could see he had expected her to do nothing. Briskly she reminded him of the mention of responsibilities that had given her hope.

"In our chamber you said we must *all* do our part to see preparations finished in good time." Gold sparks burned, and Elysia's chin tilted upward. "I *am* the lady of Wroxton and I take seriously the responsibilities you once suggested I'd failed to meet. I demand you allow me to play a role in the defense of my people and home."

Mark's black brows met in a slight frown above eyes gone a cloudy gray. Though he could admire Elysia's sentiment, what task for battle was there that a *woman* could do?

"I would deem it a fine accomplishment if you could rally the women and children whose men will accompany me into battle. See that the mothers' minds are occupied with else than apprehensions that could only succeed in frightening their children."

Elysia's lashes settled in black crescents on pale cheeks to hide the mutiny burning in her eyes. Plainly the man she loved had listened but not heard the meaning at the heart of her request to be of aid. Nay, mayhap he'd heard but couldn't believe her able to perform such deeds. Ah, well, he wanted her to *organize* the women and children? Fine. That was precisely what she would do—organize them just as Mark's garrison already was and all the men of Wroxton soon would be. And while Mark met with the men, Elysia meant to meet with the women and children of the castle and village who could be summoned without dispatching an army of messengers.

Though so crowded that men standing shoulder to shoulder could barely shift their feet, the waiting hall was so quiet that the sound of Mark's footsteps as he climbed to the dais was near as startling as a clap of thunder.

Mark took his time, pausing to look out over the multitude of faces. Once these men had viewed a new lord with wary suspicion of promises they hadn't trusted. But in the time between his personal visits to their homes and this day, they'd come to accept him as an honorable man who'd proven his worth by holding oaths made to his serfs as dearly as those given to a man wellborn. He had earned their trust, and in return they now waited to learn what assistance he needed from them.

The trust Mark saw on the open faces of these men he'd come to know and respect won from him a warm smile completely devoid of its usual cynicism. But his expression went solemn again before he started to repeat for them the news of a looming invasion and the part Duke Robert intended for Wroxton to play in a scheme for wresting the English crown from his brother.

However, in this telling, Mark dwelled upon the greater inland threat from Kelby Keep. Although it wasn't possible to further blacken the savage reputation of Robert the Devil Belleme, he shared news just given him of this morn's arrival of the dangerous man's many, equally brutal mercenaries. These heartless men would of a certainty be added to Gervaise's garrison and together form a daunting army.

After raising that fearsome specter, Mark went on to detail the strategy he'd formed to prevail in the coming struggle. He had no difficulty in convincing his supporters that it would be foolish to weaken their strength by splitting their force into two inadequate armies in order to simultaneously fight assaults from both land and sea. The men who must follow his lead also agreed with the wisdom of his decision to keep their two enemy forces as far apart as possible. Toward that end, they would depart Castle Wroxton before the dawn and lie in wait for Gervaise and Belleme. They would seize the advantage by catching approaching foes unprepared and by that superior position be better able to prevent the Kelby force from ever drawing near to the duke's force intending to land on the beach at the base of a sheer cliff.

Chapter 18

*T*hough stars had faded, dawn had yet to cast its first glimmer across the eastern horizon and the sky above had brightened only to a dull gray. That the heavens seemed free of clouds, boding fair weather, Elysia chose to see as a good omen for the sweet prospect of victory in the imminent battle and future peace for Wroxton.

After leading a quiet party of carefully selected and determined women to the bailey wall at castle back, Elysia reached out to press a hidden latch that swung wide the concealed postern door through a seemingly solid barrier.

A soft gasp was heard as the daunting view of a sheer cliff's abrupt edge was revealed to women who, though warned what to expect, were unprepared for the sudden shock of seeing. While several strangely armed female warriors crossed themselves and word-lessly prayed for courage, Elysia peered into the hazy distance. She could barely make out the indistinct shape of a ship apparently anchored and rocking atop distant waves.

Elysia wordlessly pointed toward the expected but unpleasant sight before motioning her companions to again follow her lead. This time, however, the women shifted into a preset order for a single file descent of this treacherous path.

From a point midway between cliff top and the cave that had been Jamie's haven after his desperate leap from the lord's bedchamber window, a soft call was heard. The woman first in line behind Elysia broke off to carefully pick her way to the deep crevice where her son waited, a moving shadow barely seen. A few steps lower the action was repeated with the next woman in the line, then again, and yet again until a score of brave mothers had joined sons already prepared for the challenge soon to be met.

Elysia alone of the original party continued on down the path until it broadened out to disappear amidst a hundred sea-carved clefts on the rocky shore.

In the colorless but growing light of predawn, as if prearranged, two opposing armies met to wage mortal battle on the border between Kelby and Wroxton.

At the outset an unmoving Mark faced a coldly grinning Belleme, both with bared broadsword in hand. Only after the passage of tense, silent moments while Belleme's red-haired ally constantly glanced toward an unblemished sky, did their conflict break into open hostility.

"We wait no longer," Belleme snarled. Mark heard the statement as an impatient challenge to King

Henry, but the speaker's supporters recognized its warning not to turn back now for the sake of a missing hawk.

The clash of steel against steel echoed through the forest while shafts of sunlight glittered over well-honed blades slicing wide arcs through air and flesh. Men skilled in the arts of war struggled in deadly earnest yet no more so than the villagers, farmers, and household serfs of Wroxton who Belleme had been shocked to discover were willing to risk their lives for a lord so newly arrived.

Indeed, it was the latter who in the end turned the battle's tide. With the fervor of loyalty a more powerful motivation than a mercenary's mere monetary gain, Wroxton's forces slowly but inexorably overcame their opponents. And as it became clear which way the day would end, Belleme's men were most influenced by terror of their master's brutal punishment—not as an impetus to fight more fervently but to flee before it befell them.

As Belleme's men began steadily melting into forest shadows, his rage exploded into a brutal retaliation against the one of his two allies who remained loyal.

Gervaise found himself suddenly turned upon by the man he'd been struggling to protect moments earlier. With the strange feeling that time had slowed to a crawl, he realized the Black Wolf and his men had gone still, expressions of disgust frozen on their faces. This while Belleme took the hilt of his broadsword in the joined grip of both hands and began to swing it in a mighty circle.

"Pray God, n-n-n—"

Gervaise's horrified plea for mercy was literally cut off half-spoken.

Pandemonium followed. With this ghastly demonstration of what payment would be given for defeat, the battlefield was quickly cleared of Mark's foes— even Belleme fled into obscuring shadows. And Mark hadn't the heart to force men who'd courageously fought for him into pursuing the fiendish man too likely to wreak upon any who found him the same fate he demanded from his pitiful friend.

Drawing back the bowstring and holding it steady, Elysia took careful aim at the large black hawk soaring against the near colorless sky of early morn. It circled ever closer to the shore. Still Elysia held steady, waiting until at last it flew sufficiently near. Her breath caught while the loosed arrow zinged through still air.

The bird abruptly plummeted from the sky and disappeared into the sea below. This was the first time Elysia had ever killed a living creature. And no matter the honorable purpose for it, she was horrified by the deed.

Irritated in the next instant for wasting precious moments while her foes rowed ever nearer and nearer, Elysia dashed toward the cliff path. Racing feet slid dangerously on loose pebbles. She couldn't possibly reach her intended safe haven before the boat carrying Duke Robert's advance party reached shore.

By necessity adjusting her plan, Elysia dodged into the nearest shallow cavern as the unpleasant sound of men jumping into water and hoisting their boat ashore rose to her ears. But as booted feet hastened after her, a loud, discordant din of clashing and banging started to echo from everywhere. And as if the rock face was itself threatening to quake and crumble, a hail of stones began to fall.

Peeking down, Elysia grinned to see the confusion on the invaders' faces turn to horror as they ducked beneath shields held overhead to fend off well-aimed missiles. The duke's men had landed with the smooth speed lent by fine training and long experience. But, although their departure lacked for such refined skills, it was accomplished with far greater haste.

Though elated by their victory, the joy of Mark's warriors was tempered by their ghastly memories of a human devil's brutal deed. They were pleased but not surprised to be met at the drawbridge by a welcoming party. However, no man among them had reason to expect being regaled by those who greeted them with a merry tale of triumph that brightened the spirits of everyone.

Indeed, they all agreed the bold adventure was destined to live on in folk legends for generations to come. How could it be elsewise when an exceptional group of mothers and young sons, led by their noble lady, had driven Duke Robert from Wroxton's shores without the aid of a single blade!

On hearing this remarkable story and the strategy attributed to his spirited wife, Mark's smile was as mocking as ever, but sincere admiration glowed in silver eyes. "Did you really defeat that famous warrior, Duke Robert of Normandy, with nothing more dangerous than pots pounded with sticks and a rain of pebbles?"

Soft cheeks went bright, but Elysia beamed and nodded. "Mayhap next time you'll not discount a woman's strategies for war so blithely?"

"I pray Wroxton need never be defended again." Mark grimaced but it turned into a grin as he placed a hand on his heart to fervently declare, "But if it does, I swear I'll remember that we've been blessed with our very own Boadicea, warrior-woman beyond compare."

Several of Mark's guardsmen heard his proud statement and added their admiration before curiously asking their lady who her female warriors were.

Elysia was embarrassed that she'd failed to formally assure that these women receive their just acclaim. And not the women only but their courageous sons as well. To promptly rectify that lack, Elysia called out their names and gave to each their lady's public thanks.

Because Elysia had been a prisoner at Kelby Keep the night a nasty scene occurred, Mark wasn't sure how much she knew of it. But he was pleased to learn that among those mothers and sons chosen for the defense of Wroxton's shore, his wife had included the pair he had forced to confess a lie and apologize to Eve.

"Tonight in the field between castle back and bailey wall, we'll celebrate our victory," Elysia joyously called out. Smiling people went still to listen as she added, "There will be a fine feast meant for everyone although I ask that my defenders of the shore come to be served as honored guests."

Elysia's audience enthusiastically cheered both feast and choice of honored guests. With all that had hap-

pened, it seemed a lifetime must have passed between
the day's beginning and this end to their peril, yet the
afternoon was far from over. And the people clearly
remained too excited to easily return to the quiet rou-
tine of cottage or castle. They milled about exchanging
stories of what remarkable things they'd done and
seen during the hours just past.

"How will you arrange so large a meal so quickly?"
Mark tried to hide his doubts but failed.

"It's not quickly." Elysia grinned. "With Eve's help
to direct a second army of workers, Ida has been laboring over our feast the whole day long."

"But a *celebration* feast begun this morn ... before
the battle commenced?" Dark brows arched.

"Hah!" Elysia scoffed. "It was you who suggested
that I organize the women and keep them occupied."

Mark looked confused, but with a teasing grin Elysia shrugged and explained. "From a list I prepared
of duties for the day, everyone had their choice. The
feast was Ida's although it was I who volunteered
Eve's assistance."

Elysia didn't mention that the latter arrangement
had been necessary since the other women had refused to have the witch in their company. Nor would
she tell Mark that a reluctant Ida had agreed only
because her lambie pleaded. That was the challenge
met in laying plans. Fortunately her actions had also
led to a private conversation with Eve, one in which
Elysia learned of Belleme's role in her friend's past
and of the newly affirmed bond of love with Hugh.

"But a *celebration?*" Again Mark questioned Elysia's logic.

"Tch, tch." Elysia shook her head and against brow

and cheeks bounced a dark halo of ringlets loosened from braids by the day's trials. "Surely you didn't think any of us would plan for anything but success?"

Mark immediately responded. "I think anyone who'd wager against *our* success would be a fool."

In the gloom of a deserted stable, Dunstan crouched inside an empty stall and nervously peered around its opening. His talents lay in practical matters. He had never claimed to be a warrior nor even wanted to be one. So, how was it that he'd come to be allied with a warrior like Belleme? And not an honorable warrior, but a demon who dealt brutally with *friends!* Dunstan shivered at the too vivid memory of the scene he'd witnessed. It turned his stomach anew.

Dunstan had run from Belleme in panicked terror and without thought of what to do or where to go. But when exhaustion forced a halt, he'd had time to ponder the matter with a measure of his usual shrewdness. He daren't go back to Kelby Keep for fear that Belleme would return to that site for the sake of retrieving valuables left behind. Nor could Dunstan wander aimlessly forever, certainly not without a horse. With that thought had come the image of Wroxton's fine stables. Surely the last place anyone would expect to find him was here?

The sharp crack of the stable door being thrown open startled Dunstan so badly he fell backward into a pile of musty hay. But fortunately for him, the two boys who'd stepped inside were laughing so hard they didn't hear the thud of his hefty body hitting the floor.

"Did you see when I landed a good wham on the big arse of the oaf with a boar on his shield?"

"Aye, Thad." Jamie grinned at the younger boy. "And what fools they looked with shields over their heads, leaving us bigger targets to hit!"

The boys thought they had the stable to themselves. Everyone else, even Jamie's closest friend David, was in the courtyard refighting the forest battle, but these veterans of the cliff assault had slipped away to find a place where they could relive their own triumphs.

Rounding the corner to a stall that personal experience told them was empty, the boys came face to face with a most unpleasant surprise.

The crowd between drawbridge and castle entrance eventually began to disperse, the better to prepare for their evening's festivities. But before anyone had wandered far another desperate confrontation began to unfold.

"Thad!" The piercing scream sliced through a balmy summer afternoon and froze cheerful expressions on the faces of many in the crowd into a parody of warmth.

The lad's mother hurtled herself from the bottom of castle stairs toward the stable constructed of wood and leaning against a long, towering stone wall. Of a sudden she went utterly motionless as if, like Lot's wife, struck to a pillar of salt for some wrongful sight.

Elysia and Mark stood not far distant and could see that although seemingly paralyzed and mute, the woman's horror-widened eyes streamed with tears. Their attention followed the path of her unblinking gaze to make a miserable discovery in the stable's open door.

"If you come closer or hinder my way, I swear they

both will die!" Dunstan's words, so strained they shook, were soft yet clearly heard amidst the unnatural stillness.

Plainly panicked, Dunstan held not only Thad but Jamie at dagger's point. With a two-handsbreadth difference in height and bound together back to back, the boys would find it exceedingly difficult to move far in any direction without tripping. That fact left them at the mercy of one overwrought man with a single sharp blade.

In the gloomy structure behind the dangerous tableau, a silent shadow moved.

Though Mark dared not betray this welcome development by permitting a close scrutiny, from the corner of silver eyes he saw a useful action taken. As encouragement, he permitted a wry smile whose meaning Dunstan would be certain to misunderstand.

Returning with a full basket from Ida's likely unnecessary errand to fetch fresh greens from a garden far behind the stable, Eve had happened upon the threatening scene from the back. With long experience of moving noiselessly through the forest, Eve had slipped into the stable from a rear door. Now she slowly sank down to rest on her heels while with great caution first lifting one of the shovels used to muck out stalls and then maneuvering its handle into a horizontal position directly behind Dunstan's ankles.

Recognizing the brave damsel's intent and anxious to help it succeed, Mark purposefully deepened his mocking smile to claim Dunstan's full attention and hold it by unsheathing his own dagger with deliberate care.

"So, for the price of two negligible boys"—Mark

idly motioned to the bound pair—"I can claim *your* life?"

The depth of Dunstan's fear was revealed when he inadvertently stiffened, which in turn caused both a jerk of the boys whose bonds he held curled in one hand and the trembling of his dagger's tip. It intensified when Lord Mark took a small step forward.

"But do you truly want the blood of two innocents on your hands when you go to meet God's fearful judgment ... soon?" With the last word Mark moved another slow step nearer.

"Stay away, I tell you!" Dunstan's snarl was half a plea while he tried to take a step back.

He stumbled over the shovel handle firmly held. As he fell clumsily backward, Eve rolled to one side and the boys in tandem to the other. Mark took a long stride forward to see the fallen foe restrained, but another was quicker. And as he deemed the other man's right to retribution stronger than even his lord's, Mark went motionless.

Thad's burly father, the village ironworker, launched himself upon his son's captor and seized the hand still gripping a knife. The weaker Dunstan fought with the unnatural strength of terror, but the furious father would not be denied. Dunstan died unmourned.

While the final scene in a day of wildly fluctuating emotions played out, Elysia watched with a curious detachment. Until she saw her friend behind the desperate Dunstan, she'd assumed Eve was busy aiding Ida's endeavors. Had Ida failed to keep her promise and put Eve to work? No matter now. For whatever strange errand that had sent Eve on a path so near the stable, Elysia would thank God—as should Thad and his parents. It was only unfortunate that Hugh's duties as guard captain had kept him busied elsewhere.

Thad tried to meet the disbelieving green eyes of the nervous damsel he and his friends had come to the castle kitchens seeking.

"This time"—he uncomfortably shifted from one foot to the other and cleared his throat before stating the simple but heartfelt thing he'd come to say to the woman who'd likely saved his life—"I *really* am sorry."

Lord Mark had once forced Thad to offer the witch, nay, Eve, a sham apology, but this time he meant it. What was more, he'd convinced his friends of their wrong in thinking her responsible for what she couldn't help and goaded them into joining him here.

"Aye, me, too," a taller boy added his apology. And then another chimed in ... and another ... and another, until it sounded like the plainsong of monks in the abbey.

Having no idea how to respond to this action she'd never before experienced, Eve merely smiled and nodded. It seemed to be enough as they responded in kind and turned to leave.

As the boys filed out, Hugh stepped from the shadows and moved to gently draw his confused love into a tender bear hug.

"Did you make them do that?" Eve asked, tilting her head back to send him a gently accusing glare.

"Nay. That was sincere and done of their own accord."

Eve shook her head in disbelief until Hugh tucked

her face beneath his chin and kissed the top of her head.

"I knew that one day the people would have to see beyond the scar to the sweetness inside—like I always have." The words were a velvet thunder that warmed her heart. "And its time they did when as a knight's wife you become the Lady Eve. And more, anyone witless enough to insult the beloved wife of the garrison's guard captain might wind up in the dungeon."

Eve pulled a whisper away to gaze up into Hugh's face for fear that he was teasing in offering an outcast witch the future from an impossible dream.

The sight of wary hope and painful fear in green eyes shook Hugh to the core. He meant to spend a lifetime replacing past pains with a multitude of joys and told her so with tiny kisses over eyelids, cheeks, and lips.

"Should we go and join the feasting?" he asked between kisses gone slow and deep. "Or should we slip away and arrange our own celebrations?"

Eve blushed, but no other words were necessary after she buried her face into the curve of his neck and whispered, "I love you."

The feast that night was a great success and far merrier than any gathering in, as the village elders liked to say, "living memory." They felt justified thrice over by their threefold reason for this extravagant celebration. First, for the marriage of their lord and lady; second, the Black Wolf led victory over Belleme; and, third, the triumph of Lady Elysia and her honored guests in preventing Duke Robert from setting foot on Wroxton's shore. After the toasts were made and the mountains of food consumed, the pleasures continued with music, dancing, and indulging in barrels of wine and kegs of ale.

Once the evening entertainments settled into a rollicking series of dances, by tradition Elysia was constrained to dance for hours with the many vassals, guards, or serfs who asked. Yet, in the end, it was always the figure of her incredibly handsome husband who held her attention. And no one could gainsay them when he came to her with a request to slip away with him and grant a weary Ida the boon of a meeting before she retired. Elysia wondered what Ida needed of her that was so important it couldn't await the morrow.

While the people outside continued their joyous festivities, in the solar where privacy was assured, Elysia discovered that it was not merely Ida who waited but Jamie as well. She looked to Mark for explanation.

To Elysia's surprise, Mark smiled tightly and motioned toward Ida instead.

"There's something I ought to have told my two children a very long time ago."

Elysia's confusion was growing, and Jamie looked as curious as she to learn the explanation for this cryptic statement.

Ida took a deep breath and stared blindly down at fingers she'd tightly weaved together. "I always thought of you as my daughter, my lambie ... though you were not."

Although Ida wasn't looking at her, Elysia nodded. It had ever seemed their natural relationship. Ida had always been more her mother than the one she didn't remember.

"And because of that," Ida continued, still without glancing up, "I hoped you and Jamie would think yourselves siblings, ... which in blood you are."

A slight pucker drew Elysia's brows together as she looked between Ida and the boy whose frown was much fiercer than her own.

Thoroughly tired out by the busiest day of her life, Elysia suspected her weariness was responsible for this difficulty in understanding. To solve the problem, she calmly asked for a simple explanation. "What does that mean?"

Ida drew a deep breath but met Elysia's gaze steadily as she answered. "That your father was Jamie's father, too."

"But you were wed to ..."

"Aye," Ida fervently nodded. "I was that, but Cyril couldn't have been Jamie's father." Her lips had become a tight line.

Startled, Elysia and Jamie gazed across the table and directly into each other's eyes. Now that they'd reason to look, for the first time each saw traces of themselves in the other.

"No wonder we've always been such great friends." Elysia smiled. It took Jamie a brief while longer to acknowledge a blood bond with the beauty he'd long adored. Yet the moment he did, a beaming smile broke across his face.

"Leastways as my sister you can't ever be rid of me."

"Tch!" Elysia chided. "As if I'd ever want to be without my childhood friend."

"Well, you'll have to be ... for a time."

Two shocked faces instantly turned toward Mark.

"Sorry, my love," Mark murmured to his wife. "But no matter your great talents as a tactician for battle, only boys can be fostered in Henry's royal court."

Brother and sister continued gazing at Mark in confusion until, at near the same instant, comprehension dawned on them both.

"Really?" Jamie demanded, brilliant smile returning. "At the *royal* court? With King Henry? How soon?"

While the friend who was brother asked a litany of questions without pausing to wait for answers, Elysia's own grin appeared and grew ever brighter. A glance toward Ida proved she was already aware of this plan and pleased for her son. To foster in a royal court was the pinnacle a boy could hope for and near always brought fine positions for his future.

Elysia knew they had Mark to thank for this and thank him she would—in very private ways.

After Ida led her son away for quiet talk of matters he'd never known, Elysia turned to look up into her husband's face, imprinting every line of his handsome features in her mind—as if the image hadn't been etched there the very moment she'd first viewed it. Handsome, but so very much more to respect ... admire ... love.

Mark returned his lady's steady scrutiny, letting the liquid silver of his gaze brush over her delicate, adoring face even as a low voice of rich, dark velvet whispered, "I love you, Elysia."

This was the most precious gift that could ever be given, and one she immediately returned with equal fervor. "And I love you."

"You are the most unique woman I have ever

known," Mark murmured against the smooth skin of her throat, while the black strands of his hair brushed her chin. "And that is a treasure far rarer than great beauty, although you have that in abundance, too." He pulled back but only a breath away. "I doubt that I'll ever be able to fathom all your complexities but will gladly spend a lifetime trying."

He bent his head as she lifted her face and their mouths joined in a soul-binding kiss before he swept Elysia off her feet to carry her through the empty hall, up the spiral staircase, and into their bed's sweet comforts and blazing love.

Epilogue

Autumn of 1103

*O*n a journey to the barbaric hinterlands of the Welsh border how would you manage the twins alone?" Standing next to a mound of trunks and baskets, Eve was horrified by the prospect of such a trip at all. But the notion of her friend braving the trials of travel without Ida to help manage the exhaustingly energetic sprats, which the toddler sons of Mark and Elysia were, was more than daunting.

"Alone?" Elysia grinned. "Mark wouldn't appreciate having the value of his company so completely dismissed. And I would caution you not to let him hear you disparagingly describe his birthplace and childhood home as the *barbaric hinterlands.*"

For her part, Elysia was looking forward to seeing these wilds about whose beauty Mark had told her so much. And she was anxious, also, to meet the members of Mark's family although nervous about their possible opinion of her. In anticipation of this first visit since their marriage, Mark had repeatedly listed his half siblings and cousins for her. There was his brother, Alan; sister, Linnet; and her husband, Rhys, the prince of Cymer, who was also Mark's cousin.

By actions King Henry had taken, England was now blessed with a measure of peace that made traveling safe enough to undertake. The king had not merely tamed his older brother's ambitions, but only months earlier had stripped Belleme of his English title and lands before exiling him to the Continent. Mark and Hugh had been pleased, agreeing that for the haughty, avaricious Belleme such losses would be a more painful and appropriate punishment even than death.

On seeing Elysia blithely go about making travel plans, Eve could only grimace. That Elysia would even consider departing without another woman's aid left Eve to shake her head in amazement. She had difficulty enough in taming a single, squirming baby girl and was always grateful for the help of Ida, the experienced mother who'd become a second one to her.

"Of course, I'm traveling with you, lambie," Ida firmly announced, sailing into the solar with a packed satchel in hand. "And don't you fret about Eve. Why that new babe of hers won't be here until next Lent. And for all that little Maudie is a scamp, she's also a sweet-tempered babe."

"And there you have it from one who knows far better than either you or I." Eve nodded toward the older woman who'd become mentor to her as well as to her lambie.

Ida complacently smiled. She wanted to be helpful and, despite her age and expanding size, was curious to see new places. So long, that was, as they'd be home in time for Jamie's next quarterly visit with his proud mother. Soon to be knighted, Jamie had been offered the opportunity to choose between positions either in Wroxton's garrison or in the royal guard. One offered the stability of loved surroundings and well-defined expectations while the other beckoned with the excitement of wide-ranging travel and challenge of ever-changing duties.

"I agree with Eve," Mark announced as he stepped from the shadows of the entrance tunnel.

Wondering how long he'd lingered hidden there, Elysia glanced suspiciously at the darkly handsome man who still took her breath away every time he walked into the room. No matter, much as Elysia might teasingly warn others to beware her husband's temper, no one who knew the powerful man—least of all her—would believe him ever to be an unjust threat.

Mark moved to stand behind Elysia in the long rectangle of first light falling through a long arrow slit. Gently pulling her back to lean against his chest, he directed the men who'd entered after him in outloading of provisions and personal luggage.

Though they were off for a visit with family and friends to whom he wanted to introduce his beautiful, ever more beloved wife and mischievious twin sons, they would always return to this home they'd *both* fought to protect. Since that day of victories, rather than the half-hidden truths and lies of the twilight-hidden secrets of their past, the future hovered on the horizon with the fresh beauties and bright possibilities of a new dawn.

Judith McNaught
Jude Deveraux

Jill Barnett
Arnette Lamb

A Holiday Of Love

A collection of new
romances
available from

POCKET 1007-01
BOOKS

New York Times bestselling author of
SWEET LIAR, A KNIGHT IN SHINING
ARMOR, and THE DUCHESS presents a
timeless tale of a remarkable woman and the
one man who was to be her destiny. . .

JUDE
DEVERAUX

REMEMBRANCE

Available in Hardcover
mid-November from

POCKET
BOOKS

1014-01

THE ENTRANCING NEW NOVEL FROM THE
NEW YORK TIMES BESTSELLING
AUTHOR OF *PERFECT*

Until You

by

Judith McNaught

AVAILABLE IN HARDCOVER FROM
POCKET BOOKS

POCKET
BOOKS

987-01